SILENCER

Also by James W. Hall

Hell's Bay (2008)

Magic City (2007)

Forests of the Night (2005)

Off the Chart (2003)

Blackwater Sound (2001)

Rough Draft (2000)

Body Language (1998)

Red Sky at Night (1997)

Buzz Cut (1996)

Gone Wild (1995)

Mean High Tide (1994)

Hard Aground (1993)

Bones of Coral (1992)

Tropical Freeze (1990)

Under Cover of Daylight (1987)

Hot Damn! (2001)

SILENCER

James W. Hall

 Minotaur Books ☓ New York

SILENCER. Copyright © 2009 by James W. Hall. All rights reserved. Printed in the United States of America. For information, address St. Martin's Press, 175 Fifth Avenue, New York, N.Y. 10010.

www.minotaurbooks.com

Library of Congress Cataloging-in-Publication Data

Hall, James W. (James Wilson).
    Silencer / James W. Hall. — 1st ed.
      p. cm.
    ISBN 978-0-312-35959-1
  1. Thorn (Fictitious character)—Fiction.   2. Family secrets—Fiction.
I. Title.
    PS3558.A369S55 2010
    813'.54—dc22

                         2009039820

First Edition: January 2010

10 9 8 7 6 5 4 3 2 1

For Richard, Charlie, and Sally,
a great team

Disaster does not always enter the house with thunder, high winds, and a splitting of the earth. Sometimes it burrows under the foundation and, like a field mouse on tiptoe, and at its own deliberate speed, gnaws away the entire substructure.
—William Kennedy, *Very Old Bones*

SILENCER

ONE

THE RAPPER AND HIS GIRLFRIEND, Janiqua, stood in the sunny corral, paging through the color brochure, selecting the animal they wanted to kill.

With the Remington twelve-gauge tipped against her shoulder, Claire Hammond drifted away, letting her husband, Browning, walk the couple through their choices. She waited in the shade of a cabbage palm, listening to him work his sales pitch, pointing out the Manchurian sika deer, the blackbuck antelope, the wildebeest, the eland, and the rest, describing which might be most challenging to stalk, which horns or heads would make the most impressive mount on the rap star's living room wall.

An hour earlier, DirtyX and Janiqua had arrived without reservations at the front gate of Coquina Ranch on a day Browning was scheduled to go down to Miami for business. So the way it was shaping up, once these two made their choice, it would fall to Claire to supervise the hunt.

After another minute of conversation, Browning broke away from the couple and came over. He put his arm around Claire's shoulders and steered her to a wedge of shade near the far side of the barn.

"Ten thousand bucks," he said quietly. "How could I say no?"

"Ten thousand?" It was five times their daily rate.

"I took one look at the limo, the way he was dressed, I said ten grand. The guy didn't flinch. He's doing a concert tomorrow in Miami, wants to bag something big to impress his homies back in L.A."

"What am I supposed to call him? Mr. Dirty?"

"Come on, Claire. Ten thousand bucks. Be cool."

Thirty yards away, over at the lodge, Earl Hammond, Browning's grandfather, stepped outside into the sun, paused for a moment on the deck to stare across the corral at the would-be hunters. From that distance Claire couldn't read his expression, but his disgust was unmistakable as he turned sharply and slipped back inside the lodge and shut the door.

The rapper wore a magenta jumpsuit, a bright yellow pirate scarf wrapping his skull, and big white shades like early Elton John. Janiqua had on a tight green dress that shimmered in the October sunlight. Scooped low in front, barely restraining her breasts. Not exactly regulation hunting outfits. Normally their customers, beer-drinking good ol' boys with their cheeks full of chaw, favored fatigues and camouflage.

Earl Hammond didn't much care for those fellows, either. He'd never approved of the whole hunting preserve venture. Thought it was cheesy and disreputable. A violation of the time-honored traditions the ranch stood for through the generations of Hammonds. But Earl didn't have the heart to deny his grandson anything, so he silently endured this desecration.

"Look, Claire, I have to get going. I'm late as it is. If you don't want to do it, say so. I'll send them away. But you know we could use the money."

"I'll do it," she said.

"Thanks, babe, I owe you one." He kissed her cheek, then stood back and gave her the hangdog grin he'd charmed her with in their college-sweetheart days. Though lately its magic had been waning.

Claire climbed into the back of the open Jeep, settled the Remington on her lap. Browning strolled back to DirtyX and Janiqua to close the deal.

"Cute couple," Jonah Faust said.

Behind the steering wheel, Jonah sat erect, giving Claire a grin in the rearview mirror as if they were in on the joke together. Jonah had a shaved head, a sneaky manner, and a bleak glitter in his eyes. She'd never liked him, felt a creepy vibe, and didn't understand what Browning saw in him and his brother, Moses. A couple of moochers, as far as Claire was concerned. They bunked in the primitive cabin on the game preserve and guided hunting parties now and then, did a few odd jobs around the ranch, but mainly they loafed. Old college buds of Browning's still hanging out six years after graduation.

It was a warm morning, cloudless with just enough breeze to stir the tops of the live oaks, the pines and sabal palms, and riffle the tall grass beyond the corral. In the barn the horses were nickering as Gustavo Pinto mucked their stalls. From a stand of palmetto near the lodge came the tetchy call of a scrub jay, and filtering through the yellowed light was the scent of brittle grass blowing in from the sun-baked rangeland. Early October in central Florida felt a lot like midsummer anywhere else.

Across the corral, DirtyX raised his hand and gave Browning a jive-ass, three-part handshake, then came strutting over to the Jeep, his girlfriend tagging behind, plugged into her iPod. Browning waved good-bye to Claire and headed for his car.

The rapper was a skinny man, short, with dreadlocks, unimpressive till he got close, removed his shades, and gave Claire a look at his fierce glare. Then, yeah, she could picture him up on stage, swaggering and chanting for an arena full of screamers. The harsh brown eyes of a man whose secrets outmatched anyone he met.

"I didn't see no rhinos or elephants in your pamphlet," he said to Claire.

"We don't have any of those."

"Your husband says to ask you what's the biggest baddest monster you got? I'm after something nasty, with fangs and shit."

Right there, Claire was ready to cancel things. Climb out of the Jeep, march back to the lodge, get busy with her chores. Screw the ten thousand. They didn't need the money. Not this bad. Browning would be pissed, but he'd get over it.

"Baddest thing on the ranch is the Watusi bull," Jonah said.

"Watusi?"

"Biggest horns you ever saw," said Jonah. "Eight feet tip to tip. Fucker gores you, you stay gored."

"Don't be scaring my little boy," Janiqua said.

"Ain't nobody scaring me." DirtyX gave his girl a snarly look. "They ain't nobody been born could scare me."

Jonah Faust glanced in the rearview mirror again, sent Claire a wink.

"Not the Watusi," Claire said. "We're not hunting that one."

"Why not?"

"It's old and slow. There's nothing sporting in going after Immambo."

Janiqua plucked one ear bud out.

"The thing has a name?" she said. "Like what, it's a family pet?"

DirtyX leafed through the brochure until he found the photo of the Watusi bull. He tapped the page with his skinny finger, held up the picture.

"I want this fucker," DirtyX said. "That's what we're going for."

"Then it's twenty thousand dollars, nothing less," Claire said. She was pissed, just wanted to spin this guy around and kick him back where he came from.

"Boss man said ten for anything on the preserve."

"Okay, forget the whole deal. I don't negotiate. Case closed."

Claire started to climb from the Jeep, but the rapper said, "Okay, twenty."

Then he settled his butt in the passenger seat and that was that.

"Twenty K is lunch money," he said to Jonah. "Lock and load, bitches. Let's go whack this beast."

"Last I saw," Jonah said, "the Watusi was in Crook's Meadow."

"Big-ass horns, right?" Man to man, leaving the women out.

"Eight feet tip to tip," Jonah said.

"That's what I'm talking about."

Claire settled back in her seat.

Last month the vet from Miami had visited to check on Immambo. The bull had been stumbling around, lethargic. After running tests he'd determined it was nothing infectious, nothing that might spread to the other animals. Just a failing heart. The time had come to put the old boy down. Jonah knew the story. Probably thought it was a big goof, suggesting the Watusi. Taking the man's money for doing what they had to do anyway.

It took almost an hour to travel from the lodge to the game preserve, crossing a hundred acres of Hammond ranch land, all the rutted roads, gates to open and close, passing through cattle pastures and the tomato fields. Janiqua jiggled with her music, making little peeps of song.

On a bumpy jeep trail crossing Telegraph Prairie, DirtyX put his elbow on his seatback and cranked around to face Claire.

"What is this place, the Everglades?"

She shook her head.

"Everglades is half an hour south, a shallow river, eighty miles across. This is pine flatwoods. Completely different."

DirtyX shrugged, whatever.

They made it to Crook's Meadow by eleven. Immambo was standing in the shade of a grove of loblolly pines, grazing on knee-high wire grass. So old and weary, the bull didn't even look up when they arrived.

Jonah stopped forty feet off, cut the engine. Claire had been battling with it the entire way and had finally resigned herself to the inevitable. The twenty thousand didn't tip the scales one way or the other.

5

Immambo had to be put down. The fact was, she'd been stalling for the last week. That's how she was going to look at this: euthanasia by rapper.

"There's your monster," Jonah said.

The Watusi gazed across at them blankly. He was no bigger than an average feedlot cow, but his horns extended four feet from either side of his head, thick and unwieldy, more burden than menace.

"Fucking horns, man." DirtyX's face shined with sweat. "Those are some big-ass horns. Got to weigh four hundred pounds, horns like that."

"You have a wall big enough for those puppies?" said Jonah.

The rapper took off his white sunglasses, and he and the Watusi checked each other out. A staredown that seemed to wake Immambo from his stupor.

"You ever used a shotgun?" Claire said. "You need a lesson?"

DirtyX grinned back at Janiqua.

"Fired a sawed-off once or twice. Believe I can manage."

"That's one strange-ass animal," Janiqua said. "It's staring at us funny."

"Give me the gun." DirtyX got out of the Jeep, never looking away from Immambo. "I'm shooting this bad boy."

"No," Claire said. "Forget it. This is wrong."

"What's wrong?" Janiqua said.

"That's a gentle creature. It's sick and dying. This isn't hunting. I've changed my mind. I can't let you do this."

"Gentle?" the rapper said. "I don't fucking think so. Watusi, man. I never heard of no gentle Watusi."

"Those horns keep him cool," Jonah said, off in his own time zone.

The rapper grinned uneasily.

"Hey, Niqua, you hear that? Horns keep him cool. Just like my horns."

"I don't know about this, baby. Maybe we should go shoot something else."

"How those horns keep him cool?" DirtyX asked. "Like a hat in the sun?"

"There's blood vessels inside them," said Jonah. "Blood flows through the horns, gets cooled by the air, flows back into the body. Like a radiator."

"Like a radiator."

"Go ahead, baby," Janiqua said. "Do what you gonna do. I'm sweating through my clothes, all this sun."

The rapper couldn't take his eyes off Immambo. And the bull seemed to sense this was a showdown like none he'd experienced before.

"I think we got us a chickenshit," Jonah said.

"Who you calling names?" The rapper didn't look away from the bull.

"I don't see anybody else around here pissing all over himself."

DirtyX tramped around to Claire's side of the Jeep and held out his hand. She took a long breath, let it go, then handed him the Remington.

A couple of years back Immambo had been the first exotic Browning brought to the ranch. In the two years since, Claire had witnessed many large and remarkable creatures tracked down and shot. She'd learned to blunt her sentimental attachments to most of them. But there was something about Immambo that still stirred her. She supposed it was the dignified way he endured the weight of those oversized horns. Rambling around as if the load he carried was of no consequence.

Until today she'd managed to steer all the hunters away from the Watusi. Even when the bull was younger and healthy, it was hardly fair game. A ten-year-old child could outrun the thing. There were no Watusi females on the ranch for it to protect, so it had never shown aggression of any kind. Though what she saw in Immambo at that moment was clearly different. Its hackles rising, a forward shift in its stance.

"Shoot him in the brain or what?" the rapper said.

"Don't mess up his face," Jonah said. "Taxidermist hates that shit."

"Go get him," Janiqua said. "Do it, baby."

Claire got out of the Jeep. She looked back at the sandy road they'd followed out to this meadow and thought briefly of hiking back to the lodge, just leave these craven children to their blood sport, let them assume the moral consequence. But of course she couldn't. This was her own weight to manage.

She'd never heard Immambo's bellow before. It startled her. It startled all of them. Beginning as little more than a wheeze but deepening quickly into a throaty rumble, then rising in pitch to a bleating scream that sent the rapper stumbling sideways into the Jeep.

He swung the shotgun up and aimed from his waist, the barrel wavering as if he couldn't locate his target. The Watusi had caught the scent of peril and started forward in a shaky canter, its massive horns cutting from side to side.

Janiqua squealed and spilled from the Jeep into the dry grass at Claire's feet.

"What the fuck!" the rapper yelled.

"Not in his face," Jonah said.

DirtyX dodged to his left as Immambo trotted toward him, the rapper waving the shotgun from side to side as if simply brandishing such a weapon had always worked for him in the past.

Claire circled the Jeep, and cut in front of the rapper, putting herself in the path of the Watusi, waving her arms back and forth for it to halt. But the bull had disappeared into its dream of combat, eyes as vacant and sightless as chips of coal. Claire yelled its name, a futile and silly act, losing a second and another as she waited for Immambo to respond. The bull trotted onward as though the rails it was mounted on ran directly through the Jeep and shot west across the farthest prairies.

"Get back!" she yelled to the others.

Claire kept her focus on the closer horn, waited till it was a foot away, then cut to her right, ducking below the slash, feeling a hot rush of air as the Watusi passed.

Immambo rammed the Jeep just above the front right wheel. He twisted his head and dug the point of his horn into the rubber tire and gouged away a fist-sized chunk. He rooted under the chassis as though whatever demon he'd conjured might be hiding in the shadows there.

The rapper dropped the Remington and backed toward the sandy trail, his girlfriend huddled at his shoulder.

Immambo jimmied his head beneath the carriage of the Jeep and seemed intent on flipping the vehicle onto its back. Some imaginary rhino armored for battle must have been flickering in its head, a squat adversary sheathed in metal. The Watusi found the leverage it was after and the right side of the Jeep rocked a foot from the ground.

"Get out of there, Jonah! Get out!"

"Hey, fuck this, okay."

Jonah bent forward, dug beneath his seat, and came out with a compact automatic weapon with a banana clip. He climbed atop his seat, lurching once, then grabbed hold of the windshield with one hand and aimed at Immambo with the other.

Before Claire could order him to stop, Jonah fired twenty rounds, then twenty more into the back and shoulders of the furious bull. Another dozen were required before Immambo gave up the battle it must have been anticipating for years, sinking silently to its belly in the yellow grass.

TWO

"COQUINA RANCH," RUSTY SAID. "YOU ever heard of it?"

"Up near Lake Okeechobee? That place?"

Rusty said, "Yeah, that one. The Hammond family, seventh-generation Floridians, here before Ponce de León."

It was a sheer afternoon in early November. A few minutes earlier Rusty Stabler had returned from a business trip and located Thorn in his customary spot, on the dock by the lagoon, tying bonefish flies. Selling those handcrafted lures to Keys fishing guides and a few long-time customers brought in a meager income, though it was the only income Thorn had ever required.

After they kissed, Rusty began to pace along the dock, a twinkle in her smile.

Thorn watched her for a minute, then went back to work on his bristle worm.

"So what about Coquina Ranch?"

She halted, her back to the water and the early-morning sun.

"Okay, but not until I have your undivided attention."

Thorn knotted the thread, snipped the end, and turned away from the fly-tying vice. Rusty was wearing one of her new business outfits:

olive twill pants, a white linen blouse, and a burgundy jacket. Around her neck was a gold chain with a plump antique pearl her mother bequeathed to her.

In the last year, as her corporate duties consumed more of her time, Rusty had been forced to supplement her wardrobe of shorts, sandals, and T-shirts. Since most of her adult life had been spent on fishing boats, she'd never even owned a steam iron or coat hanger, much less a business suit. Which was one of the many things she and Thorn had in common.

With so little fashion sense, Rusty chafed and squirmed in those first store-bought outfits, and for weeks all the skirts and blouses seemed to fit her angular frame as awkwardly as starched cardboard. Little by little she discovered a style that suited her—clothes with a sporty grace, just proper enough to allow her to slip in and out of the boardrooms and the wood-paneled chambers of various elected officials that were now on her appointed rounds.

It was only one part of Rusty's makeover in the last twelve months. Using two decades of business smarts she'd acquired from running her own charter fishing operation, Rusty Stabler was now very skillfully managing Bates International, the third-largest privately held corporation in the United States.

Last winter, Abigail Bates, the matriarch of the Bates family, a grandmother Thorn didn't know he had, left her large and complicated estate to him, including the corporation and all its subsidiaries, which were valued in the billions of dollars, a sum so staggering it never seemed quite real. At Thorn's urging, Rusty agreed to oversee the board of directors, select new members, and take a shot at converting BI from a profit-driven monster that trashed large swaths of Florida into a good citizen and a constructive force. In other words, turn Genghis Khan into Henry David Thoreau.

Though he'd always known Rusty was exceptionally bright, Thorn was boggled to see how undaunted she was to be swimming in those deep waters. She'd learned the lingo fast and well. Nowadays she spoke fluently about balance sheets and global platforms and short selling and supply chain management and metrics for functionalities. The gibberish of the marketplace.

She was a lean woman with ash-blond hair that she kept so short it barely required a comb. Her hazel eyes were wide set and tenacious. Her narrow face highlighted the slope of her cheekbones, and in relaxed moments her generous lips tended to soften into an artless smile. In the right light Rusty could pass for mid-twenties. She liked to tell the story from last summer when she'd set a six-pack next to the register at a 7-Eleven, and the twenty-something kid behind the counter carded her. She didn't have her license and the kid flat refused to sell her beer. Best damn beer Rusty never bought.

"I'm ready, Rusty. What about Coquina Ranch?"

She looked out at the riffle from a passing school of mullet, then took off her jacket and hung it carefully on the back of the Adirondack.

She smiled.

"Oh," Thorn said. "So this is good. Something big."

"Very big. I think it fits your guidelines perfectly. Turning shit into gold."

"Our new mantra," Thorn said.

"So here's the nutshell. We're going to sell the entire Bates tract east of Sarasota and use the money to buy Coquina Ranch."

"How's that work?"

"It starts with the state of Florida, their land-preservation program."

"Okay."

"It's called Florida Forever. They buy land, take it off the table."

"Rings a faint bell."

"Here's the story. I was talking to some of our people in Tallahassee, Bates attorneys and lobbyists, sketching out the goals we had in mind, and someone suggested I go to the Division of State Lands, talk to the Florida Forever people. I was there a couple of hours, brainstorming with the director of the program, and little by little we shaped the outline of a deal. Maybe at that point I should've called you and gotten your go-ahead, but I didn't."

"You don't need my permission for anything, Rusty. Nothing. Ever."

"Well, this is a big deal," she said. "Probably bigger than anything you had in mind. You can say no. Nothing's set in stone yet."

"Go ahead."

"In exchange for the eighty-eight thousand acres along the Peace River, the phosphate mines, the state is going to pay you five hundred and thirty-four million dollars."

"That should buy a few cases of Dos Equis."

"Yes, it should."

Last year after Thorn inherited the Bates holdings along with that parcel of land, he and Rusty and Sugarman had driven up to Summerland and spent a few days exploring the back roads of the region, then tramped on foot for miles along riverbanks and through scrubby pinelands to get a feel for the property that now belonged to him. It was huge. It was desolate. It was a long way from the coast, and it was dense with wildlife, including some rare crested caracaras and wild hogs. It was a different Florida than the one featured in fashion shoots and the slick TV shows. This was the rugged heartland of the state, a good hour from the sandy coastline and blue waters and neon-drizzled hotels, a landscape still as harsh and inhospitable as it had been when the first cutthroat Europeans on horseback pushed into its matted underbrush seeking the Fountain of Youth and bricks of gold.

"So I filled out a stack of paperwork," Rusty said, "ran everything by the Bates lawyers, then went back and negotiated like hell with Division of State Lands. They're fast-tracking the environmental-risk audit. The state's required to see what contaminants on the land need to be cleaned up before they take possession. They know about the phosphate pits, the gyp stacks. That's factored in. But even if they find something they don't expect, we should be able to get waivers. I agreed in principle to pay whatever costs might be incurred in a clean-up. Margaret

Milbanks, the director of State Lands, she's ecstatic. This is a huge deal, a career maker. It's so big it depletes the fund."

"Wait a minute. Why do we want to sell land to Florida?"

"So they'll preserve it. So nothing will ever be built on that land. So it'll be green forever. A flyway for migrating birds. So the rivers will never be polluted or pumped dry. So the trees will never be harvested."

"Who needs the government? We could keep it that way ourselves."

"As hard as it is to imagine, Thorn, someday you won't be here. And depending on how you write your will, if you ever get around to that, the land could still be up for grabs in the future. Now it won't be. Ever."

"We could give it to the state for free. No reason to make the taxpayers cough up five hundred million and whatever."

"Five hundred and thirty-four million dollars."

"Why?"

"The taxpayers have already anted up. The money's set aside in the Florida Forever fund, just sitting there waiting for the right offer. If you hadn't claimed the pot, someone else would. Normally it's some real-estate sharpie, he unloads a chunk of property that's not commercially viable, no utilities, too costly to develop, bad zoning, so he pawns it off on the state, then turns around and uses those millions to buy other land and develop golf courses and condo communities or strip malls."

"The old shell game," he said. "Con men picking the citizens' pocket."

"Exactly."

"But we're not going to do that."

"Well, this is where it gets tricky."

"Give it to me. I'm a big boy."

"The day after I signed the initial agreements, Earl Hammond showed up at Division of State Lands and offered them Coquina Ranch. Almost two hundred thousand acres. If he'd come in one day earlier, he could have had the deal we got."

"But we depleted the fund."

14

"Right."

"Only we don't really want all that money."

"No, we don't," Rusty said.

"So you tore up the deal, stepped aside, and let him take the five hundred million. Which means we're still stuck with the Bates land."

"No, I didn't do that," she said. "The attorneys for the state are drafting the arrangement. I don't understand all the ins and outs. But essentially everyone gets what they want. In about three weeks we're all going to sit down in a room, pass some papers around a table. The state of Florida hands you a check for five hundred and thirty-four million dollars, you endorse it over to Earl Hammond, which leaves us with zero, and when everything is signed, the state of Florida takes a shit-load of land out of circulation. You wanted to use Bates International to do some good, well, this is something very good."

Thorn took a swallow of the breeze coming off the water. Feeling a quick tingle of righteousness.

"Coquina Ranch," Thorn said. "That's the safari operation, right? A thousand bucks to shoot a penned-up wildebeest. That Earl Hammond?"

"Yeah, that's the one."

"And we're going to take this guy's land, put him out of business?"

"That's one way to look at it."

"Better and better."

"Minor point, but old man Hammond is holding back a few hundred acres to leave to his two grandsons. Even subtracting that, bottom line, your land plus the Hammond land, that's four hundred fifty square miles of Florida real estate. Which is larger than all five boroughs of New York City."

"Out of circulation forever," he said.

"Exactly."

Thorn looked out the mouth of the lagoon where the Atlantic was slick as ice. Today its color was more Irish green than blue. Maybe there was some chromatic aberration at work, particles in the upper atmosphere diffracting the sunlight in some oddball way. Though he could be wrong. It might be sorcery, not science. That deep green might be an upwelling at the ocean floor, a rare release of emerald water from the secret vats of Neptune and his boys. Yeah. He liked that idea better.

"You're a very smart woman, Rusty Stabler. Anyone ever tell you that?"

"I never tire of hearing it."

"Can we keep my name out of this?"

She looked off at the treetops for a moment, then came back.

"Well, Margaret and a couple of her legal team in State Lands will know, but yeah, I stipulated that you wanted to remain anonymous."

"If it can't be, I won't sign anything. We keep this thing between you and me and Sugarman. That's it. No big hoo-hah, pictures in the paper, any of that."

"Understood."

He leaned out and kissed her on the lips. When the kiss was done, her eyes stayed closed for a fraction of a second, then drifted open.

"I had a feeling you'd like it."

"It's better than anything I imagined. You're an amazing woman."

"I am," she said. "I'm damn amazing."

"I'll tell you what else I want to do," he said.

Rusty touched the pearl at her throat with an inward look as if briefly communing with her departed mother.

"Thanksgiving is in a couple of weeks, right?"

"Two and a half."

"The deal will be done by then?"

"If nothing snags it. That should be about right."

"Then I want to have a party."

Her eyes came back to him, first puzzled, then amused.

"A party?"

"A celebration. You, me, and Sugar, we'll know what it's about. To everybody else it's just a bash."

"Thorn's going to have a party? Hermit crab leaving his shell?"

"Yeah, the new and improved Thorn. Dance on the table. Toast the smart woman I'm lucky enough to live with. A big, loud, drunken, shit-faced party. Invite everyone we know. Everyone they know."

At that moment, Sugarman came walking around the west end of the house, wearing a jaunty Panama hat, faded jeans, a red polo shirt. Looking at Thorn, then at Rusty, sensing something, getting a quizzical look.

"What happened?" he said. "Who got pregnant?"

"No one around here," Rusty said. "Thank God."

"Rusty just made five hundred million dollars. We're rolling in loot."

"Five hundred million?" Sugarman said. "That's almost half a billion."

"More or less," Rusty said.

"What do you want money for, Thorn? A new pair of flip-flops, a safety pin to hold up your loincloth?" Sugarman smiled innocently.

His buddy had been giving him the same raft of shit forever. As a couple of ten-year-old misfits, they'd struck an immediate bond that hadn't faltered over the turbulent decades.

"Go on, Rusty, tell him the story. I'd like to hear it again anyway."

Sugarman eased into one of the rattan rockers and Rusty ran through it one more time. Giving him the abbreviated version. Sugar rocked, looking off at the indigo sky above the mangroves. Nodding as Rusty spoke, not interrupting like Thorn had, but simply absorbing it, a slow smile taking shape on his lips as the scope of the deal came clear.

To strangers, Sugarman could come off as dull, a plodder, lacking in ambition. But Thorn knew the flip side of that surface appearance. He'd never met anyone as resolute, persistent, and loyal as Sugar. This man whose self-indulgent parents had betrayed him the moment he was born had set his course early in life and had kept an unswerving focus ever since. He was determined to be the opposite of his own parents. Steadfast and dependable to a fault.

Sugarman was only a week old when he was deserted by his Nordic blond mom and his badass Rastafarian dad. He'd been raised by a granny in the Key Largo slums and grew up polite, soft-spoken, but with uranium at the marrow. With his sharp-angled good looks and cinnamon skin, Sugarman had long been a target for bullies of both races. "Pretty boy," the jerks would call him, "dandy man." Sugarman was slow to anger, but if the taunts ever got physical, he wasn't shy about shutting them down. Long-limbed and nimble, he could flatten a shithead's nose quicker than most men could make a fist.

After high school he spent a few years living his childhood dream, though he eventually discovered that working for the Monroe County sheriff's department was far less gratifying than he'd imagined. When he grew weary of writing speeding citations and stepping into the middle of snot-slinging bar fights and domestic chaos, he went private. "Security consultant" was what he was calling himself lately.

As Rusty reached the end of her story, Sugarman shook his head and whistled in admiration.

"And that's not even the most incredible part," Rusty said. "Get this: Thorn wants to have a party to celebrate. On Thanksgiving."

"Thorn? A party? Mr. Anti-Social?"

"I said the same thing."

"Hey," Thorn said, "a guy can change. Give me a chance."

Sugarman looked at Rusty and shook his head.

"Boy, oh, boy," he said. "This I gotta see."

THREE

ON THANKSGIVING NIGHT, CLAIRE HAMMOND was in the tack room skinning a wildebeest when Earl wandered in and sat down on a bench nearby. Just the two of them—the first time they'd been alone together in weeks.

Earl Hammond sighed, took the unlit pipe from the corner of his mouth, and tucked it in his back pocket. She waited in silence while he rolled up the shirt sleeves of his blue work shirt, then cut a look her way and gave her a bashful smile.

"How you doing tonight, Miss Claire?"

She said she was fine, just fine.

He chewed on that for a minute, nodding to himself, building up to something, but not quite there. A moth circling the Coleman lantern stumbled in Earl's direction, and he raised a hand and waved it on its way. For half a second his eyes darted to her, then cut back to the darkness beyond the barn door.

She wiped her bloody hands on a towel and came over to him.

"So," Earl said. "You have time for a story?"

"Another one about the good old days?"

"What? Do my stories bore you?"

"Come on, Earl. I'm kidding. I love your stories."

Earl Hammond was a big rumpled man whose silvery hair was still luxuriant. Though he was in his eighty-seventh year and there was some stiffening in his gait, he showed no loss of vigor, no wasting of muscle, no fading of the sharp light in his eyes. An unbowed six-foot-six, he could still ride a horse at full gallop, could fell a mature pine without setting aside the ax to catch his breath, and was still the best marksman on the ranch. Men were drawn to his cast-iron vigor, women to his reserved gentility.

Staring off at the shadows, Earl Hammond told the tale straight through, altering his deep voice here and there to mimic the various characters, and narrating the rest in that slow, resonant manner she'd heard him use a few times before, a tone he reserved for cherished memories, rare glimpses into his storied past.

Earl Hammond had been ten years old that winter in 1930 when Henry Ford and Thomas Edison arrived at Coquina Ranch early in the afternoon on a Friday. Clara Ford and Mina Edison stayed behind in Fort Myers, where the two families wintered in adjacent homes.

Young Earl had met Mr. Edison on previous visits but had never seen him so pale and feeble. Mr. Ford had to hoist Edison out of the passenger seat of the Model A Tudor Sedan, then assist him across the bridge and into the lodge.

After dinner the men were seated in the dining room enjoying their cigars when Ernest Hemingway lumbered in, his arm bandaged from a recent accident. He was red-faced and joking in Spanish with Juan Miguel Pinto, the ranch foreman. In the two hours it took Juan Miguel to chauffer Hemingway from his Miami hotel, the writer and the ranch hand had apparently forged a friendship.

It was to be a quick stop for Hemingway, enroute to Key West, making this detour to shake hands with two of America's great geniuses, gab a little around the bonfire, and drink some first-class whiskey with the legendary Earl Hammond Sr.

Earl Junior could have cared less about the lightbulb man or the manufacturer of the Tin Lizzie. But he was enthralled with Hemingway and dogged him all evening. At the campfire he sat on a log behind the great man and memorized his every move.

President Hoover appeared well after dark, accompanied by a single federal agent. There was a one-bodyguard rule at Coquina Ranch, for otherwise Earl Hammond feared the place would be overrun with Pinkerton men and gun-toting thugs, and the camaraderie between the guests would be compromised. Hoover saluted the others, and they returned the greeting with affection—all but Hemingway. By then well drunk, he began to fume about the fatheaded Quaker and his prohibitionist policies, until Earl Senior stepped in and quieted the writer down.

The logs burned and young Earl watched the vines of sparks twist up into the dark sky as if they meant to take root in the heavens. The discussion ricocheted from topic to topic so quickly the ten-year-old could barely keep up. Earl's father congratulated Hemingway on his new novel, which he believed was the best war story he'd ever read. The praise sent Hemingway rambling on about his exploits on the Italian front in that long-ago conflict. Everyone listened politely to the familiar narrative until finally the writer paused to take a long swallow of whiskey.

President Hoover cleared his throat and remarked on Mr. Edison's many contributions to the war effort, perhaps less well publicized than Hemingway's but of critical importance in the ultimate victory. The president ticked off a few of Edison's wartime inventions: a ship telephone system, an underwater searchlight, anti-torpedo nets, and navigational equipment. The list seemed to come as a surprise to Hemingway. After that young Earl caught the author giving the half-deaf inventor respectful glances.

Prohibition took its turn as a topic, and Hoover had his say, mostly religious tripe. Ford, a teetotaler, chimed in with a homily about the devilish effects of liquor on his workers. Sulking in silence, Hemingway sipped his drink and stared into the fire, his cheeks flushed as if the flames of the log fire were singeing them.

Finally the matter that lurked in the background all evening broke forth. The stock-market crash of the previous October, the rising rate of bank failures, and the economic misfortunes that were spreading poverty and gloom across the land.

In a somber voice, President Hoover described a certain gala that Henry Ford had hosted the previous fall in honor of the fiftieth anniversary of Edison's invention of the lightbulb. Hoover, along with the major political and financial leaders of the country, showed up in Dearborn, Michigan, for the event. It was Hoover's view that in the fifty years since the lightbulb first flickered on, Edison, Ford, Firestone, and Durant had transformed America from a third-rate power into the world's industrial giant. Then, tragically, only seven days after those festivities in Michigan, Wall Street crashed and the Great Depression was under way.

"Well, there's a pretty picture for you," Hemingway said. "A gang of Neros fiddling while the world catches fire."

Nobody had a response for this cynic of the new generation. Young Earl shifted uncomfortably as the other men looked away from his hero and stared into the flames or into the dark woods that surrounded them.

Hoover broke the silence with a short address on the need for voluntary and local responsibility when it came to feeding and caring for the growing population of poor. It sounded like something he'd lifted from one of his speeches.

"This is not the time to grow the government larger. This is the moment for churches and neighborliness."

In Ford's opinion, the downturn was going to be a very good learning experience for the country . His only concern was that it might not last long enough, in which case people would not have ample opportunity to learn enough.

"Oh, for fuck's sake." Hemingway got to his feet, waving a dismissive hand at Hoover and Ford. "What we need is a big goddamn war. That would put things straight. And send everyone back to work in a hurry. Maybe Mr. Ford can put a word in with his buddy, Adolf."

"What did he say?" Edison asked Ford.

Ford leaned close to the old man's ear and gave him the sanitized version.

It was then that Earl Senior motioned to his son. Time to be off to bed so the men could speak freely.

Time for young Earl to dutifully march back to the lodge, climb up to his bedroom. Time to lie on his cot and sniff at the wood smoke clinging to the sleeves of his shirt, to stare at his own palm, which had touched the big paw of Ernest Hemingway. Time to lie awake and imagine what extraordinary things were being said around that campfire on the edge of the wild Florida pinelands.

When he finished the story, Earl rose, drew a handkerchief from his pocket, and swabbed the sweat from his brow. He stretched his arms and blinked at Claire as if surprised to find her there. He smiled, turned his eyes back toward the darkness.

"So why that story, Earl? What's it mean to you?"

"Just some ranch history, how it used to be."

"But Coquina Ranch is still that way. Great men passing through, sitting around the campfire, having their mysterious talks."

"We've been a little short of great men lately, wouldn't you say?" Earl looked at her with curiosity.

Claire rubbed her palms on the legs of her jeans, cleaning off the sticky film of the wildebeest's blood.

"That's what you're saying? You'd like to improve the guest list?"

He flinched as if such a thought was painful beyond imagining.

"Dad, if you don't like how Browning's running things, sit down and discuss it. He listens to you. He respects you."

He shook his head as if somehow she was missing the point.

"That creature you're skinning," he said. "How do you feel about all that?"

It was Browning's idea to convert two hundred acres of the ranch into a safari-style hunting preserve and import exotic African game. A scheme to wring more profit from the ranch. He'd selected a remote area of pastureland, pine forest, and scrub on the western edge of Coquina Ranch. It was the natural place, since the tract had been fenced decades before to hold German prisoners of war—a plan the war department canceled just weeks after the vast fence was completed.

These days corporate hotshots used the Hammonds' landing strip, bunked in the primitive hunting camp on the preserve, and chased the game in dune buggies and ATVs. Most returned home with an exotic trophy. But because the initial outlay for the imported game had been far costlier than Browning had expected, so far the enterprise had failed to turn a profit.

Though neither man discussed it openly, Claire knew the safari scheme had created discord between Browning and Earl. Not because it was a bad investment, but because those exotic creatures violated the longstanding tradition of the Hammond clan of maintaining the natural history of the ranch, keeping the land unspoiled and the flora and fauna as close to native as possible.

"That story," she said. "Were you suggesting Hemingway and Henry Ford and the others somehow cooked up World War II?"

Earl smiled.

"No, nothing that dramatic. But we did get a pretty nice lake out of the deal. That levee around Okeechobee, you might say that was Hoover's gift to my dad."

When she first arrived at Coquina Ranch and was acquainting herself with the area, Claire had driven over to the lake several times and hiked up the steep banks of the levee. It was only forty feet high, but it towered above the flat landscape, allowing for an unbroken panoramic view.

Over a hundred miles of embankment circled Okeechobee, making it the second-largest freshwater lake in the United States. Only Lake Michigan was bigger.

The Hoover Dike had been built to prevent another flood like the one after the '28 hurricane, which had drowned thousands of people in that farming region, but over the decades that dike's unintended consequence was to fuel the explosive growth of Miami and the rest of South Florida. These days seven million souls relied on that reservoir for their drinking water.

"What I was getting at," Earl said, "is that over the years a lot of good came from those campfires. Things that had nothing to do with profit or power. Positive things that wouldn't have happened otherwise. It pains me to see that go."

"You think there's a risk of that?"

He looked out into the murky night, his silver mane glowing in the lantern light, his brown eyes weary and evasive.

He swallowed, braced a shoulder against the doorway.

"Browning's had six years to find his way," Earl said. "I've tried to steer him the best I could, but I think we can see where he wants to take the ranch. The kind of men he's surrounded himself with, and where that's likely to lead."

"Is this about that rapper and his girlfriend last month? Because that wasn't Browning's fault. The guy just showed up out of nowhere. I agreed to take him on a hunt. So blame me."

"No, Claire. You're missing my point. It goes much deeper than that."

"Well, what're you saying?"

"I've made a difficult decision, Claire. Coquina Ranch is about to change. It'll be a radical new direction. There'll be those who won't like these changes, but that can't be helped. I'll leave it to your husband to explain the details, but I wanted to tell you face-to-face why I did it. Because as I see it, my duty is not simply to you and Browning and the children you'll have someday. I have an obligation to my father, and the generations of Hammonds who have been faithful stewards of this land, working hard to preserve its traditions and natural beauty. I can't let all that just disappear. I've tried to do what I thought best for all of us and for the land we love. One day, I hope you'll come to agree."

"What kind of change, Earl? What's going on?"

He closed his eyes for several moments. When he opened them again, he drew a long breath as if he were hitching an enormous burden back onto his shoulders.

"I've said enough. Browning will have to explain the rest."

She moved closer to him, opening her arms to embrace this man who was more father to her than her natural one, to give him what consolation she could provide. But she was a second late, for Earl Hammond missed the gesture and stepped away into the shadows of the corral, heading back toward the faint light of the lodge.

FOUR

ON THE SKINNING TABLE, THE wildebeest was spread-eagled on its belly. Blood drizzled into the stainless-steel gutters and drained into the spouts that disappeared into the concrete floor. Claire Hammond worked with quick, efficient strokes, slicing first at the middle of the rib cage an inch before the front legs and continuing up and across the shoulders.

When she'd finished that radial cut, she cleaned the blade on her towel and moved around the table to make another incision above the animal's knees, then sawed the blade around the tough hide until she met the first cut. She wiped the blade again, then slid the tip into the back of the leg and carved downward to intersect with the incision above the knee.

The wildebeest was an African antelope with a long tufted tail and upturned horns curved inward like parentheses. The one lying before her was nearly four hundred pounds, its coat a bluish gray. The vapors rising from its pelt were funky with the manure scent of the marshland, and its dark blood was as plummy and sweet-smelling as a lush Merlot.

After she completed the knee cut, she stepped to a side table, switched on the grinding wheel, skimmed the blade against it, and bent into the shower of sparks.

Twenty-seven years old, Claire Hammond had a lanky build and shoulder-length hair the color of ripe peaches. She had her mother's brown eyes and her dad's prim mouth and fine, straight nose.

At least the nose started out that way. Now there was a pearly crimp at the bridge where she'd broken it playing volleyball on the university team. Her side lost the game, got knocked out of the regionals. Though, as her roommate, Sabrina, used to say, Claire scored big that day.

Lying on the gym floor, blood spilling from her broken nose, she was scooped up by none other than Browning Hammond, who whisked her off to the campus infirmary, then hung around till she was released two hours later.

Wild Dog Hammond, as he was known in those days, was cocaptain of the Miami Hurricanes, second team All-American defensive end, famous for batting down passes and body-slamming quarterbacks. Turned out he'd had a crush on Claire forever and came to all her home games. On several occasions her teammates had spotted him in the stands. How could you miss the guy: six-seven, two-eighty, shoulders out to there. But none of the girls had a clue who he was coming to watch. Until the day Claire went up to block a spike, her hands spread a little too wide.

After that day, Browning courted her with unstinting devotion. He arrived with bouquets at every date, Russian chocolates, books of sonnets. He had a round, boyish face with pale skin, bright red cheeks, and hardly any beard at all. He blushed easily and often. He was simple, plainspoken, calm, and unhurried. It was a steadiness she believed he'd acquired from growing up in a stable farming family and living close to the measured cycles of the land.

He was majoring in business and intended to take his book learning back to the ranch and run the place more efficiently when it came his turn to take charge. Not a sophisticated thinker or an intellectual in the usual bookish way, but smarter than any of the assorted jocks and college smoothies Claire had dated.

Socially he was backward, slow to hold her hand, slow to kiss her, slow to move beyond kisses, clumsy in bed at first, but enthusiastic and open about his lack of skill and willing to be tutored. Happy to go slower, use a lighter touch, read her rising cries, and try his best to time his orgasm to hers. He threw himself into learning about her body and its responses with the same dedication he'd used to master college football.

Though she kidded him about treating lovemaking as a sporting event, she did admire his devotion and his belief that with enough hard work there was nothing he couldn't accomplish. Unlike Claire, he was not a natural athlete. On the football field, where he could have traded on his strength and bulk alone, Browning never slacked, but worked tirelessly to master the subtle spins and feints the best players in his position used to slip past blockers and attack the ball carrier. He was, in Claire's view, a coach's dream: physically gifted, hardworking, coachable, and a faithful team player.

Browning was so strikingly dissimilar to any man she'd ever been with, so dedicated to his family and its traditional way of life, so sentimental that at times he could be downright corny, so formidable in body and spirit, that against all reason she found herself falling for him.

After Browning Hammond entered her life, her careful career plans whipsawed in a new direction. A Connecticut girl, premed major, her idea was to return to New Canaan and partner with her dermatologist father. Now at odd moments, looking around Coquina Ranch, it still astonished her, the person she'd become instead. A Florida rancher's wife who employed her limited surgical skills on creatures she hadn't known existed six years before.

As a college girl she'd explored every nook of South Florida and indulged in its full array of diversions. The sugary beaches, the decadent clubs, the ethnic cafés, the tiki bars with reggae booming out across the bay. In four years she'd mastered the gaudy landscape, the overheated driving, the spicy salsa of cultures and languages, and the triple-espresso pace. She'd earned her South Florida green card. Sand on her bare feet, gold American Express tucked in her string bikini. Fluent in the glib and jaded lingo of her generation, and with just enough Spanish to get by.

But on those first trips with Browning, driving an hour beyond Miami's fringe to visit his grandparents, Claire was blown away to discover another Florida a century out of step with the urbanized coast. Rodeo gals and shit-kickers and migrant laborers in cowboy shirts. Pickup trucks plastered with pissed-off decals and shotguns racked in the back window. Lettuce fields, sod farms, and black plumes of dust rising from pastures of muck. Rundown Dairy Queens, RV parks, abandoned sugar mills, and roadhouse bars with no signs out front. Men gathered in parking lots wearing sweaty work clothes and snakeskin boots, reeking of cigarettes and malt liquor and pesticide. Country music twanged on every radio, at every gas stop, and the endless scrubland was as flat and unforgiving as the plains of Texas.

Then came her marriage into the Hammond clan, followed by a crash course in ranch life, full immersion in rural Florida. Year by year the culture shock wore off and Claire became a convert, sincere in her admiration for Rachel Sue and her husband, Earl, both still hardy in their eighties after a lifetime spent cultivating the land and making do with its austere pleasures, thriving in its brutal heat and isolation.

Their life's greatest challenge had been the loss of their only son, a grief from which they never fully recovered.

Earl Three, as they called him, was a reckless child of the sixties. From the looks of the photos hanging in the dining room, he was part playboy, part hippie, a dashing young man with a careless smile, while his wife, Deidre, had the waifish body and stoned eyes of a teenage runaway. She, in her long flowered dresses and silky hair, and he, wearing paisley tunics and a shaggy Beatles mop, seemed younger and more lighthearted than Browning or Frisco ever were. The young couple named their two sons for the cities where they were conceived—

Frisco during their flower-child phase, and Browning christened for the town in Montana where Deidre and Earl Three had gone to ski. In their middle thirties, the couple perished in an avalanche on a downhill run on Mont Blanc, leaving behind their two boys for Rachel Sue and Earl to raise. Frisco was seven at the time, Browning barely a year.

"Earl and Rachel Sue didn't raise me," Browning liked to say. "Everything of value, I learned from my football coaches."

Claire Hammond set the sharpened knife aside and touched the ragged edges of the wound at the wildebeest's chest. This one hadn't been a noble death.

Hours earlier, during the twilight hunt, Herbert Sanchez, governor of the state of Florida and Browning's frequent guest at the ranch, had botched his first two shots, then squeezed off a grouchy third that nicked the wildebeest in the rump. The wounded buck folded to its knees, then promptly rose and stumbled toward a stand of slash pine. Claire ordered the governor to shoot before it disappeared.

"That's enough," he said. "I'm done. We'll pick this up tomorrow."

With darkness only minutes off, there was no option. No way in hell was she going to spend the night tracking the creature through two hundred acres of pinelands and hard plains.

She peeled the rifle from his grip, aimed, and fired. When the wildebeest dropped, the governor huffed at her impertinence. But ten minutes later after they'd hiked to the fallen animal and he'd tossed back two slugs from his flask, the big, fleshy man had recovered his good cheer.

He kneeled beside the buck, and jacked its head up for a photo—in that moment making it plain he was claiming the kill as his own. Claire was thereby sworn to secrecy about who'd actually bagged the wildebeest. Which was fine. In the last year on Coquina Ranch, her code of honor had grown flexible on this point.

Now as she looked down at the carcass spread before her, she took a calming breath. For no matter how many of these big animals she prepared, her hands always quivered at this final moment, the unveiling.

She stepped around the table, curled her fingers under the edge of the hide and tugged the skin off the meat of the wildebeest as one might peel a tight shirt off the back of a lover. When she reached the neckline, she picked up the capping knife and made a deep laceration in the throat, working the blade down till it severed bone.

All but done, she halted, listening to the night sounds beyond the barn, the field crickets, the tree frogs and bull frogs, a group of barred owls echoing one another in the pinelands, and louder than any of that were the men's voices at the lodge. She heard the governor's belly laugh, a whiskey wheeze at the end, then the sound of Browning and his friend Antwan Shelton joining in the laughter. But the voice she didn't hear was Earl Hammond.

She considered again Earl's story of Hemingway, Edison, and Ford, hearing the mournful echoes in his voice, his reproachful view of Browning. Wondering why, of all the stories of the ranch's history, he'd chosen that one to share.

She set the knife aside and walked to the head of the dressing table.

Most skinners wore cut-resistant butcher gloves. Not Claire. She knew full well the dangers of working bare-handed around the razory blade and of the probability of stabbing herself on a splintered bone. She'd been tutored in her craft by several old-time skinners with missing fingers, and a couple who'd contracted infections that almost did them in.

Those were risks she accepted. These animals had been sacrificed so men like the governor could decorate their walls with trophies and fill their scrapbooks with grinning displays of manliness. The least she could do was send the wild beasts on to the pastures of afterlife without the alien touch of synthetic yarn.

In the last few years she'd learned to skin each of the exotic species on the preserve: ibex goats, gemsboks, Asian water buffalo, eland, sika deer from China, a small herd of African scimitar-horned oryx, even a few dozen American bison and Florida wild hogs. Call her foolish or

New Age silly, but Claire Hammond took it as her sacred duty to keep this last rite as natural as possible.

She gripped the horns, one in each hand near the points, then jiggled them lightly as though guiding a motorcycle along an icy roadway. Testing the tension of the meat, the remaining grip of tendons and vertebrae.

When she had a feel for what was left, she set her feet and twisted the horns, leaned back, increasing the pressure until she heard the crackles of the last strands of gristle giving way.

Then she tore the head off the body.

FIVE

IN THE FIZZY LIGHT OF the propane lantern, Claire held the wildebeest's head away from her stomach. A portion of the creature's hide
trailed behind the head like the cape of a magician who has vanished
after his final trick.

Straining under the weight, she hobbled across the concrete floor
and settled the head into a black plastic garbage bag. She tucked in
the hide and closed the bag, then carried it in an awkward embrace to
the icebox.

Freezing the hide stopped the growth of bacteria. Hides not frozen immediately after skinning risked hair slippage and rot. She'd
done a decent job on the skinning, left enough cape for the taxidermist to work with. Excess could always be cut away, but too little cape
sometimes meant no mount could be made at all. Governor Sanchez
was not a man who'd easily forgive such a blunder and he sure as hell
wasn't a guy she wanted to be indebted to.

When she latched the freezer door and turned back to the cleaning
table, the sudden silence stopped her. An icy prickle washed across her
shoulders. The frogs had ceased. No owls, no voices from the lodge.
Even the bugs had gone quiet.

She moved to the open doorway and peered into the darkness. Coquina Ranch observed a strict dark-skies policy. Outdoor lighting wasn't allowed, no porch lights, no spots, not even ground-level solar lights. Ranch workers and guests used low-volt flashlights to move around the grounds at night, and even indoor lighting was muted. Earl Hammond Jr. was a fascist about starlight. Don't mess with his Milky Way.

Claire stepped out of the barn. She cocked her head and peered at the soft light spilling from the lodge.

Over a hundred years ago the two-story bastion was constructed from slabs of coquina quarried along the coast of northern Florida, then hauled by wagon down the state so Hartwell Hammond, the family patriarch, could pay homage to a Spanish fortress he much admired, Castillo San Marcos, which conquistadors constructed on the shores of St. Augustine four centuries before. Coquina was Florida's only native stone, a pulverized blend of clamshells and oysters and snails and fine quartz sand cemented together by acidic groundwater and forged for centuries beneath the crush of sedimentary layers. It was yellowish white, the color of a winter moon.

The thick coquina walls gave the lodge a fanciful air, more like an oddball tourist trap than a family residence where generations of Hammonds had laughed and quarreled and celebrated together. Though Claire had been slow to warm to the structure, she'd gradually come to see the virtues of coquina stone. Those heavy walls kept the interior spaces cool even on insufferable August afternoons, and the howling gales of hurricanes and tropical storms hardly registered within the lodge. Then there was the incense that permeated the interior spaces. She supposed it was some trace of the marine life that once inhabited the shells, releasing into the air the musky smolder of the sea, even though the Atlantic was sixty miles away.

Claire stared at the dark lodge, seeing no movement at the windows. Gone were the laughter and voices. Filling the night air was a stillness that bristled the hair on her arms.

Wary and uncertain, she walked across the corral, through the sandy parking lot where the governor's black SUV was parked. Beside it was the Faust brothers' Prius with the silly camouflage paint job.

Antwan Shelton's white Mercedes sedan was parked there, too. A flashy running back, Antwan had been a teammate of Hammond's at the U, and after college he had been drafted by the Dolphins. One championship ring and a blown knee later, Antwan had parlayed his sports fame into a career as a celebrity pitchman, hawking luxury cars in TV commercials or posing shirtless on billboards with skinny fashion babes draped on his muscular body while he sipped a shot of Grey Goose vodka.

At the south end of the lot, Claire spotted a truck that must have arrived while she was absorbed in skinning the wildebeest. Gustavo Pinto's rusty Nissan pickup. As ranch foreman, Gustavo hired the seasonal help, the fruit and vegetable pickers, the sod crew, and the loggers, and it also fell to him to oversee them after hours.

In her six years, Claire had never seen Gustavo inside the lodge. Even for such a high-ranking employee, and the son of Juan Miguel Pinto, who'd served in the same capacity for decades, these grounds were strictly off-limits. No one was permitted at the lodge except the Hammond family, a few invited guests, and their security men.

If Gustavo was at the lodge, there was serious trouble somewhere on the ranch, most likely with one of the workers.

She relaxed, caught her breath. That had to be it. At that very moment Earl or Browning was probably on the phone with Sheriff Prescott. A tomato picker had gotten into a scuffle with a townie from Palmdale or Clewiston, drunk versus drunk.

She halted at the threshold of the bridge that spanned the alligator moat. She'd caught herself just in time. She'd been about to break into the lodge wild-eyed over nothing, disgrace herself in front of that gang of good old boys who'd have a few hoots at her expense. And she could picture the look on Browning's face as he added this episode to the list of grievances against her.

Coquina Ranch traditions were established more than a century earlier, and those rules were still rigidly upheld: no women permitted around the campfire bull-sessions or inside the lodge when the elite gatherings were under way. No women. Period. The sexist rule pissed her off mightily, and for her first year she campaigned for Browning to discard it, but he claimed it was beyond his authority. So grudgingly she abided by the anachronism, another concession she made out of respect for Earl Hammond and the ranch's fabled traditions.

As she turned back to the barn, the toe of her boot stubbed something in the grass and Claire stumbled against the railing.

Only later would she realize how that fractional deviation in her stride would forever alter the world she'd come to know. If she'd simply walked back to the barn to wait for the gathering to break up, the night would have swung a different way, another outcome with consequences beyond her reckoning.

But no. When she righted herself, she stooped to peer into the darkness and spotted an odd gleam at the base of the oleander bush. More than odd. She passed this way dozens of times each day and could navigate the pathway blindfolded. Knew every rock, stump, outcropping of roots.

Claire squatted down and stretched her arm into the snarl of limbs, brushed her fingertips across the object. Not metal.

She pried open the branches and waded deeper into the foliage.

Lustrous in the soft light was the toe of a highly polished shoe. Claire took a breath and forced herself farther into the bush and made out the khaki trousers and white polo shirt the guy had been wearing earlier in the afternoon.

His name was Brad Saperstein. Heavy-jawed man around fifty with graying haircut in a GI flattop, he was an officer with the Florida Department of Law Enforcement, assigned as the governor's single bodyguard. A smug bastard who'd openly eyed Claire like she might be on the evening's menu.

She spoke his name. When he didn't respond, she touched his bare arm and found the flesh as cool as the slaughtered wildebeest's.

A bubble of acid broke in the back of her throat. Claire flopped backward on the path, crawled on her butt away from the body. She groaned, then struggled to her feet and swung around to stare at the silent lodge.

Its two-story windows were glowing faintly. Tonight, as on most nights, there was only that muted halo radiating a few feet from the structure. Maybe a couple of table lamps illuminating the big den where the men had gathered to socialize.

Calling 911 wasn't an option. The only landline was inside the lodge, and her cell was upstairs in the master suite. Even if she'd had access to a phone, police assistance would've been a long time coming. As far as she knew, not one of the county deputies had ever been to the lodge, and she doubted any were experienced with the maze of unpaved roads that crisscrossed the vast tract of prairie, scrub and pine flatlands. Few landmarks, no road signs, dozens of gates to open and close, dead ends and dusty, rutted Jeep trails that went on for miles. Navigating at night was even trickier. Veteran farmhands sometimes lost their way.

These were the seconds that Claire would have to account for. What she saw, what she heard, every word spoken by her or others. She would explain how she'd managed to regain her composure and from that moment on stay resolutely calm. Why wasn't she paralyzed with fear? The investigators were suspicious. A young woman finding a security guard dead in the bushes outside a strangely quiet house. Why hadn't she run for help? It simply wasn't credible. They would treat her as if she knew more than she was saying. That she was covering up, or involved somehow. Doubt would be in their eyes, skepticism lacing every question.

She'd explain how that flush of terror dissolved and everything downshifted to slow-mo. She couldn't account for it. It was a knack she'd had since childhood, and it served her well as a college athlete.

Claire went cold and quiet. Saw every detail frame by frame. A sharp focus, eye on the goddamn ball.

She sprinted back to the barn, ducked into the tiny office, pulled down the twelve-gauge, loaded it, and trotted back to the house. See the dead guy, go fetch the shotgun. A handful of seconds to race back to the lodge. Less than a minute. No thoughts buzzing through her mind. Not a trace of the earlier panic.

There'd been no drills for such a moment, though given the steady stream of politicians, sports stars, diplomats, literary lions, painters, musicians, and movers and shakers of every stripe, and all those grim-faced bodyguards, more than once Claire had considered a worst-case scenario. Still, nothing like what was unfolding. Nothing that put her dead center.

In a light-footed crouch, she crossed the bridge, went up the steps. Pressed her ear to the door. She made out one low voice. It was Browning's, but she couldn't distinguish the words. His tone was stern, like the voice he used on ranch hands who'd screwed up, a stiff restraint that barely masked his disdain.

She thumbed the latch, shouldered the door open an inch, set her feet, then barged into the foyer. Two minutes max since she bumped Saperstein's shoe.

With the shotgun at her shoulder, she stepped forward into the den.

Twenty feet away Gustavo Pinto held a pistol in his right hand. A silencer was attached to the barrel and the handgun was aimed down at the floor. Gustavo's cheeks glistened and his eyes were red. Ten feet in front of him, Browning and Earl stood stiffly at opposite ends of the big burgundy couch.

A long oak coffee table separated the two of them from Gustavo. Rolled out on the table was a survey map dotted with red circles. Governor Sanchez stood paralyzed behind the couch, Antwan Shelton at his shoulder.

"Gustavo. Listen to me," Claire said. "I don't care what's going on here, but you need to set that pistol on the floor and you need to do it right now. Do it now, Gustavo. No debate, no mistakes."

Claire stepped closer, the cherry stock of the Remington cool against her cheek.

"Shoot him," Browning said. "Shoot the fucking bastard."

Browning glared at the small man. Tears sparkled on Gustavo's cheeks.

"For your family!" Browning yelled. "Shoot him!"

Less than three minutes since she'd discovered Saperstein in the oleander. Three minutes. Everything frame by frame. Her finger tightened against the trigger.

"I'm sorry," Gustavo said. "Mr. Earl, I'm sorry. God forgive me."

"Shoot him, goddammit!" Browning roared.

If Claire hesitated for a few seconds, it was because Gustavo's right arm was slack, his handgun aimed harmlessly at the floor. And because she knew him to be a gentle soul, with a wife and several grown children. Like his father before him, he worked his ass off alongside the pickers and ranch hands. Once in her early days on the ranch, Gustavo rescued Claire when she'd become hopelessly lost while driving around the ranch, trying to familiarize herself with her new home. Night falling, she was on the brink of despair. Gustavo appeared in his pickup and guided her back to the lodge, never mentioning the incident again. Unfailingly polite, Gustavo was the one employee on Coquina Ranch she considered a dear friend.

Seconds passed. Claire waited for her order to register with Gustavo, waited for him to drop the pistol, waited as any reasonable person would. That was all. With Browning yelling, commanding her to open fire on the gentle soul.

Gustavo's pistol rose, Claire saying no, no, as that long cylinder wobbled upward toward the men across the room.

There was no choice. No time for pleading. God help them all. She tensed her finger and set off a blast that seemed to rattle the foundation of that house.

Though she'd fired that shotgun hundreds of times and knew its kick, she was staggered and spun awkwardly to her right. When she swung back she saw the spray of pellets had blown out the twenty-foot window and a cascade of bright needles was raining down on Gustavo's body.

She dropped the shotgun on the stone floor and turned to the couch. It was then she realized that in those seconds of delay she'd lost more than a friend.

Earl Hammond, who'd been born on Coquina Ranch and spent decades nurturing the land and the people under his care, strictly maintaining the customs of his ancestors, Earl Hammond Jr. was sitting oddly erect on the leather sofa. His head was turned to the side as if he were watching the scenery pass outside the window of a car. The expression on Earl's face was too serene for this world.

Browning bent over him, felt for a pulse at his throat. He kept his hand there for half a minute, staring up at the ceiling. The governor and Antwan Shelton emerged from behind the couch.

"Holy Jesus," Sanchez said.

Browning removed his hand from his grandfather's throat. He straightened and looked at the governor and Antwan.

"Aw, shit," said Sanchez. "Mary mother of God."

Antwan was holding himself erect, eyeing Claire with a grim fascination, like one gladiator marveling at another's deadly skills.

Browning walked over to Gustavo's body, glared down at it for a moment, then drew back his boot and kicked the small man in the ribs. Gustavo's limp body rose from the floor and flopped back down, his arms slinging loose. The front of his blue cowboy shirt was ripped open, exposing a meaty mess.

Browning stood above the body and raised his hands to his head and slicked his fingers through his brown hair, once, twice, a third time. Eyes closed, blue veins rising at his temple. A moment later, he turned his eyes to the ceiling and howled till his lungs were empty.

When he'd gathered himself, he wiped his lips on his sleeve. Looking at Claire, his face was pale and shrunken, but his eyes had the fierce glimmer from his football days when he trotted through the stadium tunnel onto the field, readying himself for the clash of bodies, the bruising hits.

Claire came to him and he opened his arms mechanically. Pressing into his warmth, she felt his massive body tremble with such force it seemed the house was quaking around them.

In that moment, in her husband's shuddering embrace, Claire felt an ache of dread and desolation as the enormity of the moment settled. Because she had been the instrument of Earl Hammond's death, however justified her slowness to act might have been, it was very likely she had committed the one unpardonable act that would forever alter her marriage and her life at the ranch.

"Sweetheart, I'm sorry," she said. "Forgive me please. Oh, God."

Gradually his trembling subsided, and with a long sigh, he released her from his arms. She reached up and smeared the tears from his cheek. With dawning recognition, he stared at her as if she were just now emerging from a heavy mist.

"Call Frisco," he said. Nothing in his voice she could read.

"What?"

"Call my brother. He should hear it from family."

"Frisco?"

"We'll need him out here. A cop talking to cops, it'll go better."

Claire swallowed but found no words.

"He can run interference. Do his cop thing. Give us advice."

"What kind of interference?" she said.

Browning didn't reply. His eyes had come unmoored from the moment.

"Where's Saperstein?" the governor said.

"Outside," Claire said. "He's dead."

The governor winced and flipped open his phone and began to punch, calling in the rest of the FDLE eight-man security detail stationed at the eastern perimeter of the ranch in compliance with Earl's one-bodyguard rule.

"Call Frisco, Claire."

He flexed his jaw. Those brown eyes she'd fallen in love with, so boyishly adoring, so simple and kind, had narrowed to slits, as though a vengeful resolve had taken possession of him, his mouth assuming a scowl so fearsome, so devoid of mercy it seemed the very act of gazing upon the world had become all but unbearable.

"All right," she said. "All right. I'll call him."

She glanced past Browning at the bodies of the two dead men. One, a trusted friend, the other, her surrogate father, a man of such quiet dignity he'd been Claire's inspiration and her lifeline these last six years.

More glass tinkled against the stone floor. Claire looked up at the high sill where the last shards were breaking loose and dropping like sleet from an unearthly sky.

SIX

"THORN? WHAT KIND OF GODDAMN name is that?"

"It's his name. His last name. What difference does it make what his name is? The other one's named Rusty. That bother you, too? They cohabitate."

"She's a girl?"

"A woman, forty-five. Middle-aged."

"Rusty's a boy's name," Jonah said. "A girl with a boy's name—I hate that kind of freaky shit. It's aberrant. Rusty and Thorn. I don't like these two already. They piss me off, names like that."

Three in the morning, Jonah and Moses Faust were in the Prius rolling onto the last exit ramp as the turnpike petered out and dumped them in tiny, redneck Florida City, a good hour's drive from their base at Coquina Ranch.

Moses drove. Jonah had his hand out the window, doing wing-dips with his Glock as they passed through the franchise strip. McDonald's, Burger King, all closed up, the gas stations dark and shuttered. He'd been plugging away at speed signs, mile markers, and billboards whenever one flashed into view. Hitting about as many as he missed, which was damn fine shooting at seventy-five miles per hour.

His iPod was connected to the sound system, pumping out a Navajo death chant, the kind of transcendental eerie shit he listened to after a kill.

"That's inviting trouble," Moses said. "State trooper sees the muzzle flash, we're busted."

"Like I'm afraid of some hick cop? Bring him on. Let's see what he's made of."

Jonah let off two more rounds at a Budweiser billboard. Drilled the top of the twenty-foot bottle. Two other bullet holes already marked the sign from some rival sharpshooter.

Moses snapped up the phone, the silver one with international coverage. Pressing it to his ear with his left shoulder, using both hands to scribble on the pad that was clipped to the dash, steering with his knee.

"Too low," Moses said. "The Danny Rollin is already at three hundred." He waited while the client weighed the new price. Then Moses said, "Okay, you're down for three seventy-five. Bidding's over at noon tomorrow. Check in around ten."

Six phones in all. Five items being auctioned at any given time. Most of the bidding happened on their website, new offers streaming in all day and night from keyboards around the world. But there were some clients too paranoid to trust the Internet. Nut jobs who favored the phone. So Moses accommodated them. As it turned out, a lot of the phone freaks were their biggest buyers.

The MoJo brothers made their living purveying murder memorabilia. Specializing in Oldie Goldie shit, like the Danny Rollin item, a crime-scene photo smuggled out of the police files up in Gainesville. Color shot of one of the decapitated coeds, her head posed in front of three mirrors, syrupy goo dripping down the front of the dressing table. A twisted smile on her dead lips.

In all, Rollin, the sick fuck, confessed to killing and mutilating eight victims. Probably there were more, hacked-up scraps of them buried in the Florida woods.

The Faust boys paid two-fifty for the photo from a crime-scene technician who was funding his meth habit by stealing photos from case files. They had a dozen sources like that spread around the United States and Canada. The rest of their product arrived word-of-mouth, people calling at all hours. "Hey, dude, you want to buy an unedited video of the cops at 8213 West Summerdale Avenue, prying up the floorboards and digging in the crawl space beneath the house of John Wayne Gacy?" Moses and Jonah sold that video last month, $284 to some waitress in Omaha. She was a phone-in. Kept yacking away like she thought Moses and Jonah shared her twisted addiction for serial-killer paraphernalia.

Just because they sold gruesome shit didn't mean they were whack-jobs. It was a business, like collecting garbage, hosing out Port-o-Johns. Didn't mean you wallowed in the product. Yeah, okay, now and then Jonah glanced at the photos and shit that passed through his hands, purely professional curiosity, trying to see what the clients got all hot about. And yeah, it happened once or twice, his fantasies kicking in, he found himself looking at a photo, wondering how it felt, cutting off a cute blonde's head, placing it neatly in front of those mirrors.

Jonah didn't see how it automatically made you a twisted fuck if you wondered a little, let your imagination play.

Business kills, like the one Jonah did earlier in the evening, that was different. Nothing psycho about it. Bang, it's over, collect your pay. Quick and slick. None of that creepy weirdo shit, playing with the bodies, having sex with corpses. Jonah was a straight-ahead bad boy, certified outlaw, nothing twisted about it.

Moses ended the silver phone call, dropped it in the cup holder, got the blue phone to his ear, scribbled on the pad some more, taking down the new bid.

Twenty-eight years old, two older than Jonah, Moses Faust was a fine-looking man in the classic *GQ* mode. He went six-one, one-ninety. On that score, Jonah got shorted by a few inches and fifty pounds. Moses was ripped from pumping iron in their home gym. He had the abs, the biceps, the quads. Not Jonah. No matter how many protein shakes he guzzled, how much iron he cranked, he stayed slinky as a coyote.

Cool Moses got his thick black hair styled. While Jonah went with the shaved, Dalai Lama, end-of-days look. A minute with the razor, he was done, ready to roll. No shampoo, no comb. Bing-bing-bing.

All right, so Jonah didn't have the slick-cool thing going on like Moses, and dammit, he didn't have the gaunt, weathered tough-guy face he truly, deep down craved. Newman, McQueen, Eastwood, one of those. What he had was his dead mother's bone structure, way too delicate. Narrow face. Lips puffy and red. So puffy, he'd once investigated lip-reduction surgery to bring his mouth in line with his straight nose, sharp cheekbones, the Aryan ideal. But after he saw the medical brochure, he dropped it. Jonah Faust was not into pain.

Not like Moses. Hell, you could drive nails into his brother's fingers and the guy wouldn't flinch. Hang him on a cross, go ahead, crucify his ass, he'd just look at you with those quiet blue eyes and be like, "What's the big deal? How's this make you a god, hanging on a cross?"

Absorbing punishment was a skill Moses acquired as a kid from standing up to their old man. Putting his body out there to protect Jonah from the drunken abusive prick. Moses, the shield, getting thumped and bloodied so Jonah didn't have to.

Moses, Moses, Moses. Total opposite of Jonah. The guy was deep down tranquil and unruffled as a stoner on a bong full of hash. He never sweated or fretted, just breezed along with a free-flowing, untroubled cool. Today on their mission of homicide, Moses had on a blue button-down no-iron shirt, creased khakis, woven leather belt, and shiny loafers like here he was, some stockbroker driving to a bed-and-breakfast in Vermont for the long weekend.

Moses Faust was the dapper ying to Jonah's rat-fuck yang.

Jonah dressed like a scumbag. Wore the same black jeans day in, day out, till they got crusty and impossible. Same gray sweatshirt with the arms hacked off. Bought a fresh one when the armpits went rank. White high-tops, no socks, a long green bungee cord for a belt. His fashion statement to the world: Fuck if I care.

As the car zipped south into the Keys, Jonah drew the Glock inside, reloaded from the ammo box between his legs. Barely got it out in time to blast at a couple of speed signs. Missed the first, clipped the second.

"I didn't tell you," Moses said. "We can't just drill these two and walk off. Thorn and the lady, they've got to evaporate. Can't have a crime scene, a big investigation. Keep this one below the radar."

"Thorn and Rusty—just saying their names makes my stomach go nasty."

Moses looked his way, eyes calm, staying in the zone.

Jonah said, "Please tell me this doesn't involves digging graves, 'cause I hate to break it to you, dude, you can't bury bodies in the Keys. The ground, it's coral rock. There's no fucking dirt."

"Yeah, but there's boats," Moses said. "Lots of deep water."

Jonah leaned forward to see if Moses was yanking his leash, but no, he was serious.

"Get real, Mo. I'm not taking any boat ride. That's the end of that story."

Jonah was cursed by his name, its Biblical aspects. Since he was five and first discovered he was named for a guy famous for being trapped inside a stink-ass whale, Jonah'd been having nightmares, waking up gasping, clawing at the air.

A name could fuck you up. It was predestination. Nothing you did to deserve it. You just got up one morning when you were an innocent kid, and you discovered this weird-ass name stuck to you forever. Shaping your fate.

That name was why he stayed away from the ocean, boats, all that nautical bullshit. If you didn't go near the water, you stayed out of the whale.

Moses scribbled down the bid he'd taken on the blue phone, and dropped that one in the ashtray.

The red phone warbled. The badass phone, a text message coming in. The guy loved texting.

Jonah picked it up.

"Let me guess," Moses said, " 'WTFUB'?"

"Yeah," Jonah said. "You want me to hit him back?"

Moses nodded, and Jonah shot him a "Jstaboutthr."

The phone trilled and another message sprang up.

"What now?"

Jonah had to squint in the bad light. "Says skip the woman, just do the guy. Thorn only."

Jonah thumbed him back: "Ys dat?"

Waited for a minute, then the phone warbled.

"What'd he say?"

" 'FAF.' That's a new one. You know it?"

"Fire and forget," Moses said. "It's military. Refers to one of the new missiles. Damn thing's so accurate you press the button, send it on its way, get back to your bowl of cereal. He's telling us to do the job, stay out of his business."

"I like that. FAF."

The phone trilled again.

" 'MOS,' " Jonah said. "Mom over shoulder. He's got to go."

"Now he's fucking with you. He's not going to tell you anything."

Another warble and he signed off with his usual: "BEG."

"We work for one pissed-off primate," Jonah said. "Fucker has blood-pressure issues, needs some good Navajo flute music to calm his ass down."

"It's his deal, Jonah. We're just his crew. That's how he works."

"It's bullshit. Treating us like punks. We need to tell the asshole we want to see the big picture or no job."

"Oh, yeah? You want to negotiate? Go in the man's house, have a face-off? That man's tough enough to wear pink."

Jonah thought about that. Picturing a showdown, Jonah muscling up close, getting into the guy's breath. But he had to close his eyes and shake off the image because the man's giant hands were reaching out to wrap around Jonah's throat, lifting him off the floor.

To clear his mind, Jonah aimed out the window, fired twice into the darkness. That fucking goliath was cold and cruel. A big evil fuck with the morals of a zombie.

The silver phone rang again and Moses nabbed it, flipped it open, got the bid down on the pad, and snapped it shut.

"Offered six-fifty for the Manson drawing," he said. "Wants the prison envelope, too."

"What do we have in it?"

"Paid a hundred." Moses shook his head. "These people continually amaze me. Charlie Manson, that soda's lost its fizz. Hippies, dopers, bunch of Hollywood bimbos. Cobwebs all over that shit."

"No, man, you're missing the point here. Manson is fucking Elvis. Guy never goes out of style. Those eyes, hell, nobody has eyes like that anymore. Not Dahmer, Bundy, Speck, Berkowitz, Hannibal Lechter. They're all putzes. One look at their gummy eyes, Jesus, they're not in Manson's league."

Moses glanced over at him.

"Hannibal Lechter is fiction," he said. "You know that, right? You know the difference between real people and people in movies?"

"I was talking about their eyes, man. Their freaking eyes."

"You're still wired, aren't you?"

"Maybe a little, sure. Whacking cops, that cranks me up. Cops, all big and tough. I didn't like that guy's name either. Saperstein."

"You didn't need to empty the clip. That was excessive."

"I was making sure. Little gun like that, big FDLE man, coming on so bad."

"I worry about you, Jonah. The way you are after. Like you dig it. It lights you up."

"No worries, man. It's work, that's all. I take pride in it." Jonah looked out his window for a few seconds, then turned to his brother.

"Okay, maybe there's some afterglow. But it's like Shaq post-game. He takes a while to come back to Earth. Hits the bars, chills with his boys, has some pussy. I'm like the Shaq of whack."

"Don't start enjoying it. That's all I'm saying."

Then Moses went silent. That's what he did sometimes. It used to drive Jonah nuts, the way he'd pull the plug and go quiet. Now when he did it, Jonah pretended to zone out, too, like he was doing the same thing, going off into a cloud of nothingness. Except he wasn't. It was fake. Jonah didn't have an off button. He couldn't do the calm thing. Hell, he could barely do the sleep thing. He was wired funny. It was next to impossible to shut down the turbine inside him.

A couple of miles blew past, with the GPS speaking in a woman's voice, guiding them through the darkness. Jonah did banks and dives with his Glock, getting off a few fruitless shots. Blowing the bark off some mangrove bushes out in the dark.

"How much we getting for this?"

"Two thousand."

"You're kidding me," Jonah said. "The FDLE guy, too?"

"Two thousand for the whole thing."

"That's piss poor."

"People do worse shit for free every day of the week."

"Yeah, but Moses, we need to get our asses into the entrepreneurial mind-set. Been like five years the man's stringing us along. We do his heavy lifting, take the risks, and we're still a couple of dumbass wage slaves. Guy's taking advantage. Team MoJo deserves better."

"That two thousand will buy some groceries."

Jonah curved the wing of his hand so it came skidding back into the car. He upped the window.

Beside him, Moses braked hard and cut the wheel. Ahead, springing up in the halogen glow, were all the tacky dive shops of Key Largo—the gas stations, seashell stores, sub shops, everything closed up, the highway empty—then Moses swung left, making a U-turn onto another road, this one darker and surrounded by woods on either side. Snake country. Crazy-ass armadillos, frogs big as pumpkins, and other unspeakable creatures lived out there in the mangroves and weeds.

The GPS told them to turn right in one mile.

Jonah said, "I'm catching the vibe. Approaching mayhem."

They went a quarter of a mile, a thought coming to Jonah all at once, a flash of otherworldly inspiration.

"Listen, Mo. I got a what-if for you."

Moses was silent, waiting.

"What if we don't kill this guy?"

"Then we don't get paid."

"But, I mean, what if he disappears the way our man wants, but he's not actually dead? We got him prisoner."

"And why would we do that?"

"So we could grill his ass till we find out what the deal is. Then we figure a way to leverage that into a major payday."

Moses was silent. He drove, ignored two phone calls, drove some more.

"Screw our benefactor? The man's been good to us."

"He's exploiting us. Using us for scut work. We're his bitches, man."

"No way. Too dangerous."

"Just think about it. We interrogate this guy. Find out what kind of scam he's into, why our guy wants him terminated. Turn that into a bargaining chip. For once in our fucking lives we negotiate from a position of strength."

Moses was silent. Driving slower.

"That could work, right? How's the big guy know the difference? This Thorn creature disappears. We get our two grand. Once we have the lowdown, we use what Thorn tells us to better our position."

"You talking about blackmail?"

"I'm talking about finding a way to cut ourselves into whatever's going down."

"What if Thorn doesn't know why he's being whacked?"

52

"He'll know. Shit, everybody knows why they're being whacked."

"But if he doesn't?"

"Okay. So if he comes up empty, I snuff him later, and nobody's the wiser."

Moses continued to slow. Then he looked over at Jonah.

"This from some TV show you saw?"

"It came from my own freaking creative lizard brain, man. I'm no plagiarist."

Moses was down to five miles an hour. The electric motor kicking in. The whir of it humming through the floor.

"Maybe you're not crazy," Moses said. "Or maybe I'm losing it."

"So you like it?"

"Keep him where?"

"You want to work those phones the rest of your life, Moses? 'Cause that's what I see. Scribble down this bid, that bid. A hundred here, a hundred there. Paying our room and board from taking those hunters out to shoot big dumb animals. Just scraping by."

"Keep him where?"

"The pit," Jonah said.

"The pit?"

"Place I found near the cabin, back in the second pasture. I told you about it. I cut a hatch in the wood cover to see what was down there, you know that place."

"Put him in the pit."

"Yeah, dump him down there, we can interrogate the guy to our heart's content. Our own private Guantanamo."

The voice on the GPS told them to turn right in two hundred feet. Moses slowed the Prius, made the turn, heading up a dark bumpy road.

"Say yes, Moses. Come on. You know it's a good idea."

There were a dozen cars parked along the shoulder. Junkers and a few nicer models, a couple of pickups, some Harleys.

Ahead about a hundred yards the night was lit up. There was the thump of a heavy bass, rock music, loud speakers, a band maybe.

"Somebody's having a party," Moses said.

"Thought this guy was a hermit, just him and the girl out in the woods."

"Apparently hermits have parties."

"Your destination is in one hundred feet," said the GPS.

"This could be a very dumb idea," Moses said. "This could come back to bite us in the nutsack."

"You have arrived at your destination," the GPS woman said.

"We've arrived," Jonah said, grinning, and put his fist up for a bump.

Moses shook his head one more time.

Then he raised his fist and went knuckle to knuckle with his kid brother.

SEVEN

THORN WAS DUMPING ICE FROM plastic bags into the washtub where the last of the Red Stripe bobbed in tepid water. He was in the kitchen next to the tile-covered island where all the chips and dips and carrots and celery and burgers and buns and fried grouper fingers and shrimp and fish tacos and condiments had been set out neatly a few hours ago. Now the kitchen was in disarray. Since sunset dozens of people had wandered in and out, helping themselves to food and drink—not many neat freaks among them. Friends, and friends of friends, and complete strangers who heard about the party on Key Largo's coconut telegraph.

Thorn was an hour past tipsy. The walls were not yet rotating, the floor was still solid beneath his feet, but there was a wavery blur at the edge of his vision, and he was no longer capable of complex sentence structures. Not that they were ever his forte.

Outside, next to the lagoon, in the golden glow from a dozen mosquito torches, Rusty was doing a courtly waltz with Sugarman. Three guys were swaying around them like moths worshipping a flame. This was Rusty Stabler's Circe routine, turning a lot of reasonably intelligent males into snorting goofballs. Everyone was smiling. Good for her. Good for Rusty.

An hour earlier, Thorn had stepped up onto a chair and clinked his beer bottle with a spoon, and when the rabble quieted down, he toasted Rusty's incredible smarts and good looks and good humor and good everything else he could think of. A long list of fine attributes.

It went over well, with people interrupting, making fun of him, making fun of the idea of a toast, making fun of his speaking publicly in the first place. Everyone laughed a lot, and Thorn finished the toast to a wild cheer and whistling. Rusty came over to him and gave him a full-frontal wet kiss, and there was more hooting and poking fun at Thorn for the public display of affection, for being sentimental, and for being happier than anybody had seen him in quite a while. Thorn had been toying with the idea of making a public marriage proposal, getting down on one knee. He had the two-carat diamond solitaire ring in his pocket, something Kate Truman, his adoptive mother, had left him. It was there just in case he worked up the nerve.

But everything was so helter-skelter, with so much ridicule, jeering, whistling, and hooting, Thorn believed it might be better if he saved the proposal till later, when he and Rusty were alone. More romantic. And just in case she said no. Given Thorn's history, all the disasters and upheavals he'd attracted, a woman with any sense would turn him down. And Rusty had a lot of sense. So he decided to wait. Sober up, do it in the bedroom with the lights low. If she refused, she refused. They could work out some other kind of arrangement. It didn't have to be marriage. Nothing magical about a legal document. Thorn didn't have a single legal document to his name as it was. Another good reason to wait and do it later.

After his speech he danced with Rusty. They danced slow, and they danced fast, then slow some more and even slower. Sweat soaked through his blue-and-yellow shirt with the oversized hibiscus flowers on it, his one and only party shirt. Sugarman broke in to take his turn, not with Rusty, but with his pal Thorn. Thorn went with it, the two of them putting on a giddy show, spinning and dipping. Sugar and he pranced around for about half a minute before someone shoved Thorn from behind and sent him splashing into the lagoon. He swam around out there and took more shit from his friends and their friends and a lot of complete strangers who'd shown up for the free beer.

He guessed it was a good party. He hadn't thrown a lot of parties over the years, and this was by far the loudest, the biggest. As the night wore on, more people were pushed into the lagoon, including Rusty.

All those wet dresses and blouses and T-shirts clinging to those pretty breasts and rounded hips changed the atmosphere. A few couples slinked away into the shadows and came back later, smiling and holding tight to each other. Someone cranked up the music, which seemed to drive the mosquitoes back into the mangroves. A couple of Monroe County sheriff deputies showed up, not to shut down the party, because Thorn's nearest neighbor lived a long way off, and that neighbor, a retired math professor, was at the party enjoying himself with a couple of younger ladies, but the deputies were off duty and had heard about the party and wanted to visit with Sugarman, their old buddy. And they wanted free beer.

So it went on like that. Good music, a lot of old favorites, country and classic rock. That reggae tune Thorn liked, "Bad boys, bad boys, whatcha gonna do when they come for you?" Some Mary Chapin Carpenter, Dixie Chicks, a few ancient Beatles, Stones, Bruce Springsteen, Marley. Some more country, Lucinda Williams, that daughter of a poet and a poet herself. A few cuts of Crosby, Stills, and Nash and a little ZZ Top. Around midnight a Jimmy Buffett number came on, a song from back in the day when the guy still had that gritty edge, before he got so slick he became the John Denver of the Keys. For three minutes everyone became parrotheads and sang along to that one.

Now Thorn was ready for all of them to go home. It was nearly three in the morning and he believed he'd celebrated just exactly the right amount.

He liked his friends and he liked the strangers and he liked all the noise and commotion, but now he was ready for it to end, but the party wasn't thinning out and had the look of one that winds up with everyone sitting on the edge of the lagoon, or swimming in it and watching the sun come up over the Atlantic. A party where you had to wake people up who'd passed out in the grass and the beach chairs and on the living room couch, wake them up tomorrow at noon and hand them aspirin and a glass of water and send them on their way. Probably better than forcing them out on the overseas highway drunk in the middle of the night. Probably better than that.

Thorn dumped the remaining bags of ice into the washtub and opened another Red Stripe, definitely the last he was going to allow himself that night, and he was headed outside to join the fray when two guys blocked his way, then came into the kitchen, making him walk backward three or four steps.

One athletic, good-looking guy, the other was slinky with a shit-eating grin. He hadn't seen them around Key Largo, and he was pretty sure he hadn't seen them earlier at the party. Arriving too late for anything good to come of it.

The shit-eater was blinking against the kitchen lights like some troll who'd just emerged from under his dark bridge.

"You Thorn?"

Thorn said yes, he was in fact a man by that name.

"Girl outside said you were in here. Blonde with tits big as Ohio."

"That's Squirrelly Shirley," Thorn said. "Runs a dress shop. You in the market for a dress?"

The shit-eater grinned and looked over at the big guy.

"Oh, boy, this one's cute."

"You, on the other hand," Thorn said, "are not so cute."

Thorn was watching the athletic one amble around the kitchen, searching for something. He was looking at the appliances and the knickknacks with a possessive air, like a shopper who could afford anything in the store.

"Party's winding down," Thorn said.

"No, it's not," the runty guy said. "We just got here. We're the party now."

The athletic one, muscular shoulders, dressed like a schoolteacher on the first day of class, picked up a notepad that Rusty used for grocery lists.

He took a pen from the glass jar on the kitchen counter.

"What's going on?" Thorn said.

"Name's Moses," the big one said. "You have permission to call me that."

Moses set the pad on the counter in front of Thorn. He set the pen beside it.

"And I'm Jonah," the other one said. "Like the fucker in the whale."

"You need to write a note," Moses said.

"A note?"

"Yeah, a note to your friend Rusty. Apologize. Tell her you'll see her later, maybe a few days from now. You went on a trip or whatever."

"What do you guys want?"

"I know what he should write," Jonah said. "Yeah, yeah, this is perfect."

He picked up the pen and held it out to Thorn.

Thorn was drunk, prickly, ready for bed, not focusing a hundred percent. Maybe not even fifty. He'd taken an instant dislike to these two but was trying to remind himself he was the master of ceremonies. The host of a party and he'd assumed all the responsibilities of that position. The primary responsibility as he saw it was to be tolerant of friends and strangers, whoever showed up.

So there he was, trying to be polite long after he'd stopped feeling polite.

"A girl left me this exact note one time," Jonah said. "It's good. It's just right for this occasion."

"Take the pen, Mr. Thorn," Moses said.

Thorn took the pen. For an instant he thought he should stab the big guy in the face with it and see where that led.

"Now write this," Jonah said. " 'I just need some time alone to think.' Use those words. 'I just need some time alone to think.' Then sign your name."

"What the hell is this?" Thorn said.

The slinky guy, Jonah, lifted his gray sweatshirt with one hand and whipped a chunky black handgun from his waistband and showed it to Thorn.

"Write those words."

"I just need some time alone to think." Moses was looking out the kitchen windows, checking the crowd. "Do it, Thorn. Do it now."

Thorn bent over the pad and scribbled the words. This wasn't a joke. That was clear. But his reasoning skills were so impaired, as hard as he tried, he couldn't think of a good reason not to write the words he'd been ordered to write. So he did.

"The bitch that left me that note," Jonah said, "I never heard from her again. She's out there somewhere, still thinking."

"Now, where's the back way out of here?" Moses said. "So nobody gets hurt. We wouldn't want that. People getting shot through the heart at a nice party like this. People dying left and right."

Thorn led them through the length of the house, out the front door, outside into the darkness. No longer quite so drunk. Looking for an escape. Looking for a way out of this that wouldn't endanger anyone at the party. Shoved along by the slinky guy, poked in the spine with the unfunny end of a pistol.

The two men with Old Testament names marched him away from his house. Outside in the shadowy drive Moses told him to halt and to raise his hands. Thorn complied and Moses patted him down and found nothing in his pockets—no guns, no knives, no leather saps, not a wallet or a key chain.

As Thorn was lowering his hands Jonah made a huffing noise like the chuckle of an addled child, and a second later he cracked Thorn in the skull, and Thorn's knees sank, while far away Springsteen crooned on behalf of all the ordinary Joes.

Floating about ten feet above the scene, the part of Thorn that was still conscious watched his body lifted and carried, then wedged into a tight place. For some indeterminate period he viewed a spool of the evening's events, disconnected images and snatches of conversation, the lagoon, the mosquito torches, his friends and some strangers splashing drunkenly in the warm water, Thorn giving his speech in Rusty's honor, suffering the good-natured ridicule. He saw himself writing a note, words on a pad of paper. A note for Rusty. Though he couldn't remember exactly what he'd written.

Sometime later he came awake in the cramped backseat of a small car.

He might have been missing in action for five minutes or an hour. His head was hooded by rough material that smelled vaguely like a feed sack. The hood was held in place by an elastic cord lashed around his throat. Behind his back his hands were so numb he could not tell what material the cuffs were fashioned from. Plastic, steel, leather, or something else entirely.

For a while he tried to focus on the turns the car made. That's what you were supposed to do when you were kidnapped. He remembered that much.

They seemed to travel in one direction for many miles, maybe as long as an hour. No doubt heading north on US 1 back to the mainland, then after that, there were too many choices to be sure.

The passenger window was open and the rush of wind hid sounds from beyond the car. Three or four times he heard the crack of gunfire close by, then the voice of the big man speaking. Afterward there was no more shooting.

Only later, much later, when the car turned off the pavement and began to jolt across the washboard ruts of a back road, Thorn got a sense of their location. Through the rough fabric he smelled the fertile night air of the Florida countryside, pine resins and grasses, pennyroyal and sage, the faint honeyed taste of slash pine. And as the car slowed to a crawl, he made out what he believed was the jug-o-rum croak of a bullfrog and a series of low whoots that might be a great horned owl.

Impossible to pinpoint from a whiff of breeze and shred of sound, but his senses were telling him they'd landed somewhere in South Florida's interior, out in the untamed pineland well inland from the coast, a vast area north of the Everglades that was home to cattle ranches and sod and tomato farms and sugarcane fields, a region so remote, so desperately lonely that the closest shopping mall or full-sized grocery store was hours away toward the bright lights of the coastline. The only prominent structures in that wild place were the occasional church or slaughterhouse.

The car came to a stop and the men got out. Neither of them spoke as they muscled him from the car and prodded him across rough terrain studded with rocks and scratchy plants that scuffed his bare ankles. At one point he tripped over a stone and pitched forward but the larger man caught him and hauled him upright, then shoved him onward. In that brief contact, Thorn got a sense of the man's strength, and there was nothing comforting in that knowledge.

He shuffled ahead till one of them gripped his shoulder.

"My, my, Mr. Thorn, what an obedient Boy Scout you are," Jonah said. "You salute and stand at attention. So far you're a model prisoner. What do you say let's keep it that way? Get a few extra merit badges, make Eagle Scout before we're done."

Thorn was working on a snappy comeback, when the big one began to loosen the binding on his hands.

"Now," Jonah said, "here's what's going to happen."

When the cuffs were off, Thorn opened and closed his fists, trying to pump life back into his fingers.

"Thorn, you're headed into the belly of the whale, and that's where you'll stay until that big fish's digestive juices have tenderized you a bit. You following me?"

Thorn's hands tingled. Not yet alive.

Groggy, his throat so parched he wasn't sure he could speak,

Thorn squinted through the burlap hood, but all he could make out was a shadowy hulk a few feet in front of him. The big guy, Moses. Which put the shit-eater behind.

"Now we're going to take off your blindfold because I need that bungee cord back. Then you and the whale are going to get acquainted."

"What do you guys want? Money?"

"Oh, give me a break. You're not a nickel better off than me and my brother. Where you gonna get money?"

"This isn't a kidnapping? You're not looking for a ransom?"

"What do you think, Mo? We looking for a ransom?"

"Put him in the hole. Enough of this shit."

"Let me ask you one thing, Thorn. What kind of business dealings you been involved in lately?"

"I don't know what you're talking about."

"Let me give you some names, see if any of them ring a bell."

"Do this later," Moses said. "Put him down."

"Look, face it," Thorn said. "You snatched the wrong guy."

Behind him, Jonah unlooped the elastic cord holding the hood in place, then whipped it off Thorn's head.

To his left a brilliant red seam burned along the horizon. And in the high branches of nearby pines, the dim haze of dawn was spreading like pink smoke.

The breeze carried the fetid musk of bog water and the black mud of marshland. He'd been right about the approximate location. The timing confirmed it. Leaving his house in Key Largo a little after three, arriving at this desolate place at dawn. They were somewhere north of the Everglades, close to Lake O.

Thorn blinked. His vision was blurry, and numbness still prickled his hands. He faced the bigger man, maybe an inch or two taller than Thorn, and bulkier by thirty or forty pounds.

"All right," Thorn said. "You want something. I'm ready to deal."

"The whale's waiting," Jonah said from behind him.

Thorn pivoted and swung at the smaller man. He meant it to be a sharp, efficient jab, but his arm was still numb and the punch looped slow and lazy. And Jonah was lizard quick, ducking away with a foot to spare.

Before Thorn could make another move, a chopping blow against the back of his neck ignited a display of fireworks onto a black velvet sky. The ground wobbled and warped into another dimension.

In a scalding flood the long night's beer rose into his throat, and he bent forward to empty his gut.

While his head was bowed, one of the brothers planted a foot on his butt and sent him sprawling forward, two feet or three, until he stumbled onto a wooden platform, then the ground vanished beneath him and he plunged into blackness. He clawed at the air, raked his fingertips across a pitted wall, saw it was no use, and tried to soften his body for impact.

But he was disoriented and the drop was longer than he expected. His butt and left hip slammed against the floor, his lungs emptied, and his skull whacked some brutal outcropping, and in one brilliant bulb-flash of pain, Thorn was delivered from his body.

EIGHT

IN THE FRAIL DAWN LIGHT filtering into the horse barn, Sergeant Frisco Hammond walked from stall to stall, handing out peppermint sticks. He'd started sneaking candy to the horses a month ago, now there was no turning back. He couldn't bring himself to disappoint them.

Down the line he went, Apollo, Serenade, Major, Striker, the big athletic Morgan, fast and strong. All the horses alert to his arrival, expectant nickerings, each of them extending their heads, slurping up the striped cane with their gentle lips. Looking for more.

Last he came to Big Girl. Eleven hundred pounds, a big-chested beauty. As usual she hung back from the gate, observing him with those neutral eyes. He'd been married to eyes like those for two years before he admitted he couldn't awaken her. Still he tried like hell to keep it together, honeymoon weekends, counseling sessions, a fling at dirty movies. They never argued, but there was no heat either. Two long years until they both agreed it was pointless and broke off. Sheila was her name, and she had Big Girl's eyes. Bland affect, he'd heard it called, aloof and untouchable.

Big Girl was a roan Tennessee walker, seventeen hands tall, with a long neck, sloping shoulders. She fit the standard in all the physical ways. Large head, refined bone structure, small ears. She had the short back, long mane and tail, strong coupling and hind quarters, and carried herself with a gliding gait.

A nearly perfect horse, until you looked into the sad liquid depths of her eyes. The flat stare, the empty watchfulness. She wasn't rank. Not an aggressive bucker or biter like some twitchy rodeo horse. That you could fix. Enough time and training with constant reassurance. Several of the horses in the barn had been jumpy when they arrived; now every one of them was doing daily patrols with no difficulty.

Before any horse could work the street, months of training were required to make them bombproof—safe and reliable. Exposing them to sudden noises, backfires, barking dogs, car horns, siren whoops. Then came the harder tests, the visual ones. Plastic cups blowing along the ground, a tumbling sheet of newsprint, dirtbikes flashing by, a flock of birds exploding into flight, cats, dogs, other critters let loose in front of them. All the while keeping the horses calm, comforting them, dismounting to pick up the sheet of newspaper and bring it over to the horse so he could see it was not a monster. In time, even the spookiest of them adjusted. Eventually all would even learn to tolerate the shooting range, with officers firing handguns off their backs. Every single horse, in his five years as head of the mounted unit, had come around.

All except Big Girl.

None of the other officers would ride her. Something didn't feel right. She was balky, unpredictable. She reared, or backed away at some approaches, dipped and jumped sideways. The other men simply refused to trust their safety to Big Girl. The horse was damaged. Even Julia thought it was hopeless.

Down at the east end of the barn, Julia Scarborough, the stable girl, was mucking a stall. She'd grown up with horses, ran a riding school out on the edge of the Glades, and only came into the city a few hours every day to sweep up and do a few jobs around the barn and grounds to keep her medical insurance going.

Julia headed his way, eyes down, something on her mind. Kinky brunette hair, tan face and arms. She had the kind of face Frisco liked: good cheekbones, dark eyes, lush mouth. Some gypsy blood. For the last few months she'd been dating one of the homicide guys, so Frisco was keeping his distance.

"You have a good Turkey Day?"

"Whipped up some arroz con pollo," Frisco said. "Fried plantains."

"So," Julia said, done with small talk. "You're not carrying your cell?"

"It's in the office. Why?"

"What good is a cell if you never turn it on?"

"I use it to call out," he said. "Somebody wants to talk, they leave a message."

"Yeah, well, you had several of those on the office line," she said. "From your sister-in-law. First one came in last night, eleven-thirty. Ten calls, eleven. Last one was just a while ago. She said she tried your cell, left messages there, too."

Hammond nodded.

"She said it was urgent."

"You talk to her?"

"No, it's on voice mail. I saved the messages. Urgent. Code red."

"Claire said that? Code red?"

"No, I'm interpreting. She sounded desperate. Worse than the other times."

Frisco looked back at Big Girl. The horse was staring at the side of her stall, trying to ignore the two of them.

"I'll call when I get a chance."

"Is your brother smacking her around?"

"How would I know that?"

"If he is, you should go out there and kick his ass. That's a great woman he's got. She's a strong lady. Better than that moron deserves."

"Their marriage is none of my business. And sure as hell isn't any of yours."

"You're chickenshit, Sergeant Hammond. If you'll pardon my candor."

Frisco sighed. Julia and Claire Hammond had never met, but they'd bonded on the phone. Since last September, when Earl Hammond buried his wife of sixty years, Rachel Sue, Claire had been campaigning to get Frisco out for a visit at Coquina Ranch. Reunite the family at least for a Sunday brunch, something that might perk up the old man. She'd enlisted Julia to join the nagging.

"I'm just saying, Sergeant, you should listen to the damn messages. She sounded bad. Crying, verge of hysteria. Something's happened."

"When I get a chance."

"You keep your family at arm's length," Julia said. "What're you afraid of? You'll piss off your little brother, your granddad? Well, hey, guess what? They're already mad. You're not singing from the Hammond hymnal. You live in the big bad city, turned your back on that patch of earth. So see, since they're already pissed, you can't use that as an excuse."

"You're about a mile over the line, Julia. You sure you want to keep going?"

"I've been that woman," Julia said. "Crying out for help. And no one came for me, either. Nobody. And I made a few urgent, code red calls."

Frisco waited. The peppermint was growing sticky in his hand. Julia wasn't going to stop until she was done. She was on the civilian payroll, so he had no real authority over her, and probably wouldn't use it if he had.

"Okay, okay, I'll call later. All right? That make you happy?"

"If you want me happy, call now."

He waved her off. That's enough, back to work.

Julia held her ground, taking a moment to drill him with her dark eyes. When she was done, she shook her head at him, at all men, their willful stupidity.

"Oh, and Lieutenant Rizzo called this morning."

"Yeah? You speak to him?"

"I did. He says to put Big Girl on the street this week. Get her in the rotation or cut her loose. City can't afford a horse that isn't pulling her weight."

With that, Julia turned and marched back down the row of stalls.

Frisco turned to Big Girl, raised his hand slowly so not to frighten her, and held out the peppermint. He clucked his tongue, but she hung back. Eyes on his eyes. Same stare-down every day. She snorted once, holding her head high.

"It's okay, girl. It's good."

He slipped the curled end of the candy cane into his mouth and sucked.

After a wary moment, she stepped forward a foot.

He withdrew the candy, giving his lips a wet smack, then stuck his hand through the stall door a second time. Big Girl came forward another step, lowering her head. He flattened his hand, letting the peppermint lie there.

When she took it, her lips and whiskers were a brisk tickle against his flesh. Not like the gluttonous slurps of the others.

He looked back down the barn to see if the other horses were watching. None were. He snuck a second stick of peppermint through the slats and waited. Big Girl blew out a flutter and ducked her head and whisked the second bribe from his palm. First time she'd had an extra helping. That was progress.

Frisco knew more about how Big Girl got those eyes than how his ex-wife got hers. Big Girl was born on a pharmaceutical ranch in Canada. Her mother was penned in a tiny stall, unable to turn around or lie down in the straw. The mare was repeatedly impregnated and was connected twenty-four/seven to plumbing that collected her urine. That horse urine was the main ingredient in Premarin, a drug used to treat menopausal symptoms. Big Girl was taken from that Premarin mare at birth, stashed in isolation, fed, watered, but only that. Never weaned properly or allowed to learn what mares have to teach. Hence, the eyes. The empty look. An acute lack of mothering.

Big Girl had been liberated from the Canadian farm by some do-good group. Passed along to a family that found her too difficult, passed along again, then last summer she was donated to Miami PD. Hammond asked about her past, but the donor claimed he didn't know. The horse's eyes were wrong; Frisco could see that. But he was one animal short for his troop, so he accepted the gift.

At seven sharp, an hour before his men were scheduled to arrive, Frisco saddled Big Girl and let her wander around the ring while he went back into the office for a last sip of coffee and to get his Glock and radio. He looked at the blinking light on the message machine, then locked up the office and went outside.

These days it was rare for Hammond to go on patrol. He had more than enough chores in the barn. Writing up the daily work schedules, special events assignments, updating the files on stable and horse management. Confirm blacksmith visits, set up vet appointments. Check the tack and feed orders. Make sure the stock of borium-coated shoes was sufficient.

Going riding was dead last on his work sheet. Fifteen years on the force, including a five-year stint on SWAT, and this is what it came down to, making up duty rosters for the Mounted Unit.

It was seven-thirty when he headed Big Girl up Third Street toward Miami PD Headquarters. A northwest wind was kicking trash down the street. Every tumbling cup sent clenches through the mare's sides. But she was walking straight, head high, and the reins were loose in his hand.

Frisco believed, yes, they could do this. They had to do this or he'd have to find a new home for Big Girl. Hammond hated the thought of a fine horse like her going round and round the same dirt ring with squalling eight-year-olds in her saddle.

He moved her under the I-95 overpass. Even early on this holiday Friday, a few cars and trucks were booming overhead. Frisco brought

70

the horse to a halt. A good test—the wind, the highway noise, some early workers barreling into the heart of downtown Miami. The sunlight flickered at the edges of the street like a wildfire racing across the grasslands.

She held her position, waited.

Hammond's plan was to follow Third Street from Lummus Park where the Miami PD horse barn was located, go six blocks east into the skyscraper canyons, and emerge at Bayfront Park. Do a walk around Bayside Marketplace, let the early-morning tourists gawk at her, then loop back by ten or so. Nothing too taxing. With any of the other horses, it would have been a cakewalk. But nobody had ridden Big Girl beyond a block of the barn without her freezing up and having to be bullied back.

He talked to her as they went, kept his voice even and firm. Everything cool. The tension was coming and going in her flesh, but she moved steadily. Two blocks, three. Crossing into new territory.

Then shit, wouldn't you know? A couple of vagrants were crossing the street to pat the horse, make nice. He knew one of them, Jethro Kurtz, a red-haired vet from Idaho who'd wound up in Miami and had been in and out of jail for possession. Aside from being a confirmed crackhead, he wasn't a bad guy.

Hammond raised his hand to wave them off, but stopped himself. This was part of the test. Big Girl had to do this. She had to have a public face. She had to accept strangers, let them draw close, touch her.

With a sloppy, stoned smile, Kurtz held his hand out to Big Girl. She swung to her left, ducked her head, but Frisco rode the spook and got her still.

Kurtz kept coming. Big Girl watched him out of that eye, turning her ears backward in alarm. Frisco spoke to her calmly, patted her neck. She stayed aloof, watchful. No more shying back, which at that moment was about the best Hammond could wish for. Hold her ground, learn that people weren't dangerous.

All the other horses discovered quickly what magical power they wielded. Big Girl had yet to realize she was magnetic. She drew them to her as she had Jethro Kurtz the doper. Like all big horses clopping through that concrete landscape, she had a mysterious ability to awe or intimidate. Twin powers that Hammond saw registered in the faces of everyone he encountered while he was on horseback. Horses struck some psychic chord. That was a big reason the city footed the bill for the mounted unit.

When it came to crowd control, a single horse and rider could do the job of twenty foot patrolmen. Hammond had seen the crowds part, mobs of protestors or spring-break drunks stumbling away in panic. And the other side of the equation was equally important. Community service. Spreading a positive image of Miami PD. Hard to believe, but a cop on horseback ambling through the hood could convert a gang of pissed-off punks into cooing kids, at least for a few minutes. And if Frisco and the horse came back day after day, who the hell knew? One kid might be saved. What was the dollar value of that? Frisco Hammond was fairly sure his own love of horses had saved his ass from one kind of hard time or another.

"I used to have a horse." Kurtz was sliding his hand across her muzzle, then down to her throat latch.

"That right?"

"You don't believe it, but I did. A pony, and when I outgrew that, the old man got me a real horse. An Appaloosa. Big-ass horse. 'Bout as big as this one. You wouldn't know it, looking at me now, but back in the day, I was a rich little fuck."

Frisco removed his sunglasses and wiped them on his shirt sleeve, one-handing the reins. Staying cool, sending Big Girl that signal, calm, calm.

If Kurtz had truly owned a horse, he'd forgotten how to stroke one. He was as clumsy with Big Girl as a teenage boy manhandling his first breast. Thumping her neck, ruffling her forelock.

Frisco felt the horse clench, ready to get the hell away from these psychos, yearning for the safety of the barn. Before he could break away and take Big Girl deeper downtown, the radio on his duty belt squawked.

"Code three, officer needs assistance."

The address of the emergency was two blocks south of his position, a shop on Second Avenue that Hammond knew well. With Miami police headquarters only three blocks farther north, technically he didn't need to respond. There'd be at least a dozen available units in the vicinity.

Still, it would be useful to expose Big Girl to some routine street action, so Hammond reined her left. She resisted, shaking her head against the bit.

Kurtz and his buddy stepped back and Hammond muscled Big Girl around and gathered her into a slow steady walk toward the scene.

When they arrived, three squad cars were blocking the front of Nupi's Bridal Shop. The front door stood open, and one of the three mannequins whose lacy gowns had been yellowing in that window for years had been stripped bare.

Frisco was tight with the Cuban grandmother who ran the place, though he knew the store was a front for a wedding scam. Nupi made a good income matchmaking illegal immigrants with U.S. citizens. She claimed the marriages she arranged beat the national average for longevity.

"What is it?" Hammond asked a patrolman setting up a barricade nearby.

"Dog versus cop."

"Who's the cop?"

"Dominguez. Dog's holding him hostage in there."

"What the hell?"

"Dominquez saw the front door open, goes in to investigate, and a rottweiler's there, the guard dog. It's got him boxed in a back room along with the perp. Dog got Dominguez's pistol away from him. The idiot. Disarmed by a freaking dog."

The patrolman grinned. Raul Dominguez wasn't going to live this one down.

"This is no break-in," Frisco said. "That's Omar, the owner's grandson. He's into gowns, likes to play dress-up. And that dog is Ajax. It's protecting the grandson."

"Well, Ajax is about to get euthanized," the patrolman said. "SWAT's gonna give it a nine-millimeter needle."

"Hold my horse," Frisco said and dismounted.

By the time Hammond sprinted over, SWAT was staging by the front door. Lieutenant Rizzo was on the radio with the team leader.

"Call them off," Hammond said.

Rizzo turned his head and gave Hammond a sour look.

"Call them off. I know that dog. It'll listen to me."

"It's already going down."

Frisco pushed past the rear guard hanging by the door. Inside the store one of the officers swung around to block his way till he recognized who it was.

"Sergeant Hammond. What's the problem?"

"Tell them to stand down."

"Can't do that, sir. It's under way."

Hammond sidestepped a fallen mannequin, ducked past the armored squad stationed at the storeroom doorway.

Two SWAT guys were inside the room, angling carefully for a clear shot at Ajax, who stood behind a glass case full of costume jewelry. Ajax was blocking the exit of Officer Raul Dominguez and Omar Mendez. Omar was seventeen. He was wearing a white lacy wedding gown a size too large for his skinny frame and trying to shield himself behind Dominguez's broad back.

Ajax had the Sig Sauer in his mouth, ribbons of drool hanging from his jaws.

"Hey, Ajax," Hammond said. "Drop it. Drop the gun, boy."

Ajax swiveled his thick neck and eyed Frisco.

"It's okay, boy. Everything's cool. *Tranquilo, perro.*"

"You're fucking up, Hammond. You got no business here."

Frisco walked over to the dog. A growl thickening in its chest.

"Drop it, Ajax. Put it down, boy. Put it down now."

Ajax gazed at Dominguez and Omar. He snorted, then eased down onto the linoleum, turned his head to the side and let the pistol clatter onto the floor.

"Good boy," Frisco said. "That's a good dog, Ajax. Now stay. Stay."

Hammond circled in front of Ajax, moving slow, then scooped up the Sig and handed it to one of the SWAT guys. He took hold of Omar's arm and tugged him out from behind Dominguez. The SWAT guys made room for the three of them to pass, a couple of them muttering.

Hammond led them out of the storeroom and shut the door behind them.

Frisco handed Omar off to the SWAT commander. The kid looked dazed by all the attention, but relieved to be in custody. Behind him Dominguez staggered outside to applause and wolf whistles. He shook his head and stared down at the street as he followed Omar to the patrol car, like a gloomy father of the bride.

Chief Mullaney had arrived to watch the circus and was standing at the rear of the swarm of cops talking to Rizzo. Rizzo caught Hammond's eye and waved him over. Mullaney was wearing a dark blue suit, white shirt with a red tie, but already looked disheveled before breakfast. Bloated face, wind-burned cheeks, and the yellowed eyes of a vodka enthusiast.

"Dominguez lost his piece to a dog?" Rizzo said. "Is that right?"

Hammond nodded.

"Sergeant Hammond," the chief said, "you misplace your cell phone?"

"No, sir. I got it. It's turned off."

"People been trying to get hold of you since last night. You didn't know?"

Hammond shrugged. He was looking around for Big Girl but didn't see her or Officer Maxey.

"What the hell happened to my horse?"

Rizzo said, "Two seconds after you went inside, the fucker bolted, headed north in the direction of the barn. I sent Maxey after her."

"Goddammit."

"Hammond, that horse has no business on the street. Get rid of her."

The chief put his hand on Hammond's shoulder and steered him away from Rizzo's glare.

"You should leave your cell phone on, Hammond. It's department policy."

"There some kind of problem?"

Frisco watched Nupi, wearing a bathrobe, get out of a cab and hustle over to the patrol car where Omar sat crying.

"Look, it's a shitty thing," Mullaney said. "I'm sorry as hell to be the one to break the news. But it's your granddad."

"Yeah? What about him?"

"He was killed last night out at his ranch. Along with two others, including an FDLE agent. It's all over the news."

Frisco thought he'd heard wrong. Earl couldn't be dead. Earl Hammond Jr. wasn't ever going to die. He was as everlasting as a goddamn slab of granite. He was going to outlive Frisco and everyone Frisco had ever known. It was a lie, a mistake, some kind of fucked-up joke.

"Hammond?"

"Who's the third victim?"

"Employee. Hispanic guy. Gustav something."

"Pinto. Gustavo Pinto?"

"Yeah, I believe that's right."

"Governor was there, too," Rizzo said. "His Honor made it out alive, God bless us all. But the media's already gone into major jerk-off mode."

"That's enough, Rizzo," the chief said.

Frisco stared down the avenue where Big Girl had galloped away.

"Take a few days off, Hammond. Take a week. Whatever you need."

Hammond said nothing, still not believing any of it. Earl Hammond Jr. was not dead. Because the Earth was still orbiting the sun and the sky was still overhead, the ground still beneath his shoes. No way was Earl gone. No way in hell.

He turned from the two men, his eyes on the pavement before him as he marched back to the barn.

In the guest bathroom at the lodge, Antwan checked himself in the mirror.

Looking good. Looking sleek and shiny cool. He dabbed a crumb of shmutz from the corner of his right eye, flicked it away.

Out in the hallway the governor was still groaning. Taking it hard for a country boy who must've seen slaughter before, his pet pig or goat getting its throat slashed. Antwan heard him whining to his FDLE people about ten feet from the bathroom, sounding weak and shrill like the man needed a good talking-to, settle him down, take him off to a quiet corner, get up in his face mask and tell him what's what and what's not. Which was one of Antwan's specialties: putting the fear of God in folks.

Sixty years old, a lard-ass, Herbert Sanchez had once been a Florida Gator back in the leather-helmet days. Offensive tackle, big, dumb, and slow. But point him in the right direction, spell it out, Sanchez could do a half-assed job.

And Browning Hammond, he was dumb, too, in a different way. One of those boy wonders, he could recite the phone book, but he never knew for sure if you were praising him or mocking his sorry ass. Tone-deaf motherfucker. And since taking over Coquina Ranch, day to day, the boy acted like he'd grown some big-time cojones, which meant Antwan had to do extra duty making Browning think everything was his own clever idea.

Antwan's first rule for success: Surround yourself with powerful men, but always be the smartest asshole in the room.

He took out his BlackBerry, got his thumbs dancing, shooting a text to his homies, the doofus brothers. A haiku directive. Zinged it on its way: "GTFG."

Get the fuck gone.

Signed it like always, "BEG."

He waited for a minute and nothing came back. Shitheads were offline.

He flushed the john, used the mirror for a last check of his handsomeness.

Then opened the door and headed to his first interrogation of the morning.

BEG on his face. Big evil grin.

NINE

THORN'S HANGOVER WAS WRAPPED IN a concussion with maybe a skull fracture thrown into the mix. Every heartbeat was a clap of thunder echoing off canyon walls. Piano wire coated with crushed glass was wrapped around his skull, biting tighter with every breath. Acid scalded his throat, and its fumes filled his lungs. His mouth was packed with fiberglass and cat fur.

He couldn't move. He was, to the best of his knowledge, lying on his back. Beneath him the ground rolled like a raft at sea. Above him a few slits of sunlight were stabbing through the gaps between wood planks, piercing the shadows, one of them hitting him in the face, searing his optic nerves like a sadist's laser beam.

He wanted to howl, but his own breath gagged him. He wanted to strike back at his tormentor, but there was no one there but him. Thorn, the good host. Thorn, the idiotic party animal. The man who drank himself insensible and let two dimwits abduct him and dump his body into an open grave.

He'd been hurt before, oh yes. He'd been cut and shot and beaten and gouged and sliced across the palm with a butcher's knife. But all that was dewy May flowers and tinkling harp song compared to this.

This was a hangover direct from Dante. This unspeakable gangbang of pain made death appear before him like sweet succor. A gorgeous harlot from hell bent over Thorn to kiss him with her poisonous black lips, bathe him in her rotten breath, insert her long snake-tongue down his throat.

Thorn drifted off and drifted back. From high above, the shafts of light shifted and the lasers singed his right cheek. He floated away and floated back. Each time he resurfaced, the dark-hooded maiden with the lethal lips was hovering above him, smiling down, welcoming him to her brand of love. Come along, she whispered. It's fine here. It's fine and dandy, and everything is made of candy. Come along, sweet boy, come along with me. I'll thrill you beyond any thrill you've known.

Later, an odor woke him. A perfume from somewhere long ago, a woman he once loved, or else some forgotten place or time revived by a wisp of scent. He blinked. The woman in her black cowl and inky lips was no longer attending him.

The slit in the ceiling pointed its death ray farther along the craggy wall. The smell was gorgeous, fruity and rich. He couldn't place it. Couldn't find its name in the crushed memory banks. But he knew he loved it. This wonderful, lip-smacking aroma.

Thorn lay on his back, unmoving, working on the riddle of smell. Ruling out perfumes, for this odor was not complex. No war of sweets and sours and salty tangs. This was elemental and basic and true. This was rich and good and beautiful. These were fumes that raised in him the long swoon of hope.

Then he lulled away into oblivion.

When he woke again, there were tongs digging into his ice-block skull. Someone was lifting his head, but no one was there.

He turned his head to the side and saw what first appeared to be a thick icicle. He blinked and cleared his eyes. No, it was a spike of stone. There were several of them rising like pygmy spears from the floor. Stalagmites? He remembered the word. Calcium carbonate, made from some steady drip from the roof of the pit. The one nearest his head rose more than a foot from the floor, as crooked as a witch's finger.

Then he caught the smell again, oh, God, the wafting scent from the honeyed center of the earth. The caramel nougat, the pungent bliss of the natural world. It was carrying him higher than his body, offering him a chance at salvation.

And then, yes, of course, the answer came to him in a hazy rush. It was water. Of course, the wellspring of goodness. It was green and blue and clear and it filled the air around him with clarity and precision, the scent of water.

Thorn rocked his head off the ground. Took a deep breath, drew in the aroma, drew it into his own broken, ruined body, suffused his bloodstream with it, the blessed scent of water, then he relaxed and slipped back into the melt of dream.

"This isn't Thorn. He wouldn't do this."

"It's his goddamn handwriting," Rusty said. "You know it is."

They were in the living room, Sugarman picking up beer bottles and plastic cups and plates of half-eaten shrimp and cocktail sauce and tossing the recyclables in one can, trash in another—just to have something to do while they made sense of this. It was seven in the morning. Rusty had found the note in the kitchen two hours earlier when the last of the guests were leaving.

When she brought the note to him, Sugarman was policing the area around the dock and the lagoon. He read it several times before it sunk in. Though truly, he couldn't say it had sunken fully yet.

They'd searched the house. All Thorn's clothes were still in the drawers. His shaving stuff and his few toiletries were in the medicine chest. His fishing rods and gear were all accounted for as were the keys to his VW and his stash of ones and fives and a single twenty that he kept rolled up in a rubber band, tucked into the top right drawer next to his cotton briefs. They roamed the two acres, that part of it that was not covered by impenetrable mangroves or stands of gumbo limbo and mahogany. They walked out to the highway, went a half mile in each direction, checking the tall grass for any signs of him. It seemed silly, an overreaction, but Rusty was panicky, so Sugarman went along, trying to settle her nerves.

" 'I just need some time to think.' " Sugarman emptied the dregs of two more beer bottles into the kitchen sink, then came back into the open living room. "Think about what?"

Rusty was slumped on the couch. Her face was drawn and pale, her white sundress wrinkled and stained with grease, mustard and cocktail sauce from hours of carrying platters of food, dishing out burgers and fish tacos and broiled shrimp and corncobs to the dozens of people who'd showed up.

"It's what you say when you're dumping someone, Sugar. You know that."

"You guys been having some kind of problem? Arguing or something?"

She looked up at Sugarman, squeezed out a grimace, and shook her head.

"We were doing fine. No problems. At least that's what I thought."

"Okay, so you notice him being moody or off in his head lately?"

"Just the opposite. Less grumpy than usual. He was happy about the Florida Forever thing. He talked about it all the time. He wanted to come up with more stuff like that. Give money away, become an eco warrior. I haven't seen him so motivated. I mean, really energized. I haven't seen him that way before, ever."

"Yeah, he's been a little giddy about it all."

"Something's wrong, Sugar. Maybe it wasn't the land swap he was giddy about. Maybe it's another woman."

"All right, calm down," he said. "So he could've wandered off. All these people, the crowd, the noise, it probably made him cranky. He had one beer too many and stalked off and curled up somewhere and fell asleep. He'll stumble in any time now, apologizing all over himself."

"The note, Sugar. Why'd he write that if he just wandered off?"

"Look, I saw the way you two were dancing. He wasn't about to dump you."

"I've been on the road so much lately. I've turned into a goddamn business geek. Always up in Sarasota, Tallahassee, doing Bates International bullshit. He met somebody else. Go on, Sugar, you can tell me. He met someone. An old flame. Someone new, that girl Michaela who kept looking at him last night. I saw her."

In the morning light flooding through the French doors, Rusty's flesh was sharply illuminated, and for a moment Sugarman was startled by how pale she'd become. All the hours she'd been spending lately in conference rooms had faded the golden tan she'd had for as long as Sugar could remember. Like so many fishing guides in the Keys, Rusty Stabler had spent years in the relentless sun, up on the poling platform spotting fish for her clients. No matter what she did to protect herself, the rays managed to leave their stain. But in only a few months all that was washed away. A change that perhaps suggested others not so visible.

Sugarman dismissed the thought. Not possible. He knew Thorn. He knew Rusty. They were on solid ground.

"There's no one else," Sugarman said. "Trust me. I'd know if there was. And if I knew, I'd tell you."

She stood up.

"The ring."

"What ring?"

"I noticed it was missing, subconsciously or something, when we were checking his things before."

Sugarman followed Rusty back into the master bedroom. She walked over to the oak chest of drawers that stood between two windows with a view of the mangroves and the blue glimmer of the Atlantic beyond.

"See." She held up the glass ashtray where his car keys were. "This is where he kept it. Kate Truman's wedding ring, a big diamond. It's been sitting here since I moved in. Out in the open. Always in the same place."

Sugarman looked into her eyes, looked back at the ashtray. He'd seen the ring lying there many times. He watched her eyes fumble around the room.

"Maybe someone from the party stole it," Sugar said. "There were people I didn't know. It could be that."

"Nice try," she said.

Rusty sat down on the edge of the quilt, a burgundy and yellow creation Kate Truman had designed and stitched together when Sugar and Thorn were ten years old and becoming friends. Sugarman remembered watching Kate's nimble fingers suture those geometric shapes together. He remembered that simple trouble-free period so clearly because it was the first time he'd been welcomed into a home where both father and mother presided together over an orderly routine, that happy, caring couple who had adopted Thorn at birth greeted Sugar as an instant family member.

"Okay," Sugarman said. "We need to be logical about this."

"Logical, yeah, okay, let's be logical." Rusty set the ashtray back on the chest of drawers. "You start, Sugar. Go ahead, be logical."

"We make a list of everybody at the party. You take half; I take the other half. We track everybody down, see if anybody saw Thorn leave. That's logical."

"Jesus," Rusty said. "What the hell is it with this guy? Things are going good. He's happy. I'm happy. But it never stops with him, does it? One crisis after another. I thought it was going to be different. I thought I was immune."

"Don't get ahead of yourself. There's got to be a very simple, very obvious explanation. Let's take a deep breath, sit down, and make a list of names."

They walked back to the kitchen and Rusty perched on a stool behind the counter. There was still trash and leftover food sitting out. Floating on the sunny breeze was the smell of stale beer and marijuana.

Sugarman got a pad of paper off the counter and found a pen.

"A simple, obvious explanation," Rusty said. "You're sure of that? Your gut is telling you that, Sugar?"

He'd never lied to Rusty Stabler before.

Meeting her eyes, working hard to keep his face neutral, he said, "Thorn is fine. My gut says he's fine. Now, let's stay focused and get going on this."

He slid the pad of paper across the counter and set the pen beside it.

"You can't bullshit worth a damn," Rusty said.

Sugarman sighed. She was right. He'd never had a knack for deceit. One of his many deficiencies.

"But thanks for trying," she said. "Thank you, Sugar."

TEN

THORN WAS ON HANDS AND knees, stooped over a cleft in the rocky floor. He'd found the source of the water smell. After scooping and shoveling handfuls of marl and finely powdered shale aside, he wedged his arm up to the shoulder into the opening. The hole was perfectly round and its sides were oddly slick. He could feel the air was cooler down below and knew water was only inches away. Rain runoff trapped in a pocket of limestone. Or perhaps a small pool of the surficial aquifer.

He jammed his shoulder against the floor and stretched his hand out and skimmed one fingertip across the cool surface.

To gain the extra inch or two to scoop up water, he was going to have to carve a much deeper depression into the soft floor.

He was drawing his arm out of the fissure to begin the excavation when a blast of sunlight filled his prison cell.

He scooted away from the hole and settled his back against the wall. The kettle drum inside his skull started up again, a Sousa marching band pounding out an old patriotic standard.

He squinted up at the grinning face of Jonah. Shaved head, face of a jackal.

"Room service," Jonah said. "Care to place your order?"

Shredded clouds floated against the powder blue like drifts of foam on a summer sea.

"For starters," Thorn said, "how about a plate of conch fritters?"

"What?"

Thorn drew a long breath, trying to quiet the booming.

"A hush puppy with gristle inside," he said. "Greasy little ball, like something that fell off your family tree."

Jonah blinked.

"Don't insult my family, fuck-breath."

Thorn held a hand up to shade his eyes.

"You hear me, Thorn?"

"I hear you. Your entire family is off-limits."

Jonah digested that for several seconds as if he was trying to decide if Thorn was mocking him.

"Okay, then. So how's it going? You and the whale doing some business? Bonding a little, are you?"

Ground level where Jonah squatted was roughly twenty feet above, maybe a bit more. Stalling, Thorn glanced around, using the sunlight to make a quick survey of the cavern's vertical walls. Earlier, he'd run his hands across the perimeter, searching for the source of water. The floor was coated with several inches of sand and pea-sized pebbles, the walls were rough limestone and sedimentary layers he couldn't identify. Some kind of rock or ancient shells compressed into deposits thin as wafers, while others were thicker slabs the width of mattress pads. Clumps of weeds and grass grew in a few nooks, a small fern was rooted in one shady corner and had sent runners along the wall. Signs that this deep pit had been above the water table for a while.

Now with a clear look he decided it might be a sinkhole. A collapse in the karst and limestone shelf beneath the surface of the ground. The substrata beneath the Florida soil was honeycombed with fissures and cavities, a sieve that allowed rainwater to filter through and recharge the aquifer. Steady rains could erode a crevice until it widened and eventually failed. When it did, the land above it caved in and these pits appeared. Sinkholes in Florida had been known to eat cars and houses. Sometimes they swallowed entire lakes or subdivisions or portions of the interstate. Rare in the southern part of the state, but there he was, way down inside the earth. So they weren't quite rare enough.

Over the opening of this particular sinkhole someone had fashioned a wooden cover made of heavy planks, and cut into it was a hinged lid, making it a perfect holding pen for idiots like Thorn.

"I asked you a question, dude. You still operating on your full mental faculties, or has the whale taken you off into a fugue state?"

"We're getting along," Thorn said. "I've always had a soft spot for cetaceans."

"You know about whales, do you?"

"I know they're mammals. A lot smarter than some humans."

Jonah stared down at Thorn for a few moments as he processed that.

"You getting thirsty? Need a drinkie? Maybe an icy bottle of Evian?"

"I wouldn't turn it down."

"We can trade. You give me what I want to know, I might take pity on your sorry ass and provide some liquid refreshment."

Propped against the pebbled wall, Thorn tilted his head, trying to get a better view of Jonah, to read this guy, decode his clothes. Anything that might be useful.

Jonah held up a shiny object. The sun was directly behind him, and Thorn couldn't make it out. He changed his angle again, tipped his hand to better shield his eyes, but it was no use. The sun blinded him.

If it was the pistol from last night, Thorn didn't have many choices. Throw rocks. Flatten himself against a wall. Plead for mercy.

"Okay, so what I'm going to do, Mr. Thorn, I'm going to speak a person's name and you're going to tell me the first thing pops in your head. Like a game show, you know, *Name That Tune*. You give me the right answer, I'll talk to the chef. See what he's got on special today."

Thorn ached in so many places it was hard to know what was hangover, what came from the fall. He had to give the alcohol some credit for no broken bones, the softening effect of being massively drunk at the moment of impact. A rag doll thumping against the thick layer of sand on the floor of the pit.

Several ribs felt bruised, and his butt and lower back were throbbing as though he'd spent the evening trying to tame a mechanical bull. But all in all it had been a miraculous landing. Nothing broken, nothing sprained. A few lumps and scrapes, some deep-tissue bruising, but not even a bad cut.

"So here we go, Thorn. Ready for round one?"

"I'm listening."

"You and the governor, Herbert Sanchez, you two been chummy lately?"

"The governor?"

"That's right. Governor of Florida. The entire state."

"Guy who did that publicity stunt with workdays? News cameras follow him around while he pretends to be a mailman, cab driver, pizza-delivery boy."

"That was about ten governors ago."

"I always liked that governor. Now, there was a classy guy."

"This the way it's going to be with you? Jokes? Bullshit. 'Cause if it is, 'cause if you keep this up, don't start playing straight, I'm going to nail this trapdoor shut and the whale's going to swim out to sea with you in its belly. This whale's going to be your coffin, cute guy."

"I don't know Sanchez. You got any other names?"

"How about Shelton? Antwan Shelton, black dude."

"Football player. One-Ton Antwan."

"There you go. See how easy this is. So what you and Antwan been up to?"

"Don't know him. Saw him on TV in a bar once. That's it. Dolphins running back a few years ago. Got injured, retired."

"That's all you know about him, what you saw in a bar once?"

"Running back, a real bruiser. One-Ton Antwan. I remembered his nickname. I should get extra credit for that."

Jonah shifted his position, moving away from the sun. The shiny object in his hand wasn't a pistol. It was oblong, about the size of a cell phone. Thorn let himself take a breath, relax a notch.

"Okay, next name on the list," Jonah said. "Browning Hammond."

"Hammond?" Thorn said too quickly and with too much weight.

An image formed in his mind: that butterfly in Argentina or wherever the hell it was, fluttering its wings, sending a wisp of air off into the atmosphere, then that puff travels down a long line of unpredictable causes and effects, and bingo, a category 5 hurricane swirls to life. Chaos theory—every part of the universe connected by a web of fragile pulses no one could predict. Earl Hammond. Coquina Ranch. Florida Forever. The land swap. Thorn tries to do a good deed, and a few flutters of a butterfly wing later, he lands on his butt twenty feet down a sinkhole. Detained by the karma police.

"Okay, good," Jonah said. "That name rings a bell. We're moving ahead."

Thorn debated it quickly and decided. Better to engage, take the risk, see what he could extract from the shit-eater. Not that Thorn was any master manipulator. But Jonah didn't strike him as the sharpest cheddar in the fridge.

Then there was Rusty. Her name was on the legal documents alongside his own, making her a player in this transaction, too. More reason to stay engaged. As long as Thorn was the target, Rusty was safe.

"Hammond," Thorn said. "Hammond's a pretty common name."

"Browning Hammond isn't."

Thorn's right hand closed around a stone. Then again, maybe he should take a shot at the guy, a fastball to the forehead. If he was lucky, he might crack his skull, bring the slinky son of a bitch tumbling into the hole. A tempting thought.

"Okay," Jonah said. "How about Earl Hammond? Earl Hammond

Jr. You got any connections with him? Business, personal, profes-sional, or otherwise."

"I do," Thorn said.

The smirk drained from Jonah's face.

"Don't be fucking with me."

"I wouldn't think of fucking with you. Not for all the condoms in the world."

"Talk to me, funny man. What kind of business you and Earl up to?"

"You said something about food and drink."

The angle was too awkward for a fastball into Jonah's strike zone. And truth was, Thorn wasn't all that confident of his aim. Oh, he'd skipped his share of rocks across the flat waters of Key Largo. He still had good snap in his arm. But the risk-reward calculation wasn't good. If he missed, Jonah would be on heightened alert thereafter. If he in-jured him but didn't bring him down into the pit, the guy would surely retaliate. He let the rock roll from his hand.

"See how much fun this is?" Jonah said. "Cooperation is a beauti-ful thing. So I'm asking you again, dude. What kind of deal you got going with Earl Hammond?"

"You know Earl?" Thorn said.

"Everyone knows Earl."

"You work for him? He your boss? You going behind his back? Messing in his business."

"I'm running this show, meat puppet. Don't get fancy with me."

"Just curious. I'm a curious fellow, that's all."

"Answer the question. What kind of business you doing with Earl?"

"It's complicated. Lots of lawyers, all that double-talk, you know."

"What kind of deal?"

"Real estate," Thorn said.

"Yeah? You buying or selling?"

"Neither," Thorn said. "I'm partnering with him."

"You and Earl are partners?"

"On this one deal, yeah."

Jonah laughed.

"Well, I think your venture might've got dissolved last night."

"Why's that?"

"Old Earl won't be lording it over anybody ever again. Snooty bastard's gone off to herd cattle on the big ranch in the sky."

Thorn was silent. Earl Hammond dead. Thorn in a pit. His fogged brain was clearing fast. The butterfly had done its work. News of the Florida Forever deal had leaked, and somebody didn't want Coquina Ranch donated to the public domain. Had to be that. Had to be.

"So tell me, how was that going to work, you and Earl partnering up?"

"We had a deal, Jonah. I give you something, you give something back."

"Whoa, there, beach boy." Jonah chuckled. "In case you didn't notice, you're the one wallowing in whale guts. So here's how it works. You give, I take. That simple. Only reason you're alive is because of me. You were going down, hombre. You were supposed to be whacked last night. But I gave your ass a reprieve. So you owe me. Got it? You owe me big time."

"Why keep me alive?"

"I'm asking the questions, humpback."

" 'Cause you're sniffing around," Thorn said. "You're trying to find an angle."

Jonah faltered for a second, which wasn't proof of anything. But close.

"You a college boy, Thorn?"

"A dropout."

"Then don't try to outfox me, man. 'Cause I got the degree, bachelor of fucking arts, man. I stacked the whole four years, major university, magnum cum rah-rah. I'm a certified smart guy."

"Impressive," Thorn said.

"So spare me the bullshit."

"Consider it done. Don't insult your family and zero bullshit from now on."

Jonah rubbed his hand back and forth across the stubble of his shaved head, and then rubbed it some more as if trying to sand his palm smooth. Or maybe keep the blood flowing to his meager mind.

"What kind of deal were you and Earl working on? No more cute stuff."

"Who in the world would want me dead? I'm such a congenial fellow."

Jonah's lips pressed flat as if he was fighting off some impulsive reply.

"It was one of those guys, wasn't it? Shelton, the governor, Browning Hammond? One of them is your boss. That's who put a hit on me. But you and your brother decided to weasel into their business instead."

"I'm not the guy you want to piss off, Thorn."

"Hey, where am I anyway? Is this Coquina Ranch? You got wildebeests running around here? Bison, wild boars?"

Jonah took a step back from the opening.

"You know about this place, do you?"

"Just a guess."

"As a matter of fact, yeah, you're inside the Coquina hunting preserve, my man. With the wildebeests and the axis deer and the buffalo and all that shit. That's exactly where you are. Behind a fifteen-foot fence of razor wire. So you can forget about escaping. You're here for good till I'm done with you."

"What're you doing here? You one of the zookeepers?"

"I'm running this interrogation. Get that straight, pud whacker."

"I'm done," Thorn said. "Tell the chef he can take the day off."

Jonah's shit-eating grin resurfaced. It must have been his default look.

"All right, fine. Twist yourself into a lotus position, meditate your ass off. I'll be back when I'm back. Ciao, baby."

The lid slammed shut and Thorn was again in twilight.

He leaned against the wall. Running it through, trying to unsnarl the tangle. Maybe he *was* in a fugue state. His mind still sluggish with booze. Add dehydration, throw in the bone-rattling crash into the pit. Blend at full speed and what you got was froth. Thorn, the useless head on a beer.

The trapdoor swung open again and sunlight flooded the sinkhole.

"I forgot something, party dude."

Jonah was holding up the silver object.

"Don't want you to expire before you spill your guts."

He tossed it into the pit, and Thorn fielded it with his left hand.

A small tin of skinless, boneless sardines.

"Whale food, baby. Heavy-duty protein, high in omega-3s. Think of it as your reward for being such a good little Eagle Scout. There's more where that came from, if you behave."

He slammed the trapdoor shut and bolted it.

Thorn sat in the murky light with the can of sardines in his hand. He waited a full minute before he peeled open the can, gave it a cautious sniff, then tipped it to his mouth and slurped down the contents.

He sat for a moment savoring the oily warmth spreading into his belly, until finally the saltiness registered. Not good. The alcohol, the sweat drenching his clothes, his scratchy throat, tongue parched. Now his lips were puckering from the sodium. Category 5 dehydration.

Thorn scooted back to the narrow shaft in the floor and began to dig, combing back the layer of marl and granulated limestone, pebbles and the pulverized remains of ancient seashells.

When he'd made a bowl around the mouth of the cleft, he snaked his arm into the hole again, pressing his armpit hard against the depression. Maybe he'd gained an inch, but it was only enough to tickle his fingertips across the cool surface.

He wriggled his arm free and sat up, sucked the dew off his fingers.

He tried to focus, tried to reduce this to simple geometry. Water so close. Tantalizingly near. Just a few inches beyond arm's length. There was a way to get at it. There had to be. Before he tried to scale those sheer walls, he had to have water. He had to. Take it one step at a time. Water, then escape.

Then he heard the sound. Thinking at first it was the wild skid and thud of his heart echoing in his ears. But as it rose in volume he recognized the familiar racket, the whump-whump-whump of a helicopter's rotor blades.

He peered up at the slits of sunlight showing through the planks above him and caught a flash of the chopper's passing. He had a spike of hope, then a slow deflation.

No one was coming for him. No one was even looking. He'd left a note for the only ones who might track him down. Written it word for word as dictated. Idiot drunk. He'd not even had the cunning to intentionally misspell a word, or leave some other signal the note was a lie.

"I just need some time alone to think."

Well, by God, he was going to have that. A whole lot of that.

He listened to the chopper fade. He pressed his back against the pitted walls and listened until it was gone and the only noise that remained was the cawing of a gang of crows who in their dim-witted arrogance must have believed they'd scared the giant bird away.

ELEVEN

INSIDE THE COQUINA RANCH BUSINESS offices, Claire Hammond heard the roar of another helicopter. That made three. Two had arrived earlier from TV stations in Miami, then another came, black and bulky like a military gunship. While she was outside taking a break between interrogations, she'd watched the big chopper tip from side to side, warning the news guys off.

Even the Hammonds' air space was no longer their own.

Her third grilling was about to begin. This time the tape recorder was held by a woman.

She was younger than her male counterparts, hair pulled back in a tight ponytail, white polo shirt. Eyes that gave nothing away. Broad forehead, pointy chin, a triangular face. She introduced herself. Anne Donaldson. FDLE. Stiff manner, strictly professional, disinterested. She asked Claire to sit, asked her if she wanted a lawyer, which she declined, then asked her to begin at the beginning, go through it, leave nothing out. Same as the others had.

She retold the story. Still numb, out of body, suspended up there with the helicopters looking down from a great height at the whirlwind she'd created. Claire Hammond, killer. Claire Hammond, who failed to act in time. Who caused the death of a man she revered and another who was her friend.

Okay, so she'd been in the barn. She'd heard the bugs go quiet. She went outside and stared at the lodge. It seemed strangely still. She walked over. But before she went inside, she decided she was spooked over nothing and started back to the barn. That's when she bumped into something on the path and stooped down to investigate. It was a dead man. An FDLE agent she'd met earlier in the day.

She panicked briefly, got control of herself, ran back to the barn, grabbed her shotgun, and ran back to the lodge.

When she barged inside she saw Gustavo Pinto holding a pistol. Earl and Browning were standing in front of the couch. Antwan Shelton and Governor Sanchez behind it. Gustavo's gun was pointed at the floor.

Claire ordered him to drop the pistol. But he didn't. Gustavo pled for forgiveness from Earl Hammond.

Browning yelled for her to shoot.

She hesitated until Gustavo raised the pistol, then she fired. But she was a second late. One horrendous second.

In the middle of Claire's account, someone entered the room. She didn't look up. People had been coming and going all day.

As she finished the story her eyes burned again. But this time she managed to keep them from fogging over. No tears, no choking up, simply kept staring down at the scarred pine table before her.

Like everything else at the ranch, that table had a history. A table where early in the last century greenbacks were slipped into white business envelopes and handed out to a line of workers on Friday afternoon. The same table where those workers and their wives and children sat in their Sunday finest to eat dinner in the Coquina Ranch canteen. Where the U.S. mail was once sorted for the hundred numbered boxes in the ranch's post office, which served the citizens of that part of the county. Where vaccinations had been administered during an outbreak of influenza. Where the punch bowl had been set up, and platters of food laid out for rollicking square dances held outside in the big corral. Earl Hammond told her the stories of that table, that room and building that had seen so many incarnations over the years and was now used for clerical work, bookkeeping, the mundane jobs of ranch operations.

After a few seconds of silence, as Claire continued to gaze down at that wood with her eyes muddy, Anne Donaldson leaned forward into Claire's line of sight, the woman's chin almost touching the table.

"The bugs got quiet?" she said. "Is that some kind of country thing?"

"Knock it off, Donaldson."

Claire rubbed her eyes and looked up. Frisco was leaning against the wall. In jeans and a gray Miami Police T-shirt, arms crossed over his chest.

"Listen to me, Sergeant Hammond. At the governor's request, as a courtesy to your grieving family, I've agreed to allow you to sit in. I understand you're a police officer, a street cop. I respect that. But my function here is a little different from what you're used to. So I'm making this request once, and once only, keep quiet. That clear? Or you're out."

"Don't mock the woman. If she heard the bugs get quiet, the bugs got quiet."

Donaldson shook her head and turned back to Claire.

"So after the bugs got quiet, and after you barged into the lodge with your shotgun, what was everyone doing? Were they arguing? Angry?"

"Only what I said. Gustavo pleading for forgiveness and Browning yelling at me to shoot."

"What'd he say, your husband? His exact words, you remember?"

" 'Shoot the fucking bastard.' I remember that. 'For your family.' He said that, too. It seemed strange."

" 'For your family'?"

She nodded.

"And Gustavo, his words?"

" 'God forgive me.' "

"That's all? 'God forgive me'?"

"That's all I remember."

"Okay, so let's run the tape back a little. You're running across the parking lot, heading toward the house. On that leg, was there anything unusual? In the yard, the parking lot, anything out of place? Caught your attention."

"In the parking lot, there was Gustavo's pickup truck and the governor's SUV. And the Faust brothers' Prius."

"Faust brothers?"

She looked across at Frisco. He rolled his eyes upward and stared at the beadboard ceiling, staying out of it.

"They live in the hunting lodge inside the game preserve. They're friends of Browning. They take the hunting parties out on shoots. Run errands."

"Jamokes," Frisco said.

Donaldson cut a look at him, then said, "So these big-game safari hunters, where are they when you're running into the lodge?"

"I don't know."

Donaldson thumbed through her notebook, doing it slowly, page by page. No hurry, forehead wrinkled, a hokey show of consternation.

"You're sure you saw that car? A Prius."

"Camouflage paint job. Yes, I saw it."

"You're not confusing last night with some other night? I mean, these two guys, they work here, so they must come and go, you could have it mixed up."

"Their car was there."

Donaldson glanced back at Frisco, gave him a look Claire couldn't see, but it appeared she might be daring Frisco to speak again so she could toss him from the room. Then she turned back to Claire and was neutral.

"So we're back inside the lodge. Anything out of the ordinary there? Beside the man with the gun."

"No."

"Nothing? No furniture overturned? No sign of struggle, no broken glass, nothing?"

"There was some kind of map."

"What map?"

"Like a survey map. It was rolled open on the table. It had red dots on it."

"You mention this map to the other investigators? FBI, Homeland Security."

"I don't know. I think so, but maybe not."

"Red dots on a map. Okay. You ever see this map before?"

"No."

Frisco had shut his eyes, and his head was lowered.

"This Gustavo Pinto," Donaldson said without a beat. "You friendly with this fellow? Have a special relationship?"

"I liked him. He was a good man. Courteous, polite in an old-world way."

"Is that why you hesitated, didn't shoot the second you saw your husband and the others in danger?"

"That's out of line, Donaldson."

"I'm not telling you again, Hammond. Zip it, or you're gone."

Anne Donaldson flattened her lips into a strained smile.

"You were saying?"

"I didn't shoot because Gustavo wasn't aiming the gun at anyone. It was pointed at the floor."

"Help me understand this, Claire. You've just found a dead man, an officer of the law who you knew was on duty to protect the safety of the governor of the state of Florida. So you realized a murder had been committed, and that very likely other lives were in danger, but despite that, you come in the house, find this gentleman holding a gun, and what? You thought it's some kind of parlor game?"

Claire shook her head. Nothing she could say.

"You ever see that pistol before, the one Pinto used? You recognize it?"

"No."

"It was a Sig Sauer Mosquito. Twenty-two caliber. A plinker. Maybe you saw that particular pistol around the ranch? Maybe it belonged to somebody else. Ever hear anyone mention seeing or owning such a weapon?"

"No," she said.

"Anything happen around here, anything of note, about a week ago?"

"A week ago?"

"The twentieth, or it could be the nineteenth, a day or two either way."

"What're you talking about?"

"That's the day that pistol was picked up at the Ace Gunshop in Miami. Purchased three days before that. Both the weapon and silencer bought and paid for by Gustavo Pinto, registered in his name. I'm wondering if something happened around here that might have precipitated that purchase."

"Look, I never saw the pistol before. I didn't know Gustavo owned a pistol. And I still don't believe it."

"Why don't you believe it?"

"Gustavo was very gentle, very kind and sweet. Not a violent man."

"Apparently you misread him," Donaldson said. "Last night he murdered two people. Killed a colleague of mine, then walked into the main house and put two slugs in the chest of Earl Hammond from five feet away in front of four eyewitnesses."

Claire shook her head, a bitter taste rising into her mouth.

"That gun's all wrong," Frisco said.

Donaldson tilted her eyes up as if beseeching the heavens for patience.

"Wrong?"

"He bought the Mosquito with a silencer. Gunshop in Miami."

"That's what I said."

"The gun you recovered at the crime scene had a functioning silencer?"

"That's right."

"Factory or custom?"

She sighed, got her notes, paged through them.

"Factory-made, serial number removed."

"Well, there you go."

"Goddammit, Hammond, spit it out."

"Only kind of silencer he could have bought at the gun shop would be a fake."

"Fake?" Claire said.

"Fake silencer is for the jerkoff who wants to look like a gangster. It doesn't do anything, it's just for show. To get a factory-made suppressor, the real deal, as I'm sure Ms. Donaldson knows, you have to fill out a mound of paperwork. It has to go to ATF for approval, it can take three months to work its way through. Or you find one on the black market. You don't go into a gun shop and get one with a three-day wait."

"I'm aware of that," Donaldson said.

"So like I said, the gun's all wrong. Serial number is removed from the silencer but not the handgun. Why's he spend the money to buy a fake silencer if he's got a real one lined up?"

Claire stared down at the table.

"You're really pushing it, Sergeant."

"Next thing you got to ask yourself, out in the middle of nowhere, place like Coquina Ranch, why bother with a silencer at all? If you want to kill Earl, you walk up, take out the governor's bodyguard, two seconds later you're in the lodge. Nobody inside has time to react to the gunshots. You walk in, pop the old man, walk back out. Why use a suppressor?"

"Why don't you just go ahead and tell us, Sergeant Hammond?"

"It's got to be about Claire, keeping her from hearing. The shooter didn't want her getting in the middle of it."

"But she heard something anyway."

"No, she heard what wasn't there. She heard the absence of noise. The bugs went silent. Whoever bought that gun didn't factor in that possibility."

"And that means what?"

"Tells me somebody didn't know her too well. Didn't realize how perceptive she is. What a country girl she's become. Gustavo would've known that. Clap your hands out in the country at night, everything gets quiet for a few seconds."

Donaldson dusted the edge of the table with a couple of irritable swipes.

"There's four witnesses to this killing," she said. "But you, Sergeant, keep straining to come up with far-fetched, pathetically improbable scenarios that say Gustavo didn't do it. Give it up, Hammond, stop wasting my time."

"The gun's funky, that's all I'm saying."

TWELVE

"OKAY, ALL RIGHT, CLAIRE." ANNE Donaldson waved her hand as if clearing the air of smoke. "Let's go back to Gustavo and his possible motive. Maybe he was pissed off about something. You get a whiff of that? Had a grudge. Unhappy with his pay, some new work assignment, mistreatment of one kind or another. Maybe marital problems, an affair, anything of that nature. Possibly something was brewing for a while and just boiled over."

"Nothing like that," Claire said. "Gustavo was a gentleman. He was a second-generation employee, his father held the same job. He was family. It doesn't make sense."

"Would you have known if one of the workers was having a problem with Earl Hammond? Would that be something you'd automatically be aware of?"

"Of course. Browning would have told me if there was an issue."

"You and your husband are open about everything?"

"What does that mean?"

"Business matters. Daily events on the ranch. You and him share the gossip, the goings-on?"

"I believe we do."

"You're not sure?"

"I would've known if something was wrong with Gustavo."

"But you didn't know that Gustavo had been fired. That he'd been given a week's notice to clear out of his house."

"Gustavo wasn't fired."

"Is that your statement? Gustavo hadn't been given a week's notice to clear out of his house and leave? You heard nothing about any of that?"

"It's not true."

"You're sure?"

"Fired over what?"

"Cost cutting. Could that be it? Trimming overhead?"

"Who told you that? Browning?"

Anne Donaldson sat for a moment without speaking. She tapped the edge of the tape recorder with a long fingernail. Tapped it several times.

"It's not true. I would've known. Somebody would've told me. He's the ranch foreman, for Christ's sake. He grew up on Coquina Ranch."

"Maybe you're not as aware of the internal operations of this ranch as you think you are. Maybe not everyone confides in you. Is that possible?"

She crooked a finger and looked at it with interest.

Claire sighed. Yes, it was possible. In the last couple years there'd been a growing loss of intimacy between Browning and her. In the bedroom, at the dinner table, in every phase of their life together. More than once lately he hadn't bothered to include her in a major decision. The safari enterprise was one of those. He'd presented it to her as a fait accompli, mentioning it one day in passing. She'd been shocked, angry, hurt. And it worried her, too. Browning seemed to be confiding more in his buddy Antwan than his own wife.

"I just remembered something." Claire glanced at Frisco. He was staring down at the plank floor, hiding his eyes as if trying not to coach her, or perhaps sorting out something he'd heard in her statement.

In her two previous interviews she'd forgotten to mention her conversation with Earl in the barn. She hadn't considered it relevant, but after hearing the claim that Gustavo had been fired, she was no longer so sure.

"Okay, go on."

"Earlier last night Earl came out to the barn where I was working and told a story about the old days, about a time when Hemingway and Thomas Edison and some others visited the ranch. When he was finished with the story, he told me something was about to change at Coquina and people might be upset."

"Hemingway came here? What, to hunt rhino?"

"To meet Edison and Henry Ford. To fraternize. Back in the thirties."

"So that's what happens around here? Big shots hang out, sit around the campfire. Is that right? Movie stars, politicians, like that?"

"Yes. Friends of the Hammond family. It's been a tradition for generations."

"A good-old-boys club. Power brokers. Is that what goes on, Sergeant?"

Claire was silent, looking at the corner of the table.

"Mainly it's old white guys," Frisco said, "sitting around a fire bitching about their prostates. Not a lot of power brokering I've seen."

Claire kept her head down, hiding a smile.

"Okay." Donaldson fluttered her hand in Claire's line of sight. "So back to this talk between you and Earl Hammond. What's he referring to, what's going to change at the ranch?"

"I don't know. He said Browning would fill me in. He just wanted to let me know something was about to happen, and he was trying to do the right thing."

"The right thing? You have no idea what he was talking about?"

"That's all he told me. Things were about to change. A radical change."

"He used that word?"

"Yes."

"Well, that's odd. I mean *radical*'s a pretty striking word. Kind of jumps out at you. And you're just remembering this."

Frisco shifted his feet, tipping forward like he was straining to hear.

"Is it normal," Claire said, "for someone in my position, an ordinary citizen who's just been forced to kill another human being, for that person to have perfect recall? Has that been your experience as an investigator?"

Frisco smiled.

"Don't get agitated, Ms. Hammond. It's not helpful."

"But your smugness, treating me like a suspect, that's helpful."

Frisco was looking down at the floor, concealing a smile.

"I'm sorry if my attitude offends you, Ms. Hammond. I sincerely regret that. It's good that you've let off some steam, that's healthy. Now, let's put that behind us and get back to work, shall we? This radical change Earl mentioned. Let's stay on that. You think that radical change could've been the cost cutting, trimming overhead, firing certain employees? Earl's decided to bring you into the loop."

"I suppose."

"So we're back to the disgruntled employee. A man who'd been fired after years of faithful service. He's going to be evicted from his house, family's got to move. It's something he can't accept. He flips out."

"But no," Claire said. "That's not what I witnessed."

"What's that mean?"

"I didn't see an angry man. I saw someone torn apart by what he was about to do. A man terribly conflicted. Not angry. Not mad."

"From those few seconds, standing with your shotgun, you could tell what his mood was?"

"He wasn't angry. He was broken-hearted."

"Desperate? Would that be a fair description?"

"Heartbroken," Claire said.

She lay her hand on the tabletop that was etched with the grooves, scratches, and pits of a century of hard use, keeping her palm flat, as if in that way she might draw energy, unite in some meager way with the generations of tough men and women who'd come before her, who'd broken bread here, received their wages, coped with unimaginable hardships, leaving behind their delicate scars on this wood, small traces of their passing.

"You've got enough for now," Frisco said. "The lady's been going at it for hours. She needs a break."

He came forward and put a hand under Claire's elbow and helped her rise, then guided her to the door.

Donaldson clicked off her recorder and stood.

"Okay, fine. I appreciate your help, Ms. Hammond, but let's be clear. When the protocol gets sorted out, the jurisdictional jockeying is finished, and all the badges get back to their respective desks, I'm confident FDLE will be taking the lead in the investigation, which means you and I will be speaking again." She reached into the pocket of her chinos and drew out two business cards, handed one to Claire, the other to Frisco.

"I know," Claire said. "If I remember something, I should call."

"Check the angle of entry," Frisco said to Donaldson.

"What?"

"Gustavo was five-two. Your guy Saperstein was well over six feet, and he took seven slugs around the sternum. In your haste to pin this on Pinto, I'd hate to see you whiz kids neglect something so obvious as angle of entry. Upward, downward, straight in. Might tell you how tall the shooter was?"

"Is it just you, Hammond, or are all Miami street cops trained crime-scene investigators?"

"My guess is you got two perps," Frisco said. "Whoever killed Saperstein has problems with impulse control. He was getting off, unloading that whole clip. Then there's Gustavo. Man's so weepy he could barely bring himself to raise his pistol. To me, that sounds a lot like two different shooters."

THIRTEEN

OUTSIDE, THE BLACK HELICOPTER HAD touched down in the pasture behind the barn. Surrounded by men in sunglasses, just beyond the prop wash, Governor Sanchez was listening to Antwan Shelton talk. The governor had his head bowed, hands behind him pressed to his kidneys. His big shoulders were humped over as if carrying some burden that taxed his strength.

Antwan had changed clothes. No longer in the paratrooper's pants and black muscle T-shirt of the night before. Now decked out in a gleaming white button-down shirt and black trousers, whose sharp creases Claire could distinguish even from a distance. Dressed like the other security guys but somehow more stylish, bordering on flamboyant. She wondered where he'd found the time to shower and change, and shave his bald head so it gleamed like polished obsidian in the sunlight. But that was Antwan. Always buffed. The muscles rippling, the hippest sunglasses, the gold rings and bangles and necklace, the popcorn diamond in his earlobe. How dapper, how utterly composed he seemed. Amid the turmoil, the ragged confusion. All wrong.

"Our man Antwan been hanging around a lot lately?"

"No more than usual."

"How much is that?"

"Few times a week. He and Browning are always working on some project or another. Knocking over one sandcastle, building another."

"Bad influence."

"Antwan?"

"Both of them," Frisco said. "A couple of frat boys egging each other on."

"I didn't realize you knew Antwan."

"I live in Miami. Antwan Shelton is unavoidable. TV, billboards. Always right there, that liar's smile, hustling the next big thing."

Yellow crime-scene tape wrapped the oleander bush where Saperstein's body had fallen. Men and women in paper boots and blue smocks flowed in and out of the lodge. One of them, a young man who was carrying a paper evidence bag, stopped on the bridge to take an admiring look out at the alligator moat and the slash pines and the shadowy groves before he headed back to the white van where the other technicians were assembled.

"Where's Browning?"

Frisco nodded to the other end of the clapboard-sided office building. "Telling his story for the third time."

"You sat in?"

"Couple of hours ago, on his go-round with Homeland Security."

"What are *they* doing here?"

"First thing everyone thought, with the governor being present, it had to be terrorism. I think by now they've ruled that out. DEA's sniffing around, too, got their fingers crossed it's cartel related, and you've got FBI. Hell, even Treasury sent out a Secret Service guy. Place is sloshing over with testosterone.

"Thing like this, they're looking for a conspiracy. Gustavo was the shooter, everybody agrees on that. But somebody could've pulled his strings. They'll be taking statements from everybody within a mile of the lodge. All the ranch hands, the cooks, anybody with a connection to Gustavo or Coquina Ranch, or Earl Hammond. Like I said, it'll take a while."

"And that's why Donaldson was grinding me. Like I'm part of a conspiracy?"

"Far as the feds are concerned," Frisco said, "there's no such thing as a lone gunman. Ever since JFK, it's their pet theory. Don't take it personally."

"And what did Browning say?"

"Told it pretty much like you told it. A couple of minor differences."

Frisco drew a fingertip across a wrinkle near his mouth, flattening it, as if trying to smooth away the inevitable.

"Browning says you came through the door with the shotgun before Gustavo said much. He'd only just got started. That squares with Antwan's story and the governor's. Nobody has an explanation."

"Browning say anything about the radical change?"

"Nothing."

"Then Earl hadn't told him yet."

"So it seems," Frisco said.

"Gustavo was fired? Do you believe that?"

"Is there some reason I should doubt my brother?"

Claire watched the governor board the chopper, shoulders slumped under that invisible weight. Antwan skipped well out of range of the swirl of white dust.

She glanced at Frisco, caught him eyeing her, and his gaze shied away at once. Another in a long string of awkward moments. They'd had no practice being together without Browning. From the very start there'd been a stiff formality between them, and over the years it had only grown worse. She assumed it had to do with her embrace of Coquina Ranch, a way of life Frisco had spurned. Some blend of resentment and jealousy and suspicion of Claire's motives, a young woman like her signing on for such hard duty. It was nothing he said, nothing he did outright, but whenever she was around him, Claire felt like a fraud, a city girl faking her role as frontierswoman.

"Governor's not taking it well," Frisco said. "Not his usual cheery self."

"And you, Frisco? How're you holding up?"

"I'm hanging in there."

Frisco's jaw was tense, his eyes following the rising chopper.

Claire walked across the corral to the bench just beyond the barn door and sat. Frisco followed, stayed on his feet, scanning the crime scene, the homestead where he'd grown up, overrun by foreign invaders.

In the six years she'd been a part of the Hammond family, Claire had only met Frisco a handful of times. Always in Miami, a hurried lunch while she and Browning were in town doing city errands. Joining Frisco at one of the fish joints along the river near the police department's horse barn.

Browning would complain about his struggles at the ranch, grumble over Earl's stubbornness, air the petty day-to-day annoyances, his efforts to turn a more substantial profit. With all that land, the greatest portion of it sitting unused, the payrolls, fuel bills, and other expenses ate up the meager profits from the modest herd of Angus and Herefords, some timber, a small sod operation, and fifty acres of tomatoes. Not that Browning was greedy. But he considered himself a businessman and couldn't accept the backward way the Hammond men had always let those thousands of acres lie fallow. Such a waste.

Never asking for advice from his big brother and not getting any. Frisco listened, a grunt of sympathy now and again. At those lunches, as Claire observed the two brothers interact, the seven years between them seemed more like a generation. Frisco's weighty silences, Browning's chatter and peevishness.

Back home at the ranch, Browning never mentioned Frisco, never brought up their common childhood, as if such a thing had not existed. If Claire hadn't pestered Deloria, the cook, for more information on her brother-in-law, Frisco would have remained a blank.

In his teens, he'd been a rising rodeo star. Spent two years on the

Florida circuit, did a few of the national events, Las Vegas, Oklahoma City. He rode broncs and bulls, did some calf roping, won a few silver buckles some decent prize money, even got a promotional deal with a blue jeans company. Then, for reasons he never shared, he quit the main events and spent his last two seasons as a pickup rider.

Since Browning was a rodeo fan, Claire had attended her share in the last few years, and because of what she'd heard about Frisco, she'd focused on the pickup guys, watched them work their quiet magic. If a bronc rider made it to the eight-second buzzer without being thrown from the bucking horse, a pickup rider galloped alongside to pull the cowboy off and set him safely on the ground. The pickup men had to time their approach perfectly, keep their own horse under strict control, and in a single swipe rescue the rider.

It was obvious to Claire that pickup guys were the most skilled horsemen at the rodeo, yet they stayed just beyond the limelight and got none of the crowd's applause. From what she could tell, only a few insiders and the other cowboys seemed to appreciate their heroics. On one occasion when she made an admiring comment about one pickup rider's skill, Browning laughed at her. "Those guys lost their nerve for broncs and bulls. Bunch of has-beens."

As she sat and watched the swarm of law-enforcement personnel move in and out of the lodge, Claire felt another dry clutch of air in her throat and a dark weight settling in her chest. For the last few hours these surges of despair and guilt had been coming in unexpected waves as she digested the loss of Earl Hammond, her own culpability in the matter, and stared ahead at the long, desolate stretch of days. She shut her eyes until the moment passed. When she looked up, Frisco was watching her again.

"I'm sorry. I'm so sorry."

"Nothing to apologize for."

"No, listen to me. Donaldson was right. I really fucked up."

"No, you didn't."

"I should've shot Gustavo the minute I walked in the door, saw him holding that gun. Earl would still be alive."

Frisco watched Donaldson step outside onto the covered porch of the offices and light a cigarette.

"You're a goddamn hero, Claire. Get used to it. If you hadn't come in like that, guns blazing, everyone in that room might be dead right now. That's how you got to look at it. Because you didn't fuck up. A guy with twenty years on the street couldn't have done better."

"Browning will never forgive me. He worshipped Earl."

"Browning's a big boy," Frisco said. "He'll get over it."

"I don't know if I can forgive myself."

"Cut it out. Now you're wallowing."

She came to her feet, stared sharply into his eyes.

"What'd you say?"

He looked at her, faintly amused.

"There, that's better. That's more like it."

He turned his attention back to Donaldson. The FDLE officer took a last drag, sucking the life out of her cigarette, and flicked the butt into the dusty corral.

"You know, Frisco, sometimes you can be one cold son of a bitch."

"And the other times?"

"I haven't seen any of those," Claire said.

A quick smile crossed his lips, then he motioned toward the interior of the barn.

"Need to show you something," he said.

Still stinging, she followed him into the shadowy building that reeked of fresh hay and manure and the damp rot of ancient wood. They passed down the length of stalls past the five marshtackies, small, tough horses that were descendants of those left behind by Spanish explorers. The early Florida crackers had appropriated the breed to manage their large herds of free-ranging cattle on land all around these parts. In the last century, marshtackies had all but disappeared. A shame, for those tough, tireless horses were so perfectly suited for working in the thick scrubland, pine forests, and rough and sloppy terrain.

The one time her father, the skin doctor, had visited Coquina Ranch, she'd brought him out to see these horses and explained their history. He simply nodded, beaming the same as he had all day, speechless and bewildered, like a man unable to match up the memories of his suburban Connecticut daughter with this woman in soiled jeans and shit-spattered riding boots. Claire's mother, Ellen, would have been less charitable about the ranch. Firing off catty remarks about the grungy world her daughter had descended into. Ellen, last Claire heard, was on her fifth husband, even younger and richer than the previous ones. Living on the beach in Hawaii, a yearly Christmas card with an illegible signature her only communication.

Frisco led her past the marshtackies to the last stall, where a roan Tennessee walker was backed up against the rear wall, head held high, peering at them warily. With its mouth closed, the big horse snorted twice.

Claire stopped and turned to Frisco.

"Her name is Big Girl. She hasn't adjusted to city life. I thought she could board here till I figured out what to do with her. If that's okay with you."

She took a second, then nodded.

"By the way," he said. "That story Earl told about Edison and Hemingway."

"Yeah?"

"He give you both halves?"

"I don't know what you mean."

"Where'd the story stop? When little Earl left the campfire, went back to the lodge and got in bed?"

"That's right."

Frisco nodded like he'd assumed as much.

"What's the rest?"

Shifting his gaze away from her, Frisco said, "Have to tell you later."

He drew a peppermint stick from his jeans, peeled the cellophane off, and held it out to the horse. Shyly it came over and took the candy from his hand.

"Tell me now."

Frisco looked past her, fixing his eyes on the entrance.

"Later," he said.

She turned and saw Browning coming into the barn with Antwan at his side.

"All right, then," said Claire. "Later."

FOURTEEN

THERE WERE SEVENTEEN PARTYGOERS ON Sugarman's list of names, but he knew the phone numbers for only two. He used his cell for both of those, and neither had seen Thorn leave the party. Missy Mayfield, one of Thorn's old girlfriends, volunteered to round up a search party, but Sugarman assured her it wasn't necessary.

Rusty called the only three on her list whose numbers she could locate and got the same result. Last anyone had seen of Thorn was when he gave his speech about what a great lady Rusty was. Rusty worked for a while with BellSouth information, trying to finagle more numbers, but it turned out Thorn's guests were fairly typical Keys folks who either had no phones at all or kept their numbers unlisted.

Lying low for one reason or another was standard behavior in the Keys, where a large portion of the population had come to reinvent themselves, assume new identities, or flee from one mainland nuisance or another. Messy divorces, the justice system, debts, the IRS were high on the list, though Sugar had met a few desperados determined to break away from darker forces, mafia snitches, gangbangers, and former drug mules looking to go straight. Key Largo and Tavernier and Islamorada had such a large population of those shadowy types who placed a high premium on anonymity that asking questions about someone's past was ill-advised conversational etiquette. It could even get you hurt.

The Friday after Thanksgiving was a busy workday in that island resort. Most on the party list were employed in the tourist trade. Only a few might have the day off—a plumber, two carpenters, an electrician, and the Coral Shores High School librarian.

Rusty and Sugar divided the rest. Sugarman took all the folks living below Mile Marker 95, from Popp's Motel south. Rusty took Key Largo, where the highest concentration of the party guests lived or worked.

She showered and changed. Came out of the bedroom in black jeans and a long-sleeve blue T-shirt and running shoes, hair still damp. Looking more like her old island girl self than Sugar had seen in a while. He followed her outside into the brittle sunshine. A steady easterly off the Atlantic had pushed the swelling tide high into the lagoon and it was sloshing over the seawall and onto the dock. Feathery white horsetails filled the sky. Winds changing aloft, a sign that things were about to shift below.

"It's going to be fine," Sugar said as Rusty got into her Accord.

She put the key in the ignition and looked up at him through the open window.

"I'm not superstitious, Sugar. I don't have premonitions. But this is different."

"We'll find him, Rusty. We'll find him and there'll be a good explanation and we'll all have a big laugh."

"No," she said. "This is serious. This is some very bad shit."

She started the car and backed out.

Sugarman watched her go, feeling a dark fist clenching inside his chest, a gloomy certainty that what she said was true.

No luck with Penny and Jed Thompson, who were home watching a ball game in the tiki hut behind their house. Neither Lisa Lee, who tended bar at Morada Bay, or Jimmy Hankinson, who ran the wind-surf concession at the Marriott, were any help. The last they remembered was Thorn's speech and someone shoving him into the lagoon. A strike-out with Joel Carmel, who operated the bookstore in the Surfside shopping plaza, and another with Randy Schutes, who sold tropical gewgaws and parrot shirts at Island Silver and Spice. Zero with Sharon Jenkins, the hostess at Snapper's restaurant. Two of Sugarman's old cop buddies, Shaky Means and Junior Nickerson, were out fishing together. Junior's wife hailed him on her VHS, and over crackling static Junior said, no, they hadn't seen Thorn after the speech or the lagoon episode.

Sugarman was down to his last two names when Rusty rang his cell.

"Meet me at Squirrelly Shirley's," she said. "Be quick."

"What?"

She clicked off and Sugar wheeled the Toyota around and hauled ass back up the overseas highway, twice skidding along the shoulder to pass slow-moving traffic, driving like a goddamn Miami idiot, getting some honks and a couple of flipped birds.

It was just after four in the afternoon when he swerved into the lot at Squirrelly Shirley's Boutique and hustled into the air-conditioned shop.

Shirley and Rusty were behind the cash register. A newspaper was spread out on the counter. The morning *Miami Herald,* front-page section.

Shirley was a cute blonde in her late thirties wearing a low-cut dress that revealed about fifty percent of her famous breasts. The boutique was one of the few clothing stores in the Keys that local men frequented, shopping for their wives or girlfriends, or at least pretending to. Shirley must have known those deeply scooped dresses brought them in because that was her daily uniform. For years that décolletage had paid the mortgage on a nice waterfront house.

"I saw two guys," Shirley said to Sugar before he could speak.

"They came in late, maybe an hour before the party ended. A big one and a little one. The little one was grubby like a derelict. They didn't look like they belonged together because the big one was dressed nice, muscled up, handsome face, but his eyes weren't nice. Mean eyes. Dead or something, I don't know. I've been trying to find the right word."

"What about these two?"

"I was on the porch and they asked where they could find Thorn, and I told them he was in the kitchen."

"You see them again?"

Rusty flattened wrinkles out of the newspaper.

"No," Rusty said. "Shirley didn't see them come back out. But they could've gone out the front door. No one would've noticed that."

"Two guys," Sugarman said. "One big, one little."

"I never saw them before," Shirley said. "I knew everyone at the party except those two. This was around two or three in the morning, pretty late. I was a little high. But I remember them clearly. You and Rusty were dancing by the lagoon."

"You'd recognize these two again if you saw them?"

"Pretty sure."

"There's something else," Rusty said.

She swiveled the paper around so he could see the headline: THREE DEAD IN SHOOTOUT, GOVERNOR SANCHEZ NARROWLY ESCAPES.

"What's this about?" Shirley asked.

Sugarman took the paper over to the front of the store where the light was better and skimmed the article. Thorn's name wasn't mentioned. An FDLE agent who'd been protecting the governor had been the victim of multiple gunshots; also killed were Earl Hammond Jr. and a worker named Gustavo Pinto. Short article, sketchy details. Must've been slammed together as the paper was going to press.

"Happened last night," Rusty said. "About midnight. Coquina Ranch."

"And a couple of hours later two guys show up asking for Thorn."

"What's going on?" Shirley said. "Is Thorn in trouble again?"

"We need more details, Shirley. How these guys were dressed. Anything you can remember, no matter how small it might seem."

"Okay."

Sugarman took notes on a sheet of Shirley's flowery stationery.

It seemed that Squirrely Shirley had photographic recall on matters relating to wardrobe—a job-related skill, she said with a smile of pride.

The two men were wildly mismatched. The scrawny guy dressed like he'd just crawled out of a Dumpster. Gray sweatshirt with the sleeves cut off at the shoulders. Grungy black jeans, white high-tops. A green bungee cord for a belt.

The other guy, the good-looking one, wore chinos, loafers, a blue button-down. The loafers had tassels and were cordovan.

"Very preppy," Shirley said. "Not my type. But cute."

The big guy had medium-length brown hair, stylishly cut. The other had a shaved head. The handsome one worked out with weights, deep chest, wide shoulders, with the pigeon-toed gait of a body builder. The other was more feline, and Shirley said he'd taken a long look at her as he was going in the door, leaning forward, trying to sneak a peek down her top. Smirked when she caught him.

"You see their car?" Rusty said.

"One of those teeny compacts," Shirley said. "I'm not into cars."

"Color?"

"Oh, it was weird. Same as Norm Higgins's Jeep. That military look."

"Military?" Sugar said.

Shirley came out from behind the counter and walked over to a spinner rack near the side window. She pulled off a pair of pants and held them up.

"Like this. Military."

"Camouflage," Rusty said. "A camouflage paint job?"

"Right," Shirley said. "That's what I meant. Why does somebody paint their car camouflage?"

"I don't think it's because they're trying to blend in," Sugar said.

A few minutes later, as they were passing over the crest of the Jewfish Creek Bridge in Sugar's Corolla, Rusty looked out at the mangroves islands, the watery view.

"This is my fault."

"Stop it, Rusty."

"Thorn wanted to be John Beresford Tipton," she said.

"Who?"

"A character in some fifties TV show. Back in September I was watching an episode on cable, Thorn came in, sat down, and sat through the whole thing. I don't think he'd ever seen an entire TV show before."

"Must've been pretty good."

"It's called *The Millionaire.* John Beresford Tipton is a retired industrialist. You never see his face, he's always sitting in a high-backed chair. Every week he gives away a cashier's check for a million dollars to some complete stranger. It's his hobby, what keeps him amused. He stayed anonymous, his personal secretary delivered the check to someone Tipton picked out, and the show was about how the money changed that person's life. Sometimes for the good, but a lot of times it turned into a disaster. I can't remember which episode Thorn saw. Probably a good result. He never said it, but I think that show planted the seed. You know, how he acted that day on the boat, wanting to do something big. Stand behind the curtains, pull the levers, and make the world a better place."

Sugarman looked over at Rusty. She was staring out her window, her shoulders quivering. He reached over and cupped the back of her neck. In a moment she grew still, lowered her head, then raised her arm and covered his hand with hers.

"We'll find him," Sugarman said. "I promise you, Rusty. We'll find him."

She removed her hand and he withdrew his.

"I did my due diligence on this transaction," she said, sounding like she was trying to convince herself. "I spent a lot of time thinking it through, researching the land, the people involved. But I should've known something was fishy."

"This isn't your damn fault, Rusty."

"What if these two goons came down and took him off and killed him and hid his body? We might never know."

Sugarman slowed for a line of traffic that was stacking up behind a Winnebago.

"I don't accept the premise."

"Why?"

"What would killing Thorn accomplish? He's already agreed to the deal. It's in the pipeline, right?"

"It is and it isn't."

"How's that?"

"The documents are done, but there's still the closing. It's scheduled for this Tuesday afternoon in Tallahassee. The three parties sit at the table—Division of State Lands, Thorn, and Earl Hammond. Thorn signs over the Sarasota land to the state, accepts their check, and he endorses it to Earl Hammond. Then Hammond signs over Coquina Ranch to the state. Florida gets three times more land than they would have otherwise. Hammond walks away with half a billion dollars; Thorn's divested himself of a good chunk of Bates International and done one hell of a good deed in the process."

"Okay, if somebody's trying to kill this deal, why bother with both Thorn and Earl Hammond? Remove either one of them and there's no deal."

She brushed dust off the dashboard. Turned the sun visor down, then turned it back up again.

"There were red flags. But I ignored them."

"What?"

"Earl Hammond was in a big hurry to give the land away. A real sense of urgency. Margaret Milbanks, she's the head of Division of State Lands, she said Earl got very agitated when he found out the

Florida Forever fund was depleted. He wanted the land to be sealed up in a preservation program as soon as possible. Money wasn't an issue. He seemed ready to donate it for free as long as it was preserved."

"There's lots of groups who'd be happy to take a couple hundred thousand acres off his hands."

"That's the point," Rusty said. "If Thorn's not at the table Tuesday, and the particular deal I structured fell through, Earl Hammond could still give the land to the state or find a private conservation group and make a donation. Taking that land off the table, that was his goal. So if the idea was to kill the deal, then removing Thorn was irrelevant."

"Maybe somebody doesn't have the complete picture. They're carpet bombing when they could've just done a surgical strike."

Rusty was silent. She stared ahead at the road.

"So what do we know about the rest of the Hammonds?"

"Not a lot," she said. "Earl had one son, Earl the third. He and his wife died way back, some kind of accident, avalanche, skiing or something. Earl and his wife raised the two grandsons, Browning and Frisco. Frisco's a cop in Miami."

"What kind of cop?"

"Horse cop. Whatever they call it."

"Mounted unit."

"That's it. And the second son, the younger one, Browning, he runs the ranch, day to day. Wife's name is Claire, college sweethearts. In their late twenties. It was Browning who started the safari operation. Fancies himself a businessman."

"Okay, so let's put it on Browning. Just brainstorm that."

"Go ahead."

"Well, number one, you got an obvious motive. Grandson's afraid he's cut out of the will, so he offs the old man, takes care of Thorn for good measure."

"Makes no sense, Sugar. If Browning's greedy, all he has to do is sit around a few weeks, let the deal play out, and a fortune falls in his lap."

Sugarman worked on that for a minute, watching a couple of

northbound crazies race past at over a hundred. No rules out there on that lonely stretch of road.

"Okay, all right. So is five hundred million what the land is worth on the open market? I mean, if the ranch suddenly belongs to Browning, could he sell if for more than that? Maybe that's his motivation. Screw the deal Earl was working on, make his own deal with higher numbers."

"Five hundred is top dollar. And trust me, there's not a big market for two hundred thousand acres of ranchland west of the lake."

"The grandson doesn't have his facts straight. He gets wind of Earl disposing of the land, but doesn't know about the five hundred."

"A stretch," she said.

"All right. So what's with this urgency thing? Earl was in a hurry to get this done. Why's that? Was he sick?"

"Not that I know."

"So why was he so juiced to protect the land? Protect it from what?"

"Good question."

"I mean what do you protect land like that from? Like you say, it's the middle of nowhere. No highways anywhere close. Clewiston, Palmdale, for christsakes. Trailer parks and barbecue joints. Nobody's going to build a housing development out there, sugarcane fields on one side, Everglades on the other, at least an hour from the city. So what was Earl Hammond afraid of? What's making him move so fast?"

He slowed for an RV with Michigan plates, tooling along at thirty.

He dug out his cell, scrolled through his directory, and found the number.

"What're you doing?"

"Shaking the trees, see what falls out."

"Sugar."

"Old friend of mine works in Miami PD. Twenty years ago we did a couple of tours at the sheriff's office in Key Largo. He went up the ladder, I jumped off. But he'll remember me."

"This guy might know Frisco?"

"Oh, he'll know him."

"The Miami police department can't be that small."

"Mullaney knows everybody on the force. He's the chief."

Sugarman made the call, but Mullaney was in a conference. He left a message with the chief's aid, his cell number, told her it was urgent. She seemed too brisk to Sugar, less attentive than he would've liked, so before she dismissed him, he told her he was calling in regard to the incident with the governor. That gave her pause.

"You have information about the shooting?"

"I do," he said. Somewhat true. True enough.

"Well, FDLE is handling that. Young woman named Anne Donaldson. I'll transfer you to someone who can give you her number."

"Tell Larry I called, give him my cell," Sugar said. "He'll want to talk to me."

He clicked off, slipped the phone in his pocket, and looked over at Rusty. She was on her own cell, listening intently. A few moments later, she said a quiet "Thank you" and snapped her phone shut.

"Who's that?"

"Margaret Milbanks, State Lands."

"And?"

"Other than two lawyers in her office that put the deal together, no one knew Thorn's role, his name, or any of the particulars. Except for one other."

Sugarman waited.

"Margaret's boss," Rusty said. "Governor Sanchez."

"Well, well," he said. "The circle tightens."

"Sugar," she said. "What's the plan? You and me. What are we doing?"

"Plan?"

"We're just going to cruise up to the front gate at Coquina Ranch? That what you think? Start asking questions while a triple homicide investigation is underway?"

Sugarman pulled out into the passing lane and floored it past the Winnebago.

"Sugar, you ran out of Squirrelly Shirley's, jumped in the car, headed up the highway. I thought you had a plan."

He smiled at her. She was a pretty woman, one of those lucky ladies who flourished with age. If not for Thorn . . . if not for that lucky bastard . . .

"I do have a plan. It's worked before, it'll work this time."

"And that would be?"

"We find out what that old man was afraid of, why he was in such a hurry to part with his land, that'll tell us where Thorn is."

"Do that again."

"In the heart of the heart of the trouble. That's where Thorn'll be. You watch."

FIFTEEN

WITH A TIGHT GRIP ON the collar, Thorn hauled his flowered shirt out of the cleft in the sinkhole floor. It was sopping with cool water. The oversized yellow hibiscus blooms had turned two shades darker, and the cotton was starting to shred from being dragged repeatedly across the jagged stones. It was the fourth time he'd dunked and retrieved his shirt, and he was starting to get the hang of it.

Careful not to exert too much pressure, he coiled the shirt into a rope, held it by the ends, lifted it, tipped his head back, opened his mouth and wrung the water out.

He swallowed the dribble, maybe a quarter of a cup, twisted the cloth harder, then harder still for the last drops. The water tasted metallic. Maybe fertilizer run-off or pesticide or some dissolved minerals that had leached into the groundwater. It didn't matter. Better to ingest a few carcinogens than die of thirst before sundown.

Problem was, the process took too long, wedging his shirt into the crevice, soaking up water, and wringing it into his mouth. He'd be working all night before he could rehydrate himself. He was still parched, still felt the drill bit of his headache boring into his frontal lobe, but he had to stop.

He stood up, hung the shirt from a jagged ledge about shoulder high, and took a long look around the pit. It was time to get busy, time to get the hell out of there.

It had to be near noon, which meant this would probably be the best light he'd have all day. A twilight haziness filled the space, with a few splashes of brightness projected onto the walls and floor from sunlight pouring through the chinks between the planks. Three of the stalagmites were illuminated. Spiny tubes with pointed tips, like stalks of coral on the reef.

Stepping around the half-dozen stalagmites, he circled the sinkhole again, patting down the walls, here and there poking his fingers into the crumbly sediment, exploring, finding some places as squashy as fresh plaster, pebbles breaking free, and other areas that were gritty on the surface, but tough an inch below. The bad news was that most of the walls were unyielding, an ancient limestone that had calcified over the centuries into impervious stone.

Impervious to Thorn's fingers anyway.

He retrieved the sardine can he'd pitched into a corner and found the lid nearby. The lid was curled slightly and fit neatly in his hand like a primitive trowel. Thorn selected what he believed was the western side of the sinkhole, a section not quite as sheer as the others. Maybe a few degrees beyond vertical. He and Sugarman had once watched a documentary about a group of blind climbers taking on Mount Everest. That was the extent of his knowledge of rock climbing. It didn't look easy. And it didn't fall nicely into any of Thorn's skill sets.

He was a fly-tier, a fisherman. He had excellent eyesight, fairly good hand-to-eye skills, and a degree of dexterity in his fingers, but he'd never spent time in mountains or around rock walls or cliffs. As close as he'd come to any of that was climbing trees as a kid.

He stood back and tried to calculate the geometry of the climb. How far apart the footholds should be spaced, where exactly to start. He didn't want to consider yet what he would do when he reached the wooden lid at the top of the sinkhole. He'd deal with that in due course. From this distance he couldn't tell how solid the carpentry was, whether the workmen had used screws or nails to fasten it all together. Didn't matter. First he needed footholds.

Trying to climb the wall without some kind of precut traction didn't look possible. A little menacing, too, since the wall was studded with burrs of rock and jagged edges. Losing his hold and sliding back down that rock would be like grinding his flesh across a cheese grater.

The initial foothold was simple. He dug the sharp edge of the sardine lid into a chalky spot about three feet off the floor of the pit. After half a minute he hit a patch of granular sediment, thick sand or marl. The material spilled out of the wall and left a fissure about three inches deep.

He put the toe of his boat shoe in the cranny, a perfect fit, and hoisted himself up, balancing for a few seconds with all his weight on that one foot. He pressed his stomach and chest flush against the wall and searched for a likely spot for a handhold higher up. He scratched the lid against a few places but the rock was too hard. Two or three inches beyond a comfortable reach, he found another natural fissure. He had to keep himself stretched out completely while he used the lid to enlarge the opening.

When he was satisfied, he pushed away and hopped back to the floor. He looked up at the wall. It seemed higher than before. Not insurmountable, but a lot more challenging than he first imagined. For sure, he wasn't going to be able to keep carving footholds then hopping down to catch his breath. Once he got up on the wall and wriggled a foot or two higher, jumping back wouldn't be wise.

Last night when he was shoved into the pit, he'd landed in an incredibly lucky spot. Missed by inches being gored by one of those rocky spikes. Not something he wanted to gamble with again.

And the truth was, he doubted he could absorb one more fall.

His body was a collection of lumps and nicks and deep bruises and stiff and swollen joints, but the sum total of all that was nothing compared to what waited for him if he didn't make it up that wall.

For a few moments he searched for a place to sink his second foot-hold, somewhere around two feet higher than the first. He tried two places but got nowhere with the lid. And the aluminum was already beginning to grow dull, and loose threads of metal were fraying along its edges from the rough use.

He tried brushing it against the wall a few times like a blade against a whetstone, and yes, the fibers dropped away and the edge shined a little brighter.

On the wall, at about the right position for his next step up, he spotted a brownish stone that jutted out about an inch. It was lodged slightly higher than he would've liked, but it would do. He gripped it with both hands and wiggled it up and down like a bad tooth. When it was loose he pried the wedge-shaped rock out of the wall and exposed a deep slot that was just wide enough to insert his hand into. Using the sardine lid he scraped at the hole until he had it broadened enough for his toe.

He looked up at the wall and thought of the blind climbers who picked their way to the peak of Everest, the joy in their faces, their fearless determination. All he had was a bad hangover and a knee heading south and some serious stiffening.

He went over and picked up the body of the sardine can. He wasn't sure how useful it would be as a digging tool. Not as good as the lid. But the lid wasn't going to last much longer. He didn't want to find himself nearing the top of the wall with a used-up digging imple-ment. At least the can itself was heavier-gauge aluminum, and he might use one of its corners to scoop out a cranny or two. He slipped it into his pants pocket and heard it plink against something.

He reached in and drew out the can, then withdrew the wedding ring. The idiot brothers had missed it last night when they frisked him—the diamond solitaire he was going to embarrass Rusty with in front of all their friends and all those strangers. He should have gone ahead and done it. How differently the evening would have gone. He probably wouldn't be a hostage in a sinkhole somewhere near

Lake Okeechobee. More than likely he and Rusty would still be spooned together in bed, sleeping off the party.

At this moment Rusty would be searching for him. He felt more confident of that than he had earlier. The note he'd written might delay her some, but he had no doubt she'd see through it and realize it was written under duress. She and Sugar would be doing what they could to track him down. He couldn't imagine how they'd manage it, but was certain they'd be on his trail.

The thought gave him little comfort.

Once again Thorn had put others at risk. He'd meant well. Secretly, he'd been swollen with pride over the plan Rusty concocted. Something good was going to come from his misspent life. Land would be spared from the march of urban sprawl. Habitat preserved, wildlife saved. All of that seemed hopelessly foolish now. An absurd, self-indulgent fantasy.

He dropped the ring back in his pocket along with the can. He scuffed the toe of his boat shoe at the tip of a stalagmite to try to blunt its sharp point. But that accomplished nothing. He took one last look around before he started the climb.

Something had bothered him earlier when he'd been dunking his shirt in that subterranean water. Not only the oddly smooth sides of the crevice, but something else, something he'd seen, registered, and dismissed in his haste and confusion.

He went back to the crevice, kneeled, reached in, and swabbed his open hand across slick rock several inches below ground. It was a perfect circle about a half foot in diameter. Such a thing had to be manmade. He knew of nothing that exact, that perfectly contoured and smooth that existed in nature.

Elbow below the ground, he ran his hand farther down. And, yes, what looked like an accidental fissure in the stone seemed to be no accident at all.

Which had to mean the pit wasn't a sinkhole. It was more likely the eroded remnants of some ancient well. That slick, perfectly round opening in the rock was a bore hole. With his fingertips he could even feel faint grooves that might have been the tracings of a drill bit chewing into stone.

If that was true, the opening had been carved to tap into the earth, then abandoned later for some reason, and over the years the steady rains had eroded the opening, widened it into a larger and larger pit. How long that erosion had taken would depend on how large the hole was to begin with, but it had to be many years, maybe decades.

As he drew out his hand, he noticed again several white clumps of stone lying beside the opening. That's what he'd seen. That's what nagged at him.

They were a familiar rock formation whose name and significance he'd known in his school years when he'd been under the magical sway of that geology teacher. That man had rhapsodized for hours about the lost worlds beneath our feet. Now, in the haze of his dehydration, hangover, and concussion, Thorn couldn't summon the rock's name or why it was unique. Each of them was about the size of a walnut and seemed to be the fossilized remains of a bunch of interlocking shells.

He picked one up, touched its contours, and pictured that geology teacher. He tried to recall the slow patient voice of the dogged educator who'd taken Thorn's class of smart asses on numerous field trips around south Florida so they could root in the soil, scavenge for rocks, sift through pebbles and old shell bits.

The word came to him then.

It was a rudist. A cluster of mollusks clumped together and hardened into rock, each of them shaped like a tiny human heart. Those bivalve creatures had been extinct for a hundred million years, making their last appearance when the shallow Cretaceous seas covered the Florida peninsula. During their prime, rudists had thrived for thousands of years, and when they died, their shell remains helped form the reefs where long-extinct fish and marine creatures once gathered. Thorn had only seen photographs of rudists. Their fossilized shells were so rare that even his geology teacher had never encountered one outside of a natural-history museum.

That was because the ancient seabed where they once flourished was now buried deep. And the only possible way a rudist could appear in such a place as this was to be pumped up as backwash from a drill rig that had penetrated at least two miles below the earth where Thorn stood.

Which was one hell of a deep hole to search for water.

SIXTEEN

THORN PUT THE FOSSIL IN his pocket and went back to the wall.

He didn't have time to sort it out. There were more urgent matters. He took a long breath, dug his right toe in the first foothold, and hitched himself up, raising his left foot to find the second hole. His right hand clutched for the slot high on the wall.

When his toe was lodged deep into the second hole, he withdrew his right foot and cranked himself up, shifting all his weight to his left leg. The bad knee held fine.

He realized he'd made a mistake. The handhold he'd cut into the wall was on the wrong side, his right, which meant he would have to dig out the next foothold using his weaker, less adroit left hand, and to make matters more complicated, the foothold would have to be dug out close to where his navel was pressed flat against the craggy surface of the pit. He hadn't diagrammed it correctly. Somehow in his woozy state he'd flipped the blueprint. Now he was forced to carve a divot in the rock wall while assuming a yoga position that had no name.

He set about it. Twisting himself, left foot lodged in the slot of stone, right hand gripping above, left hand searching for any yielding spot. At last he found one, dug an inch-deep channel, then came to solid rock or fossilized shell, and had to start over a few inches to the right. He was sweating, and he could hear his own breath rising from the strain of staying in place. Already his muscles had started to complain.

He worked the sardine lid deep into a mushy vein in the wall, making progress. He allowed himself a look backward. No great distance down. But those bayonets of stone worried him. If he fell clumsily he could easily skewer himself.

Still, it wasn't like he was clinging to a cliff high above some bottomless gorge, or clawing his way inch by inch up the towering peaks of a real mountain. He was simply climbing up the sheer walls of a shallow grave.

With the slot widened enough to fit the toe of his boat shoe in, he brought his right foot up and dug it into the niche, wiggled his left foot free, and hauled himself up another foot and a half.

He estimated he had about a dozen feet to go before he reached the wooden deck. Five or six more footholds, a couple more handholds. At this rate he should make it to the top by Christmas.

Jonah burst into the hunting cabin, buzzing with what he'd learned from Thorn, eager to lay it on Moses, then the two of them could brainstorm about what it meant. He guzzled some water from the tap, called out for Moses, but his brother hadn't returned from his scouting mission at the lodge.

For a moment Jonah stood in the kitchen, listening to the birds outside, listening to an airplane passing. Knowing what he was about to do, but resisting it, because Moses could return any time and catch him. But that familiar tug was too much, and finally he left the kitchen and drifted back to the storage room where they stashed the auction goodies.

They kept the door locked so none of the visiting asshole hunters would stumble in. He unlocked it, went inside. He stood looking at the shelves, five of them, mostly photos and letters, a couple of bullet-pocked shirts stiff with blood folded up inside plastic bags. Mostly though, it was prison artwork. Killers liked to draw. Like little kids on rainy days, nothing to do but play with their crayons and paint sets.

It was quiet in the storage room. He couldn't hear the birds anymore. The airplane was gone. In the warm air there were ripples of weirdness, as if the letters and drawings and poems and clothes were giving off radioactive vibes from all the grisly shit those people pulled. Superstars of American homicide. Ghouls and cannibals and blank-eyed killers.

At the moment their inventory was low. A lot of selling lately had cleared a couple of shelves. What they had at the moment was a scribbled letter with assorted doodles and a poem from Richard Ramirez, the Night Stalker. And there was a Henry Lee Lucas painting of a sunrise over a mountain range. Lucas got his start killing his mother, then went on to murder hundreds more. He claimed six hundred but cut that in half eventually, though nobody ever nailed it down for sure. They had a drawing the BTK killer did, Dennis Rader, a very graphic and detailed pen and ink that showed all the bad shit he was planning to do to one of his female victims. Bind, torture, kill. And then there was Jonah's current favorite, a topless self-portrait made by Carol Bundy. Big-titted woman wearing horn-rimmed glasses, another serial killer who first beheaded her ex-boyfriend then helped Douglas Clark with the Sunset Strip Murders, killing a string of hookers. Big boobs, little red nipples, like the tits on that bar girl in Clewiston Jonah had screwed a few times.

All told, just that single shelf of murder porn had to be worth over five K.

Their latest prize was an oil painting by John Wayne Gacy. It was poster-sized on a black background with skulls lined up, five rows of seven skulls. Each skull exactly the same, like the face a creepy kid would carve into a pumpkin, empty eye sockets, empty nose hole, shark teeth in the mouth.

Gacy painted in a bloody scythe behind each skull. One skull for each of his victims. Thirty-four boys. And in the top left-hand corner, at the head of the first row, was the face of a circus clown with big red lips and a doughy white face and a limp white-and-blue sock hat. That was a self-portrait. Gacy had done gigs at kid's parties. Pogo the Clown was his stage name.

When they got around to putting the Gacy painting up for auction, Moses was going to start the bidding at four thousand, about twice what they'd paid for it from one of Gacy's jailers.

He knew it was wrong. Knew he shouldn't handle the merchandise. You could get grease stains on them, fingerprints, lower their value. You could drop it, bump it, scuff an edge. It was stupid. Totally against the rules.

He listened for Moses, but heard nothing. He slid the Gacy out of the bubble wrap it arrived in and held it up to the light. Gacy had killed boys. Teenage boys. Raping them, then strangling them, stashing their bodies in the dirt beneath his house. Jonah thought about that as he looked at that picture, those thirty-four skulls, thirty-four dead kids. And that one clown like God up in the left-hand corner smiling down on his creations. The clown's lips were pouty and red.

Jonah had killed five people so far. Nobody important enough to make the news. All work-related, impersonal assignments handed out from the big guy. A pro like Jonah should have zero respect for a sick fuck like Gacy, who was nothing but a retard whose hobby was tormenting kids. But the truth was different. Jonah couldn't help himself. Sometimes he found himself getting buzzed from where his mind took him. Coming into the storage room, handling the items, letting his thoughts roam.

People like Gacy were famous. They were celebrities with their mug shots on TV. People read books about them, movies got made, TV shows recounted their life stories. They became legends, part of the fucked-up folklore of America. While Jonah labored in obscurity, doing his job, efficient and straightforward. At his current kill rate, he'd pass Gacy's thirty-four before he was done. But no one was going to know. He'd be anonymous to the end.

In the news photos Jonah had seen, Gacy's house was gray and shabby, his bedroom was in the back, away from the street. Jonah could picture a boy tied up on Gacy's bed, struggling, his mouth stuffed with cloth. The kid's eyes were big and he was crying and shivering. Jonah imagined walking slowly over to the kid like Gacy did, thinking about how Gacy peeled off the kid's clothes and did sex things to him. Everything Jonah had ever done to a college girl or a bar maid or a hooker, Gacy did to the kid. Did it and did it again till he was worn out and empty. Jonah pictured all that, how it would feel to choke the kid to death using the edge of a board the way Gacy did it, and watching the boy die in his hands.

He replayed in his head the black-and-white videotape they'd auctioned off, the one they'd sold eventually to that talky waitress in Omaha. Gacy's floorboards ripped up by the cops, exposing the crawlspace. All those shallow graves down in the dirt. One by one he'd buried the boys until every inch of the crawlspace soil was used up. After that he dumped his last six victims into local rivers.

Holding Gacy's drawing, Jonah saw himself down in that crawlspace, digging a hole. Working in those tight quarters with his shovel. Trying not to disturb the bones on either side of the new grave. All the while tasting the suffocating ammonia smell, the decay, the clammy air. Jonah Faust, shovel in hand, chunking the spade deep into the soft dirt, moving earth aside, sweating, hot, nauseous, and shivering with thrill. Digging that grave until it was deep enough, then grabbing the garbage bag, feeling the dead kid's weight, getting a revolting whiff of the decomposing body, then stuffing it into the earth, with one last look to remember how it felt to kill the kid, before covering the black garbage bag with dirt and more dirt. Airless down there beneath that house, as rank and dark and disgusting as the belly of a rancid whale.

Jonah heard a noise and turned to find Moses in the doorway.

Jonah was still down in the crawlspace. He hadn't meant to go there. He'd trailed along behind Gacy, looking out of the eyes of that mad-dog killer. He knew the racing heart, the wild electrified buzz. Gacy wasn't cold and empty. He was having fun. For him, the whole thing was pleasure beyond all pleasure. A black joy.

Jonah held up the Gacy painting.

"I was looking at this."

"Jesus Christ. I can't leave you alone for five minutes. You're some little kid."

"I wondered how his brain worked. How it felt."

"Put that thing away. Put it in the bubble wrap. Do it now."

Jonah slid the Gacy back into its packing material. Moses walked over to him, got up close, and reached out his right fist and knuckle-thumped Jonah's forehead.

"Anyone in there? Anyone alive?"

"Oh, come on, man. Don't go schoolyard on me."

"Jesus Christ. Jesus H. Christ."

"I'm sorry, man. I apologize. No harm, no foul."

"This was a bad idea," Moses said. "This whole thing."

"What?"

Moses swept a hand at the shelves.

"All of it, this murder bullshit. It's playing with fire. I knew better."

"What fire?"

Moses was silent, staring off. Big strong man, handsome and peaceful.

"What fire, Moses?"

"Forget it. We got to get busy."

"What fire, goddammit?"

Moses closed his mouth, looked down at the floor, and shook his head.

"Go on," Jonah said. "Go on and say it."

"It's in our blood. You and me, we could get a transfusion every day of our fucked-up lives, it'd be there still."

141

"What's in our blood?"

"Just drop it. We got to pack up and get out of here."

"You're talking about the old man," Jonah said. "The drunken prick?"

"There's cops swarming all over the ranch. We've got to move."

"The old man did shit like this. Is that it? Come on, tell me."

Moses stared at the Gacy in Jonah's hands.

"Like Gacy? With kids. He did that kind of shit?"

Moses bowed his head. It was true.

"Jesus," Jonah said.

"As perverted as any of these people we make our living off of. It's why Mom dumped his ass. She knew what he was doing. Neighbor kids, boys he found on the street. In playgrounds, all that shit."

"I thought he was just a drunk. A prick. An abusive asshole."

"He was all that," Moses said. "It was going on before you could remember. You were like four or five."

Jonah tried to say something, but there was only a black droning in his head.

He set the Gacy on the floor. Cocked it carefully against the wall.

"He fucked with you, Moses? He hurt you in bed?"

Moses didn't answer. He didn't need to. His face was slack, the way he got when he zoned out. Jonah stepped back for a better look. Hell, he'd been wrong. Wrong about his brother being easygoing, cool, and carefree. It was different than that, completely different. It was like Moses knew how to power himself down. Put himself in safety mode.

"And me, Moses? What about me?"

Moses came back from the dead zone, looked Jonah square on.

"No, he never touched you. I stopped him."

"You stopped him."

"I did. I kept him from you."

"Stopped him how?"

"Never mind."

"Jesus on the cross," Jonah said. "The prick didn't run off. That story, him packing his bags, throwing twenty bucks on the kitchen table on his way out the door, that was a lie."

Moses went over to shelves, started at one end, swept his hand along each one, knocked all the drawings and the poems and doodles onto the floor.

"He would've killed us," he said. "But we're still alive."

"Are we?"

"That lady next door, Phyllis, you remember? Did pottery in her garage, old white-haired lady."

Jonah wasn't able to reply.

"She was like seventy-five, lived alone, but she knew what was going on inside our house. I went over, told her what I did to the old man.

"I don't know why I picked her. If she called the police, that'd be the end. But no. She said it was a good thing. I was a hero. The two of us dug a hole out back in the middle of the night, me and Phyllis. She drove me to a canal and had me throw the butcher knife in. We covered that hole, planted that Jerusalem thorn you liked, one with the yellow blooms. Planted it right there on top of the prick."

"I remember that tree."

"Hadn't been for Phyllis, that old lady next door, I'd be on death row. You'd've gone into some foster family, never seen each other again."

Jonah felt dull and sleepy. Too much to absorb. Information overload.

"Look," Moses said. "We need to get our asses in gear. Put a bullet in Thorn and go."

"Go where?"

"I don't know. Miami, somewhere. A do-over."

"Why're we leaving? What happened?"

"Hammond's bitch put us at the lodge last night. We hung around too long after you did Saperstein, and she saw the Prius in the lot, told the investigators. We're on their shit list."

Jonah looked at the Gacy.

"I was breaking Thorn down," Jonah said. "He was into some kind of deal with Earl Hammond. Real estate. They partnered up on something."

"He told you that? That guy doing business with Big Earl? Give me a break."

"I believe him. They were doing something together."

"Time to man up, Jonah. Get your game face on. I'll take care of Thorn. You get whatever clothes and shit you want. Can you do that?"

"It should be me doing Thorn," Jonah said. "He was my project. That was my idea from the start."

"It's going to be okay, Jonah. You and me, we're alive, we're fine. The old man is dead and we're flourishing. No reason to get bogged down in all that. It happened and it's done. We are who we are."

"He was killing kids," Jonah said. "We were living in the same house. Our freaking mother left us with that guy."

"You were four. It doesn't count if you don't remember it."

"It counts," Jonah said. "Goddamn right it counts."

"Don't go south on me, Jonah. We're okay. We made it out alive."

"Jesus shit," Jonah said. "The MoJo brothers. Man, we're like so completely, totally, down to the core fucked. We're no different than these whackjobs."

"No way. Don't think like that. The bad shit we've done, we've done to survive. These people, they were getting off. It was a thrill ride. Not the same thing. Apples and oranges."

"It's all fruit, man. Different color, sweet or sour, it's still fucking fruit."

Jonah swung around, nabbed the Glock off the weapon shelf, checked the magazine, snapped it back, took a last look at Pogo the Clown and the thirty-four skulls, the images warped and glowing inside the bubble wrap, and he walked through the house, went outside, then marched through the back pasture where a herd of ibex goats were drifting around, munching on grass. As he grew close, one by one they lifted their heads, their ears perking as they registered his freakoid aura. In unison they bleated and scattered in a blaze of white dust.

SEVENTEEN

THORN MADE IT TO THE top of the pit, panting, knuckles busted, fingers torn. When he'd levered himself up the last few inches, he discovered a ledge not visible from below. He stared at it for a moment, thinking his vision might be playing tricks.

The depression was only a foot beneath the wood decking, and was recessed into the rock about thirty inches, roughly the width of a footlocker.

The space was so cramped that after he squeezed into it, he couldn't draw a full breath, and he wasn't certain he'd be able to pry his body out again.

The day was warm, somewhere in the upper-eighties, and felt at least ten degrees hotter in his tight space. Sweat pinkened with blood dripped off his bare flesh and trailed down the rock ledge. His throat was dry and his headache was chiming away again. He looked down at his flowered shirt hanging on the outcropping below. He should've indulged in a few more sips before he started the climb. It might be a while before he had another chance at water.

For a minute he lay there, diagnosing the workmanship of the wood decking.

The trap door in the deck appeared to be a recent addition. Its edges were cut sloppily as if by a ham-fisted amateur, and there were flakes of sawdust still clinging to the seams. Placed dead center in the cover, the hatch opened directly above the middle of the pit. Its hinges were on the upside, and it was a good yard beyond Thorn's reach. If a rope had hung from the opening, he might've had a chance to fling himself out from where he was, grab the rope, and haul himself up. But miss it, he'd drop straight down onto the half-dozen punji sticks of rock sprouting from the cavern floor.

He assumed the trap door had been added by Jonah or Moses to serve its present function. Turning the pit into a holding pen. Or maybe they'd just been exploring.

Clearly, the wood decking had been built by someone a lot more competent. That original carpenter had laid out the surface planks over a crosshatching of two-by-four struts whose ends were toe-nailed into notches chiseled out of the rock.

The planks of the flooring were nailed directly into the struts, no crossbeams, no cantilevers, no reinforcing joists as one might expect on an outdoor deck that would have to support the weight of several people. Apparently the wood covering was erected simply to prevent kids or wildlife from falling into the hole, with no consideration given to foiling someone's escape from below. Thank God for that.

The most vulnerable place Thorn could find were those anchoring nails.

Although their tips had gouged the rocks and most were sunk an inch or two into the wall, now that Thorn had gotten to know the geology of this pit, he believed those nails could be loosened.

The rock's composition was mostly limestone, which would crumble under enough strain. To jimmy loose the strut all he'd need to do was pull two of those nails free. Once he did that, he might be able to lever up that decking board and squeeze out of the opening.

What he needed was a good claw hammer or pry bar.

All he had was a sardine can and an antique wedding ring.

147

He took one more look at the construction, then squirmed a half turn to get at his pocket. Wriggling his right arm to his side, he dug out both the ring and the can.

He twisted to his right, tucked his shoulder, and brought his face to within inches of the two cut nails. They were flat-sided, made of steel with blunt points, and both were sunk about an inch into the chink in the rock wall.

Thorn screwed the diamond solitaire onto his left pinkie for safe keeping and got to work with the sardine can. He angled his arm under the strut and scraped at the rough stone around the entry point of the nail. He grubbed and jabbed, but after a minute it was clear that wasn't going to work. The aluminum didn't leave a scratch.

He set the can aside on the ledge.

Then took a long look at the wedding ring. He knew Kate Truman wouldn't object to his using it for this rough work. A no-nonsense, pragmatic woman, she'd gladly risk the family heirloom to dig away the limestone around the base of those steel nails. Do it, she'd say. Don't give it a second thought. Get free no matter what it takes.

He took the ring off his pinkie, found the best grip, pinched it tight and jammed a faceted edge against the dry rock. He ground it a half turn back and forth, then another grind and another. Chips of pulverized rock flittered onto the ledge. Thorn pressed harder, grating gemstone against limestone, screwing it right then left, watching the chalky rock fall away from the root of the nail.

As he worked, the diamond gave off a rosy light, and it was that light that flew Thorn back to one sunny afternoon in high school geology class—a lesson about diamonds, the way they were supposed to be cut in harmony with their own crystalline structure, a process meant to liberate the internal reflections of light, the unique brilliance within each stone. Like people, that old geology teacher said, all of us get the chance to shape our surface identities, those facets of ourselves that others see. But the trick is to craft our outer lives in harmony with what's inside, and in so doing, enhance rather than stifle the true light that burns within each of us.

With Kate's ring, it took him less than a minute to expose the first nail's root. He grabbed the sardine can again and with its curled edge he pried the steel nail free. While he rested, he took a look at the four gold prongs that formed the simple setting on the ring. That would be the weak link. The torque he was applying to the gemstone was stressing that setting in ways it wasn't fashioned to withstand. But there was only one more nail to go and no other choice but this.

He held his breath as he worked, and the prongs hung on awhile longer. They were still holding as he cleared the last crumbles of limestone from the base of the second nail. That's when footsteps shook the decking overhead.

Thorn froze for half a moment, then squirmed deeper into the burrow, fumbled the ring, lost it, swatted with his left hand as it trickled away, bouncing onto the ledge, where it rolled a few inches, bumped into a nub of stone, and spun over the rim into the pit.

EIGHTEEN

JONAH POPPED THE LID. IN no mood for talk, he aimed the Glock into the pit and fired twice at Thorn. Then twice more for good measure.

The blue-and-yellow shirt danced away from the wall and settled on the floor of the pit. Jonah stooped forward and peered into the darkness.

The shirt was empty. Just lying there.

Hadn't he seen Thorn a minute ago? Wasn't that him wearing the shirt? Getting a minor spook on, Jonah extended the pistol into the hole, making a circle around the rocky walls, then going back the other way. He felt his skin prickle. Double-spooked. Some kind of voodoo bullshit going on.

Jonah got down on his knees, squinting harder into the darkness.

"You fucker. Show yourself."

He heard something down there, soft and low like overheated breathing. Or maybe it was the moan of wind. The Navajo flute music of the dead. Departed souls whispering their secrets into the currents of air.

Jonah fired at the shirt again, spewing rock fragments everywhere, digging a pit inside the pit.

"Goddammit. Goddamn your ass."

When he got back to the hunting cabin and babbled it all to Moses, about shooting at the empty shirt, Moses slapped him. Not hard, not angry. Only to wake him from his daze. Slapped him a second time and said, "Give me the gun."

And Moses, his handsome brother, the brother who'd risked his own life to save Jonah from their depraved old man, jogged out the front door while Jonah sunk onto the edge of his bed and stared between his knees at the cabin floor.

Thorn knew he had only a minute or two before they returned. If he stayed put, they'd find him. If he jumped down they'd find him quicker. There had to be a third choice. A way to counterattack. But only if he could find a better angle.

Squirming to his right, he explored the shelf behind him with the toe of his shoe. Nothing there, just more sheer wall. As he was drawing his leg back he felt a slight dip in the ledge. He craned around to see. It was a depression about the size of a bathroom sink. He studied it for a moment, saw how it might work.

He had to inch backward, scrunch himself into a tight tuck, then pivot his legs in the opposite direction. Cuts etched his chest and arms, and blood was tacky on his knees and shins. There was a dull ache in his gut, as though he'd torn muscles in his stomach from cramming himself into such a knot.

After he got a breath, he extended his legs one at a time into the bowl and eased down, toes over the edge, hunched into a squat like a swimmer on the blocks frozen in his starting crouch. He was poised to leap, but no longer sure his legs would respond when the moment came.

Good news and bad. The bad was very bad. He was now fully

exposed to anyone who brought his face down to the level of the wooden decking. The good wasn't all that good, because from this new squatting position, Thorn had the longest of long shots to uncoil and lunge upward and grab hold of a sleeve, an arm, or maybe the pistol.

One try would be all he got. If he missed he was going to plunge back to the floor of the cavern. And then it was over. Fish in a barrel.

He waited. He waited some more. He felt a tickle of sweat or blood coiling down his thighs. What was numb before was quickly going dead.

At last he saw the shadow moving across the deck overhead. He tried to limber himself, tried to send out messages to the lightless continents of his extremities. He wasn't sure what parts of him were still awake and what parts had retired. He'd find out shortly.

It was Moses on the deck. He could tell by the louder screeches of the planks as the bigger man eased forward toward the opening.

At the hatch the same gun he'd seen before reappeared. The hand holding it was thick and dusted with black hair. The pistol moved smoothly as though the man was shining a careful beam of light in concentric circles around the cavern. A man of precision. A man in firm control of his emotions and his tools.

Thorn saw the glint of the sardine can on the ledge a foot away. He snaked his hand to it, lifted it without sound. He flicked it across the cavern, and it clanged against the far wall and bounced down the pitted stone, landing directly below the hatch.

The hand dropped lower. Moses was in a crouch, stretching out his arm as he bent forward to peer into the cavern. The pistol came first, then his hairy wrist, then his blue shirt cuff, and an inch or two more of the sleeve. When his sharp profile came down into the twilight, Thorn leaped out, both hands grabbing for the forearm.

And he got it, latched on as the pistol fired then fired again.

His hands slipped an inch on the man's thick arm, relocked on the wrist, but Moses was unyielding.

Thorn bounced his weight up and down against the man's strength and leverage, and felt him rock forward, briefly off balance. Thorn rattled the pistol, rattled it again, and it shook loose from the man's grip and fell, clipping Thorn's bare knee as it went.

Thorn bounced again, but Moses was ready for it this time. He clamped his other hand on Thorn's right wrist, and began to rise, hauling Thorn up to the daylight with the effortless power of a two-ton wench.

There was nothing rational in Thorn's reaction. If he'd had time to work out the odds, he might have decided to ride on up to the land and go one on one with Moses on that pineland prairie. But his instincts said otherwise, and he kicked his feet up, and planted the soles of his feet against the bottom of the deck, let Moses drag his arms a little higher so the big man was slightly off balance, then he thrust his legs straight and dragged the big man headfirst down into the cavern.

In the pitching tumble, their bodies collided midair, Thorn taking a futile swing at the man's face, then came another crash against the floor. This time Thorn landed hard on his right side, cushioned by the other man's bulk.

He rolled away, his lungs struggling. He was dazed, wobbling, remembering the pistol that fell somewhere close. Eyes bleared over. He pushed himself upright, rubbed his vision clear, raised his fists to block a punch or throw one.

Moses lay on his back at Thorn's feet. A few inches above his navel, a spike of stone jutted from his belly. Blood was darkening his blue shirt.

He was awake and looking at Thorn. He lifted his head and saw what had happened to him, then set his head back down. His mouth relaxed into a lazy smile.

"Fucked," he said.

Thorn retrieved the pistol. He ejected the clip, thumbed out the remaining rounds. Only two. He fitted them back in the magazine and slid it back into the Glock.

From far away he heard Jonah calling out. He was yelling for Moses, yelling his brother's name again. Coming closer.

Thorn stepped over to the side of the pit and stood beneath the ledge where the diamond ring had fallen. He scanned the floor of the cavern but saw no sign of it. He scuffed his feet in the dust, listening to Jonah's voice calling out, closer and closer.

Moses grunted and coughed. His head rocked back and he held perfectly still as though exposing his neck for a barber's blade.

Thorn continued his search for the ring. Jonah called out again.

Thorn stooped over, peering at the floor, crisscrossing the area below the ledge methodically until he spotted a gleam at the base of one of the stubby stalagmites. He picked up Kate's ring, blew off the dust, dropped it in his pocket. The diamond and the rudist. Two survivors of another age.

Above him, Jonah thumped across the wood decking, and Thorn raised the pistol and aimed at the hatch. Jonah stopped short of the opening.

Moses hacked against the pain. He rolled his head from side to side like a lover in ecstasy, then his body began to buck as if he were attempting to pull himself free of the spike. A second later when his body stilled, Thorn was certain that Moses had moved beyond the possibilities of speech.

But he was wrong.

As Thorn held his aim on the opening above, Moses bellowed, "Gun! He's got a gun!"

Thorn held his aim. He could make out Jonah's shadow through the chinks in the plank. Tempted to fire, but knowing it was a risky play with only two shots left.

"You okay, Mo?" His voice was bewildered and forlorn. "Moses, you hear me, man? You okay? You in trouble down there?"

But Moses couldn't answer. For Thorn was crouched over him, grinding a knee into his throat, bearing down with all his weight, depriving Moses of his last breaths, cutting short his final seconds. All the while keeping the pistol fixed on the opening above.

Jonah wailed his brother's name. Wailed it again, a panicked howl.

Moses' arms jiggled once and dropped to his sides.

Then the shadow on the decking moved away and the wail retreated.

Thorn lifted his knee and felt for a pulse on Jonah's big brother. None there. For a moment he took his own pulse, the moral one, and got the same result. Not a pang of regret, not even a goddamn twitch.

He retrieved his flowered shirt, put it on, still damp and riddled with holes. He tucked the Glock into a front pocket of his shorts, and climbed the wall a second time. Driven by the certain knowledge that Jonah was coming back fully armed, Thorn made it up the steep rock without a slip or hesitation, as quick and sticky-fingered as a cartoon hero scaling an office tower.

He wedged back into his familiar burrow, not wasting a second, he found the best angle for leverage, planted his hands, then heaved up against the loosened plank.

He blew a breath, blew out another, grunting like one of those stumpy weightlifters forcing the iron bar up and off his chest, straining with everything he had to raise the end of the board an inch, then another.

The plank flexed and he heard the squeal of rusty nails pulling loose farther down, and he blew out another breath and rammed his shoulder against the board, and it creaked once more and tore free.

Thorn shoved it aside, and stuck his head out into the daylight, twisted and wriggled and jammed his body through the gap and hauled himself up and out onto the land again.

Good lord it was a stunning day, with the sun high and fiercely bright, and the sky an exhilarating blue. A half mile to the west he saw a small cabin in the shelter of a dozen pines. A compact car was parked nearby. Thorn turned and headed in the opposite direction, toward the closest stand of trees, sprinting without pain, as light-footed and limber and free of gravity as a schoolboy set loose for the summer.

NINETEEN

ANTWAN DISHED UP A THIRD helping of roast beef from the serving dish that Deloria held out to him, saying, "Thank you kindly, ma'am, these are mighty fine vittles," lathering up his words with hokey southern charm, all the while grinning at the cook, Deloria Gonzalez, whose eyes were red and swollen from sobbing in the kitchen over the loss of Gustavo and Earl Hammond.

Other than Antwan's plate, the table was bare. Fifteen minutes earlier all the serving dishes and plates had been removed, but that didn't slow Antwan. Browning kept looking off toward the living room, where two crime-scene technicians were still studying blood patterns on the carpet.

For the last few minutes, Browning had been using his great-grandfather's gold toothpick to probe his gums. For as long as Claire had been on Coquina Ranch, Earl Senior's gold toothpick sat untouched in a shot glass of cut crystal on a side table next to the family Bible. Browning must've been eyeing it for a while but had restrained himself as long as Earl Junior was alive.

For a moment she tried to attribute his behavior to simple heedlessness, the bewilderment of grief. Or to the second glass of bourbon he was knocking back just now. But try as she might, those excuses wouldn't wash.

That Browning was using the toothpick at such a moment was as crude an act of disrespect as a Hammond could offer to family traditions. He might just as well have rifled through Earl's pockets before his body was stretchered away.

Frisco sat at ease, wrists on the table, fingers intertwined as though in prayer. He was monitoring the progress of a housefly as it tracked across the blue tablecloth toward a pile of sugar that Antwan spilled while spiking his iced tea.

Making this series of small observations was how Claire was keeping herself intact. Holding tight, maintaining a watchful disengagement. There had been almost no conversation at their luncheon. Antwan had asked Frisco how he'd been doing, and Frisco made some stock reply. Nothing substantial. Nothing about Earl, nothing about the grotesque tragedy of the night before or the investigation unfolding around them. Nothing about Claire, whether she was to be crowned a hero as Frisco claimed, or if she was seconds from being handcuffed and dragged away to jail by one of the armed men in the other room.

"A funeral," Claire said. "We need to talk about a funeral. Two funerals."

"There'll be no funeral for Gustavo, if that's what you mean. That son of a bitch is going to hell. No charlatan priest is doing some last-second absolution hocus-pocus on his everlasting soul." Browning's voice was directed toward the kitchen, speaking for Deloria's benefit, so she might spread the master's curse among the help. A new boss in town.

Browning downed the last of his bourbon. He clinked the cubes inside the glass as if considering another, then smacked it down.

"Ya'll have a preacher in mind?" Antwan forked in another bite.

"The Hammonds," said Frisco, "are not big churchgoers."

"Didn't think so," Antwan said. "As it happens, I know a couple of

Bible beaters in Miami. Big-time TV evangelistas. White or Afro, take your pick."

Browning cleared his throat for effect.

" 'The mirth of the wicked is brief, the joy of the godless lasts but a moment.' Man, old Earl loved to trot that one out when he thought I was slacking. It's from Job. He was big on Job. Revelations, Numbers. All the hardass books."

Everyone turned to look at him, but Browning was preoccupied with freeing a tendril of beef from his teeth.

"Do tell," Antwan said.

"And the goddamn Great Depression, that was another of Earl's obsessions. That man never got over it. Couldn't take pleasure in anything cause he thought God was going to snatch it away from him any second."

"Let's hear some more of that good Bible stuff," Antwan said.

"This is from Numbers," said Browning. "In Earl's own voice."

He glanced at Claire with a grin like a kid doing a forbidden parlor trick.

"Cut it out, Browning," Frisco said. "Show some respect."

But he went ahead with an uncanny impersonation of Earl Hammond's gruff speech. It was a talent Browning had never displayed before.

"Leviticus five, seventeen. 'If a person sins and does what is forbidden in any of the Lord's commands, even though he does not know it, he is guilty and will be held responsible.' "

Antwan put his fork down and patted his hands together.

"Like Earl himself was sitting right there speaking those very words."

"Here's one," Browning said, and brought forth Earl's voice a second time. " 'Do not pollute the land where you are. Bloodshed pollutes the land, and atonement cannot be made for the land on which blood has been shed, except by the blood of the one who shed it.' "

Browning sent Claire a sheepish smile, shrugging a halfhearted apology. She just shook her head and turned her eyes away.

"That's some god," Antwan said. "One unforgiving asshole."

"Show some manners," Frisco said. "Both of you."

"What?" Browning said. "What the hell's eating you?"

"Knock it off," Frisco said. "I'm not telling you again."

Antwan smiled to himself, picked up his knife and fork, and sliced up a few cubes of beef, speared one, then stirred it in the gravy and tucked it into his mouth.

"Come on now, Frisco," Antwan said. "You got to admit, boy's got a gift."

"Your wife is taking this hard," Frisco said. "In case you and your wing man haven't noticed."

Antwan turned and looked at Claire, then reached out and patted her on the shoulder. She stifled a cringe.

"No reason to feel bad, Miss Claire. You're the stuff of legend. Walk in with a shotgun, unload on a man in the act of homicide. It's all good. I mean, aside from the loss of Earl Hammond. That's surely an immeasurable sorrow to us all. But there's no blame on you. None whatsoever."

Claire bent forward at the waist, tipping in her chair as if she'd had the breath punched out of her.

She needed to unburden. She had to stop this churning, get out of the suffocating chambers of her mind. Browning should have been the one to turn to, but hearing him mock Earl Junior and watching him fiddle with that gold toothpick sickened and repelled her. In the overnight hours her mannerly, deferential husband had disappeared. This new Browning Hammond was behaving like some freshly coronated prince cavorting in his throne, taking practice swings with his scepter.

Now Antwan made a production of patting his lips with his napkin. He refolded the white linen square and arranged it beside his plate, and announced that it was a fine meal on a very sad day. Everything spoken with that smile tingeing his lips.

"Tell me about the map," Frisco said.

Browning pried another fleck of meat from between his teeth, looked it over, sucked it off the gold toothpick, then set the implement down and lined it up neatly on the tablecloth. A mirror image to Antwan's tidiness, as though the two of them were working in tandem, performing some kind of drill from their football days.

"What map you talking about, Frisco?"

"Last night there was a map on the coffee table. It was rolled out flat and there were a dozen red marks on it."

"Where'd you hear about any map?"

Browning kept his gaze on Frisco, but his eyes made small angry darts her way.

"So you're saying there was no map?" Frisco said. "No map of any kind?"

Browning looked at Antwan, and Antwan shrugged.

"Don't remember no map. No map at all."

"I don't either," Browning said.

"There was a map," Claire said. "I saw it on the coffee table."

Antwan slid his chair back and seemed to consider putting his feet up on the table. Then checked himself.

"Oh, she means the shopping center," Antwan said. "My project in Tamarac. That's what threw me off. It wasn't no map. It was a blueprint. The layout of the plaza, the stores, parking lot, the bathrooms. All that shit."

"A shopping center," Frisco said.

"In Tamarac," Antwan said.

"You're building a shopping center?"

"One of my projects, yeah, me and a couple of skin doctors. Don't tell me, Frisco, you're one of them tree huggers can't abide progress."

Browning was silent. He'd picked up the toothpick again and was holding it between thumb and index finger as if measuring its length. He was staring down at the tablecloth like he was waiting to see if Antwan's shopping center story held up before he was compelled to join in.

160

Claire wasn't sure how flawed her perception was. Above all, Browning had always seemed an honorable man. Though like anyone he had his flaws. A temper that could flare unpredictably. More than once she'd had to tug him out of a restaurant or bar when he'd locked eyes with a local cowboy who grinned too knowingly at Claire. That was familiar territory, boy-men finding their way. But the person who sat across from her at the table seemed a sudden stranger. A man who'd somehow managed to shrug off any trace of remorse or horror from the night before and was sporting with a plaything he would never have touched with Earl alive.

"I want to see this map," Frisco said. "This blueprint. Where is it now?"

"Out in my car, I believe. You want me to go get it?"

"It wasn't a blueprint," Claire said. "I know what a blueprint is. This was a map, some kind of survey map. It wasn't any damn blueprint. Don't treat me like a child."

Antwan raised both hands in defense, mimicking a chastened look.

"I'll go get it if you want. It's in the Mercedes."

"How about the Faust brothers?" Frisco said.

Browning was admiring the gold, angling it so it glinted in the sunlight.

Antwan pushed his plate forward and stretched his arms straight above his head and yawned.

"What about them?" Browning glanced at his brother, then cut a look at Claire.

"Were the Faust boys here last night?"

"Not that I know."

"Their car was here," Frisco said, fingers still laced, wrists against the table edge. Same steady tone of detachment.

"Those two boys come and go. I don't have tracking devices on them," Browning said. "What're you after, Frisco?"

"So they weren't here last night?"

"I said they weren't."

161

"How about Gustavo? Why was he fired? Or was he?"

Browning stared indifferently at his brother.

"I don't want to hear that man's name mentioned in this house ever again."

Frisco's eyes were still cocked down.

"Earl mention anything about some big changes coming to the ranch? Some radical changes?"

Browning dropped the toothpick and pushed his chair back.

"Goddammit, Frisco. Cops been grilling me all fucking day, now I got to take a load of shit from you. No way. You don't have any right to harass me. You don't have a fucking clue what goes on out here. You think it's all fun and games. Man, I'm busting my ass trying to stay even. Feed grain costs doubled last year, and same with fertilizer for the grazing pastures. You have any idea what a bag of clover seed or purple top turnips goes for? And Christ, our fuel bills are through the roof. We're lucky to clear one percent on the cattle operation, and we haven't started making money on the safari. I could put the same amount of cash in a T-bill and make four times the profit this ranch turns. Earl ran this place like a hobby farm. Every idea I had about improving things, he'd shoot it down in a heartbeat.

"But you wouldn't know about any of that, because you're off in your dream world, playing with your horses, riding around Miami like the Lone Ranger. So don't come out here and bully me with that law-enforcement third-degree bullshit. Don't pull that big-brother garbage on me. You know what I'm saying? I'm not a kid anymore. I'm not your goddamn punching bag."

Frisco smiled down at his hands.

"Been polishing that for a while, have you?"

"Stop it, you two." Claire rose and scooped up Antwan's dish and held it out to him till he got the message and picked up his napkin and dropped it onto the plate.

Her husband's cupid cheeks were blotched, and that vein angling toward his left eye was so swollen it seemed on the verge of rupture.

"And you, Antwan?" Frisco said. "Earl mention anything to you about a radical change around the ranch?"

Antwan produced the toothy grin he used to flaunt on the gridiron when a clear path to the end zone opened up before him.

"Much as I do love coming out here to Coquina," Antwan said, "the affairs of this ranch ain't no business of mine. I got no skin in this game."

"Good to hear," Frisco said. "Let's try to keep it like that."

Browning came to his feet, he tapped one end of the toothpick on the tablecloth as if gaveling the meeting to a close. He looked down at Frisco, at Antwan, saving Claire for last, giving her a dim meaningless smile.

"I'm going into Clewiston. Got a meeting with Lee White, Earl's attorney at First Federal. And the accountants will be there, too. We'll be opening Earl's lockbox, going through the papers, whatever's in there. You're free to come, Frisco, this might concern you, too."

"I'm not in the will."

"I can't believe that," Claire said. "You need to go."

"I'm the prodigal son," he said. "Except I'm the one that never got around to making amends. I'm not in the will. And that's just fine."

Browning gave his brother a long level stare, then pocketed the toothpick and motioned at Antwan. Antwan rose, nodding at Claire.

"Please accept my most sincere condolences in this time of im-mense sorrow, Miss Claire."

She carried the plate to the kitchen, and when she returned the two of them were gone. She stood in the doorway, looking at Frisco. He still sat with his wrists against the table, eyes down.

His gray T-shirt fit snug across his compact torso. Almost a foot shorter than Browning and leaner by a hundred pounds, Frisco had the ideal body for a bronc rider. Low center of gravity, wide shoul-ders, narrow hips, strong legs. For all Browning's physical advantages and his brute superiority, her money would be on the older, slimmer brother in any kind of brawl. A David to his Goliath.

She wasn't sure where all that came from, this sudden awareness of Frisco's physicality. But for all the years she'd hung around jocks and observed their fixation on size and the potency it implied, and for all the time she'd watched the endless one-upsmanship they engaged in, she'd never seen a man of Frisco's modest stature who so clearly had the intimidating edge.

"Care to take a ride, Claire?"

She blinked and came into the room. He was watching her with curiosity.

"A ride?"

"Horseback."

"You want to go riding? A time like this?"

"Swing by the Pintos' place. Pay our respects. That interest you?"

She drew a long breath and directed her gaze toward the living room, where the same two crime-scene techs were huddled in conversation.

"I'll need to change."

"So change," he said. "Meet you in the barn."

TWENTY

THORN WAS STOOPED OVER, HANDS on his knees, gasping. He'd run flat out for at least three miles, half an hour traveling east across open plains and rocky pastures and weaving through sparse stands of pine, coming to rest in a dense grove of cabbage palms, stumpy palmettos, and a few oaks and pines.

What stopped him at that precise spot was the patch of rare shade, and a herd of elegant antelopes that was grazing nearby on the yellowed grass in a narrow stretch of meadow. The last thing he wanted was a stampede of antelopes giving away his position.

In the grass, mingling with the herd, were a few white cattle egrets feasting on the bugs kicked up in the antelopes' passage. At least he thought they were antelopes. Their long horns corkscrewed up and back. From their withers to their rumps they were jet black, while their underparts were snowy, as if they'd once waded in a shallow river of bleach. White fur circled their black eyes. Exotic as hell. From Asia or some mountain grassland on the other side of the globe. Not more than a yard tall at their shoulders. As close to a flock of unicorns as Thorn was ever likely to see.

There were around forty in the herd. They turned as one to look him over, decided he was fine, and continued their happy snack. They seemed as docile and innocent as a troop of Brownies on a picnic. A man who would shoot such an animal for sport should be strung by his testicles to a sturdy branch and left for the rodents and insects.

He sat and rested his back against a palm. When the barrel of the Glock stabbed his crotch, he drew it from his pocket and set it beside him on a pile of leaves.

For the last half hour the midafternoon sun had been his only guide in that disorienting landscape. He'd tried to keep his shadow before him as he ran, accomplishing at least a straight line. Though he might as well have been on the Australian Outback, the pampas of Argentina, or some equally far-flung spot. Heading east was a flip-of-the-coin choice. He had no map in his mind of the shape of Coquina Ranch. He knew only that it was immense, and even if he managed to come to one of its boundaries, the land beyond it was also largely uninhabited.

Luck was going to get him out of this, bad luck or good. Maybe he could shade the odds a little, but no strategy had come to him yet. Keep moving in the same direction, try not to circle back on himself, and hope his path eventually intersected with some friendly circumstance. A public road, a house, a fellow traveler.

At the crunch of brush nearby Thorn stiffened. He swiped up the Glock and craned to the side and peered around the trunk of the palm. Twenty feet away one of the antelopes was nosing at some green shoots of grass on the edge of his oasis. It lifted its head and studied him for several seconds, its eyes so oddly large it seemed to be in a permanent state of amazement. Thorn held his position until the young buck made its evaluation, dismissed his menace, and resumed feeding.

Thorn eased back into place and delicately set the pistol aside. He was settling his spine against the tree when he felt a nudge at his rump, like a thick braid of rope tugged forward an inch. He held still, suppressing a groan. Before he looked behind him, he took a steadying breath. He already knew what it was and had gathered a sense of its size. He was only hoping it was a dusky pygmy or maybe a rare indigo, not one of their more deadly cousins.

Holding his head still, he slanted his eyes to the right but couldn't make it out because its body was hidden beneath debris and fallen fronds. What he did see was the rabbit hole five feet off. The snake he was pressed against had been staking out the entrance to the rabbit's den when Thorn sat down.

So exhausted from his sprint, he hadn't paid attention. If he'd noticed the goddamn rabbit burrow he would've steered to a less risky spot. In woods like these, it was a common configuration. Snake guarding food source.

He inched his head to the right and finally made out the wedge of the snake's head. Not good, not good at all. Hexagonal pattern, white and tawny and black and as thick as his wrist. He didn't need to turn the other way to estimate its length. Five to six feet. Seven or eight rattles on its tail. A mature diamondback. In one bite it could deliver enough venom to kill six Thorns. The eastern diamondback was a perfect fit for this terrain. It absorbed humidity through its skin, could sleep for days in ambush, wake when it smelled its prey. Like most creatures in the wild, the rattler wasn't naturally aggressive, but trapped like this one was as it waited for the rabbit to appear, it would be royally pissed. Diamondbacks only bit for two reasons: fear and food. And Thorn had both of those covered nicely.

Luckily, the snake was as straight as a staff. Hard for it to attack from that position. It would take the rattler at least a couple of seconds to coil for a strike.

Thorn was picking the direction he intended to dive when he heard the distant grumble of an engine. At the same instant, the snake edged forward an inch as though the motor's approach had stirred it into action.

So there it was. Thorn had made one more bad move in a long string of them. This grove he'd chosen was way too obvious. He saw that now. He'd taken the predictable path and invited his own discovery.

To the west a plume of dust rose off the prairie behind a red ATV with oversize tires. Perfect for navigating the marshes and gullies of this harsh land. On most days, if a crafty hunter tacked with the wind to carry away the engine noise, that four-wheeler would be an excellent vehicle to stalk a nervous herd of antelope.

But not today. This hunter didn't give a shit who heard his approach. He was bouncing recklessly across the rough terrain, his engine at full bore.

The young buck who'd been feeding nearby pricked up its ears, bleated once, and broke into a gallop. Behind him his tribe followed in tight formation.

Thorn felt the diamondback seep forward another inch. A foot of its body was out in the open, and the rattles were humming against the base of his spine. The snake had turned its head and was flicking its tongue toward Thorn, trying to suss out his potential as nourishment or threat.

Thorn didn't wait for the creature to decide, but rolled right, rolled again, and twice more until he butted against a pine sapling. He came up in a crouch, searched for the snake, and located it finally, coiled in the leaves, pine needles, and decaying fronds, forming a perfect circle around the Glock.

A swirl of prairie dust filtered into the glen.

The motor shut off.

In the steady breeze, old seed pods and dry fronds chattered, and in the high branches of the canopy the dust cloud broke up and swirled away.

The diamondback continued to guard the pistol as if it were some prized kill it had dragged back to its nest. Its head hovered a few inches off the ground and that shiny tongue worked the air.

Thorn scanned the area for a fallen branch but saw only brown and crumbling fronds. Maybe one of the palm stems would serve his purpose, but he discarded that. Too unwieldy for what he needed. He looked down at the sapling he'd collided with. Six feet tall, an inch thick at its base.

Not perfect, but it would do. He picked a spot as far down its trunk as he thought he could snap, gripped it with both hands and bent it until it broke. Filaments of the green wood held on, dozens of pine strands as tough as ligaments. He rolled the sapling back and forth against the grip of the rubbery fibers, but they didn't give. He took a step away from the base, threw his weight into it, and jerked the sapling free.

"You in there, Thorn? That you back in the shadows?"

Jonah's voice was off to his right, thirty, forty feet away.

Thorn stepped closer to the diamondback, extending the sapling's ragged end. The snake bobbed its head and glided forward a few inches, tracking the movement of the stick. Three-quarters of its length still circled the pistol, but its focus had shifted to this new intruder.

Thorn feinted the stick left, drew the rattler's head that way, then poked the blunt end of his lance beneath the diamondback's coil, hooked the snake as close to its midpoint as he could, then lifted and slung it five feet into the brush.

He snatched up the Glock and flattened himself behind the closest palm.

Maybe Jonah saw him move or heard the snake landing.

He started firing. His automatic weapon tore chunks from trees nearby, kicked up plugs of soil, put a scent in the air of pine and muck and a flowery residue. Jonah raked the cabbage palms from right to left, then back the other way. The gray rabbit that the diamondback had been waiting for darted across the glen, brushed Thorn's bare ankles, and ducked into its hole.

Jonah worked closer, spraying bursts of five or six. Tearing away branches, spinning up tiny cyclones of bark and leaf and moss, meaty chunks exploding from long-leaf pine, oak, and saw palmetto. A gash opened a foot from Thorn's face. Then more silence.

Thorn squatted down, ducked a look around the edge of the palm. He could hear Jonah tramping nearby but couldn't spot him. From the sound, he might be ten feet away or five times that. Hard to tell with his eardrums throbbing.

With only two rounds in the Glock, there was no future in a full-scale shoot-out. He'd have to be frugal. Take nothing less than a perfect shot.

The rising wind was Thorn's only ally. Kicking up leaves and broken bits of foliage, hundreds of small distractions tumbling across the ground, while overhead there was a screech of limb and the clatter of brush, and on the forest floor the sunlight and shadows flickered and flashed like some disco dance club.

Directly across from his position, he saw an old slash pine with a patch of bark rubbed away about two feet off the ground. It had the look of a scent post, a tree used by a wild hog to rub its bristly body. One of its prehistoric grooming habits. A few inches above the barkless patch were several scars in the soft wood. Another of the wild hog's endearing traits was to gash its tusks into the most prominent trees. Both the scent and the gouges were left to mark wild hog's territory, warn off rivals.

Thorn decided, all in all, to move. The scent post and the diamondback were part of it. But he didn't much like the cabbage palm where he was hiding, either. It was too exposed, and all the shooting angles in Jonah's direction were obscured. He glanced around and chose another tree ten feet away across mostly open space. He set his feet and skipped out into the clearing, staying low. Halfway to the tree, he caught a flash of movement to his right and dodged behind the trunk of a good-sized oak.

Jonah let off a burst of fire that shredded the fronds of a palmetto and dug up a trail in the forest floor ten feet from Thorn's new location. He fired another half dozen rounds. No way to count how many he'd used up and no way to calculate when he was running low on ammo. He might have brought a month's supply.

"Can't we just get along?" Jonah called out. "Just be friends." His voice was neither loud nor troubled. "You hear me, Thorn? Can you hear me?"

Thorn saw him clearly now. Close. Twenty feet to the east. He was stooped forward, aiming his weapon into the densest part of the grove. Unaware of Thorn.

Thorn stepped from behind the tree. He had no qualms about shooting Jonah in the back. Whatever moral restraint he'd possessed twenty-four hours before, he'd left behind at the bottom of that sinkhole, bearing down on a dying man's throat, watching his arms flutter at his side.

He angled his pistol slowly to the left, but with so many trees and shrubs and saplings between them, there wasn't an open shot.

Tucking back behind the oak, he pressed his cheek against the rough bark, brought the pistol up, extended it, and focused his aim on a break in the understory about ten paces ahead of Jonah. He waited, trying to time the man's gait as he disappeared behind a dense stand of palmetto and tall grasses. He estimated it would be five or six seconds before Jonah reappeared in the clearing.

Thorn counted them off, then counted off twenty more. No Jonah.

Half a minute passed. Thorn lowered the pistol. He heard only a squirrel chittering on the high branches above him and the creak of the wind through the old growth.

He was rattled. Not sure of his next move. Was he the hunter still, or had Jonah faked him out? The kid didn't seem savvy enough, but then again, this was his home turf. Maybe he knew this glen, knew its escape routes, its shortcuts and switchbacks. Or maybe it was all a bluff and he was stopping at every stand of woods and throwing out the same bait, trying to lure Thorn into the open.

Thorn was stepping away from the oak to pick his best path when a crash came from the brush to his left. He slid back behind the tree, brought the Glock up, poised to take his shot.

But the huff and grunt came so fast and from such a startling level,

Thorn had no time to fire. The feral hog was low and squat with a reddish-brown mottled coat, three feet at the shoulders, more than two hundred pounds. It was trundling directly at him, coming so fast there was no way he could dodge or outrun the thing.

It squealed at Thorn and squealed twice more at a higher pitch. The five-inch tusks jutting from its lower jaw were almost hidden by a froth of slobber. Ten feet away, the hog slewed to a stop, and beheld Thorn with its tiny eyes, red and crazed. He'd heard stories of hogs charging humans, but for all he knew, they could've been tall tales. He'd never stumbled onto one, so had no idea how much danger he was in. Still, just the look of the thing was so fearsome, his instinct was to shoot.

Thorn brought the pistol up and aimed between those demented eyes. The boar, however, had another plan. He stumbled awkwardly to his right then steadied himself and set off again, careening through the tangle of low-hanging branches. As he passed not more than a yard away, Thorn caught its trailing smell, as foul as sewer gas. Along its left flank a bloody gash ran from its front shoulder to its hip. A stray round from Jonah's weapon must have strafed him and sent him into this frenzy.

The boar plowed into the undergrowth, sent twigs and leaves spinning, and hurtled ahead until it was out of sight. Seconds later more gunfire erupted from the direction the hog had taken. Deep within the brambles, the animal screeched and squealed and screeched again. After another spurt of gunfire, the hog was silent.

Thorn listened to the branches moan and scrape against one another. He saw an owl sitting serenely on a high limb like some weary judge who has seen it all and is no longer fazed by the follies of humankind. Thorn watched the owl and waited for something to happen. Nothing did.

He stepped away from his hiding place, ready to resume his easterly marathon, when fifty feet away Jonah emerged from the dense scrub, clawing through the snag of branches and limbs, and lurched into a clearing.

His face was smeared with blood, blood on his lips, blood coated both hands and arms, and blood drenched his gray sweatshirt. He was bathed in blood. He had wallowed in blood and wallowed some more.

Overhead the sunlight brightened, putting a harsh shine on the brushstrokes of Jonah's work. Boar blood smeared on his throat and boar blood gleamed in the spiraling canals of his ears and blood glazed his skinned head. Pinwheels of light spun in the branches, and a half-dozen squirrels chased one another up and down the limbs of the oak, shrieking like a mob of ghouls celebrating one of their own.

For a full thirty seconds as Jonah stumbled past, Thorn had an unobstructed shot, but when he raised his pistol, his hand was so unsteady he couldn't bring himself to fire.

TWENTY-ONE

WHILE SUGAR WAS FILLING HIS gas tank in Clewiston, a few miles south of the turn off to Coquina Ranch, Rusty headed into the station to use the john. At the pumps across from him, two bikers with Santa Claus beards were filling the teardrop tanks on their choppers and eyeing Sugarman like he might be just the guy they'd been looking for.

They both wore black leather vests over black T-shirts and identical ratty blue jeans and black leather boots. There was mud on their boots, and the yellow stains of bug spatter and bird shit on their vests.

A half hour beyond the city limits of any Florida city, you crossed the same demoralizing Rubicon and started running into these bozos, or their redneck cousins and their Confederate half-brothers, or some other good Christian boys from the holy exalted order of the bedsheet. All these decades had come and gone, a new century and all that, a fresh generation with more accepting views taking the reins, and still a guy like Sugarman couldn't get out of his car at a gas station in the countryside of Florida without a couple of eager beavers looking to start something a lot more serious than a conversation.

Rusty came striding back as Sugar's gas pump shut off.

She saw the bikers and they saw her, and what they didn't like about Sugarman to begin with they liked even less now.

"There some kind of problem?" Rusty said to the guys.

Aw, shit. Sugarman shook his head in resignation. Running a quick estimate of how long it would take to duck into the Toyota, open the glove compartment, shuck his Smith and Wesson from the leather holster, and let these guys have a long look at its sleek and sinister shape. Too damn long for comfort.

As Rusty walked over to the guys, Sugar's cell buzzed. He drew it out, checked the Caller ID. City of Miami Police Department.

He answered, heard Mullaney's crusty voice say, "That you, Sugarman?"

"In the flesh. But hey, listen, can I call you back in five? I got a situation."

"This is your one big shot, Sugar. I have work on top of work on top of three shitloads of unreturned phone calls from people a lot more important to my career in law enforcement than your sorry ass."

Rusty was talking to the bikers. First one, then the other. They'd finished fueling up their hogs and were listening to her. Nobody was throwing any punches and nobody was screaming. They weren't making flower garlands, either.

"It's about Coquina Ranch."

"That's a toxic waste dump," Mullaney said. "Stay out of that shit."

"I got a dog in the fight. Can't stay out."

"Let me guess," Mullaney said. "His name rhymes with fishing bum."

"Thorn's made some improvements since you knew him."

"I heard he's got money now. Inherited Fort Knox."

"More money than the state of Florida."

"That ain't saying much."

"Look, Chief. I need a favor. Old times' sake and all that."

"Spit it out. There's phones ringing, my secretary's waving at me."

One of the bikers had taken off his leather skullcap and was holding it in front of his chest like he was in the presence of royalty. The other guy had his head bent to the side, listening to Rusty speak while giving Sugar a curious look.

"Frisco Hammond's cell number would be useful."

"The guy doesn't answer his phone. What's second on your list?"

"What kind of guy is he? Trustworthy?"

"Got a mind of his own, doesn't play well with others, but yeah, I'd take him along to the O.K. Corral. Last question?"

"Name of somebody on the inside. Lead investigator, maybe."

"What's this about, Sugarman?"

Sugarman gave him the bullet points. Keeping it vague. Real estate, Thorn and Earl Hammond making a deal.

When Mullaney came back he'd turned off the wisecracks.

"Look, this isn't for general consumption, Sugar. I shouldn't be having this conversation, but I got a soft spot for you, don't ask me why. Must be that second Bloody Mary I had with lunch."

Then he told Sugarman the situation, the news that hadn't hit the airwaves yet.

If Sugar had been prone to gasping, that would've been the moment for it.

At the adjacent gas pumps, Rusty was shaking hands with the bikers. Regular old-fashioned last-century handshakes. When she was done, she walked over to the Toyota and got in. Sugar listened to the last of Mullaney's explanation, thanked his friend, then took his time returning to the driver's side, keeping a watch on the good-old boys. They'd already remounted their hogs, ignoring him now. First one then the other cranked his bike, gunned it, and glided away in a swell of thunder.

Sugar got in, started the car, and pulled out onto the highway.

"How the hell did you manage that?"

Rusty said, "Taco Shine."

"I'm sorry?" Sugar looked over at her. "Taco what?"

"Back in my other life, pre-Thorn," she said. "The Outlaws, you know, the biker club. Taco was the man. I rode with them for a couple of years."

"Wait," Sugar said. "You're talking about William Shine. That guy?"

"William Taco Shine."

"He killed somebody."

"He killed a snitch," Rusty said. "The guy rode with us for a year. He and Taco were close. Somehow Taco found out the snitch was on the verge of giving up the entire club. Everybody was going down so this stooge could get a sentence reduction on a gun-running beef."

"Shine's on death row at Raiford."

"Yeah."

"Snitch have anything on you?"

"Enough," she said. "I could've had an unpleasant year or two."

"I can't believe you rode with those guys."

"Taco's my half-brother."

"Whoa."

"Older by five years, same mom. He was having money troubles, so I let him crash at my place in Tavernier for a year, and before I know it my three-bedroom became the clubhouse. I saw some pretty dark shit, got my hands dirtier than I planned on. Because I'm Taco's little sister, I was off-limits, none of the guys could fuck with me. It drove them crazy, having a woman around they couldn't gang rape or beat the shit out of."

"And those guys back there—they were in the Outlaws?"

"No, I just asked them if they'd ever run across Taco. They had."

"You're Taco Shine's sister? Jesus. That's a hard one to picture."

A mile went by before she spoke again.

"So, Sugar, when you're thinking about Thorn and me together, how difficult Thorn must be to live with, you've got to keep it in perspective. Compared to Taco, Thorn's a goddamn model citizen."

Sugarman slowed with the traffic in Clewiston. Pontoon boaters heading for the lake, migrant laborers, seven to a car, long-haul truckers, and tourists taking the scenic route up the spine of the state.

"You were on the phone back there," Rusty said.

Sugarman was still chewing on William Shine. Taco slit the snitch's throat with a Bowie knife, he remembered that. Now he was trying to see Rusty Stabler riding alongside Taco's chromed-up Harley, all that G-force and wind, all that crystal meth and the loud, violent nights. Holding her own in that rough crowd. He needed to revise his view of her. Factor in Taco Shine. It was going to take a while. He wondered if Thorn knew about Taco. But then he probably did. Rusty wasn't one to conceal her past, and it wouldn't bother Thorn. He enjoyed complicated women. They seemed to be his specialty.

"The phone, Sugar. You were talking to somebody."

"Mullaney," he said. "Yeah, I spoke with the chief."

"Do any good?"

"I got Frisco's number. Mullaney promised to call him, pave the way."

"Good work."

"And something else," he said. Then his mind strayed back to Taco and he fumbled for something to say.

"Sugar?" She tapped him on the arm. "Look at me, Sugar."

They were stopped at a light beside the Clewiston Inn. Old two-story hotel on the downtown square with a beat-up tennis court across the shady parking lot. Rusty turned her head, giving Sugar the face-on view. Ash-blond hair clipped short, sharp cheekbones, narrow face, dark brown eyes flecked with gold, a wide generous mouth. Holding still for him, like she was having her portrait drawn, allowing him to absorb her, drink it in, all those layers on display, the shrewd businesswoman she'd become in the last year, the seasoned fishing guide she'd been before that, and deeper down in the shadows was that other woman, the one who'd traveled a harsher road than any he could imagine, who'd stuck her chin out into the blasting wind, full-throttle wild and reckless.

"There's more to me than you thought. You're taken aback."

"It's okay," he said. "I think I get it now."

178

"Good," she said. "I need you to get it."

She gave him an easy smile. Then tilted her head, leaned across the center console. It probably was meant as a sisterly peck, or an air-kiss, but when her lips were about to graze his cheek, Sugarman moved too soon or in the wrong direction, or else she moved, one of those awkward bumps and dodges that are impossible to reconstruct. But their lips got flush somehow and settled.

The kiss lasted a half second longer than it should have, then both of them jerked away. She busied herself with brushing the legs of her jeans. While Sugarman looked over at her, absorbing one more version of Rusty Stabler, the one he'd never allowed himself to imagine.

An air horn blasted behind them. The light was green. All around them the world was in a hurry.

For the next mile Sugarman concentrated on driving. Rusty worked on being a quiet passenger, attentive to the scenery.

As they were leaving the franchise strip of Clewiston, re-entering the sweep of empty pinelands, she said, "You were telling me about your phone call."

"Oh, yeah, the phone call."

"Something about Thorn?"

"Herbert Sanchez," Sugar said. He was having a chill. Not sure if it was from the kiss, or because of what he was about to say. "Sanchez quashed it."

"He did what?"

"He let it be known to the commissioner of the FDLE that he wanted the investigation of the deaths at Coquina Ranch brought to a speedy conclusion. Like right now. It's done."

"Not even twenty-four hours? He can do that?"

"The FDLE is his domain. They had jurisdiction, so their work is complete."

"What about an inquest or whatever they do? Medical examiner, fingerprints, written reports, all that stuff."

"Technicalities remain, but for all intents and purposes, it's done.

Mullaney thought it was odd. He said the FBI and the state's attorney weren't happy, people with FDLE are stewing, but there it is. The governor's a close friend of the Hammond family. Out of respect for their privacy and their personal pain, the authorities will tie a bow on it and walk away. Browning's young wife blew away the shooter, and apparently the guy she killed had a long history at the ranch, he was friendly with the wife, so she's an emotional wreck. And that's the story. The governor wants it settled and done. So it's settled and done."

Rusty stared out the windshield as the road narrowed to two lanes. They'd picked up a wasp at the gas station. It sailed past Rusty's cheek and landed on the dashboard. Sugarman lowered his window and shooed it back outside.

"Jesus," she said. "The goddamn governor's in on it. He leaks Thorn's name, comes to the ranch to preside over an execution, then cuts off the investigation. He's dead center."

Sugarman drove one-handed, chewed away a flake of skin on his thumb

"How long has this deal been in the works? When was it you first proposed the land swap?"

"It all happened very fast. First of November is when I spoke to Margaret the first time. It took a couple of days to rough out a proposal, then Margaret put it in front of Earl Hammond a day after that. He agreed within twenty-four hours."

"Three weeks ago."

"Roughly."

"So let's walk it through. Probably starts with Governor Sanchez getting wind of the deal. He passes the news to the grandson. For reasons we have yet to determine, Browning Hammond decides he doesn't want the five hundred million that's coming his way. He wants all that land instead. So they throw together a scheme. Make it look like a disgruntled employee went berserk, the old man is killed, the employee is gunned down by the wife, which means she's in on it, too. You got four eyewitnesses, one of whom is the highest elected official in the state. State cop is dead, old man Hammond is dead, shooter is dead."

"Thorn is kidnapped."

"Yeah, Thorn is kidnapped, and whatever real estate transaction was about to occur evaporates."

"But you and I know there was a deal, and Margaret Milbanks knows there was one. What's to keep one of us from calling the press?"

"Oh, come on. What press?"

"The *Herald*. Hell, *The New York Times*. There's a governor involved."

"I don't think so. You looked at a newspaper lately?"

"What?"

"I don't think you can rely on a newspaper to bring down the high and mighty anymore. The days of that kind of journalism are gone. Woodward and Bernstein, there's nobody doing that anymore. Now it's press releases. Rusty Stabler calls the *Herald* out of the blue with suspicions about the governor, first thing they do is look up Sanchez's approval ratings. He was in the seventies last I heard. He's bulletproof. Thanks, ma'am, for your intriguing story, but no thanks. The few newspapers that still exist make their nut printing society-page photos."

She was giving him a queer look.

"I'm babbling," he said.

She nodded.

"It's that kiss. What *was* that?"

"That didn't happen," she said. "There was no kiss."

"Okay," he said. "That's probably best. There was no kiss."

They drove in silence. Sugarman kept his eyes on the road, but it took all his self-control not to look over.

"So now what?"

"Well, with the investigation on ice, our job is easier. Not so many cops around."

"But they're wrong. It's not about a disgruntled employee. It's about five hundred million dollars and a two hundred thousand acre ranch. And it's about Earl Hammond being in a big damn hurry to take that land off the table."

Sugarman watched a hawk slice through the windy trees, swooping down for a closer look at something in the tall grass.

"You didn't tell Mullaney about the Florida Forever deal."

"Some of it."

"How much?"

"Broad outline. I just said Thorn was involved in a real estate transaction with Earl."

"That's all you told him?"

"It was a quick conversation."

She looked out her window, swept a palm across her forehead as if easing the pressure of a headache.

"So is that how it works, being a private detective? Withhold evidence. Misdirect the cops so you can handle things on your own?"

"Only when I see no other choice."

Sugarman allowed himself one quick look, just to see if any trace of the kiss remained. She felt his glance and turned to him as if to allow this indulgence. He took several seconds to appraise the angles of her face, her mouth, which he had never considered sultry until now, her dark eyes, the faultless skin of her slanting cheeks, but he saw no remnants of the kiss anywhere. None at all.

Which he supposed was just as well.

TWENTY-TWO

JONAH CALMED HIMSELF.

He had been hunting for Thorn when he encountered a wild hog. He must have killed the hog because he was covered in blood. He calmed himself some more. Powering down like Moses used to do. Moses.

Jonah no longer knew who Jonah was. Someone else, he knew that much. Some other thing. Moses was dead, and the Faust brothers' history was not what he'd believed. Sons of a monster. Kin to Dahmer, Bundy, Charlie Manson.

Jonah was alone in the world. The old Jonah was torn up and torn up some more, and all the tiny scrambled pieces were thrown like confetti into a howling gale. He'd been brother to Moses. Now what was he? Nothing he knew. Nothing.

He found himself back at the hunting lodge. There was hog blood on his hands and his arms and all over his clothes. Hog blood.

The red phone in his jeans pocket trilled.

He took it out, looked at the screen.

"RU There?"

"Ys." Jonah got blood on the buttons thumbing back.

"WRUN." Where are you now?

"Good f-ng ?" It was. It was a good fucking question. Thanks for asking.

Then another one blinked on his screen: "LMIRL." Let's meet in real life.

Jonah wasn't sure what that was anymore. He hit back with "WUB."

"Clewstn bnk" came up.

What the fuck was he doing in a bank in Clewiston?

"RUNTS," Jonah typed. Are you nuts? Then, "O&O."

Over and totally out.

He slid the sticky-blooded phone into his pocket. It trilled again, but he didn't bother with it.

He walked to the shed out behind the cabin, went inside, and had to stand there for several moments before he remembered why he'd come. Oh, yes, the extension ladder. He carried the ladder across the pasture and into the trees and beyond the trees to the second meadow where the pit was. Where Moses was.

He stepped out onto the wooden platform over the pit and eased the ladder through the hatch he'd cut. The hatch he never should have cut. But the hatch he did cut, goddamn himself, goddamn his stupid self.

He walked the ladder forward till it was angled correctly. He turned backward and went down the ladder into the pit where Moses was. Where Moses lay on his back, a spear of stone poking through his belly.

Moses who parted the waters. Moses who led his people to freedom. Moses who protected Jonah as best he could from a monster.

Jonah stepped off the ladder. The sun was lowering and there were shadows in the pit. Jonah was going dark himself. He didn't know who he was or what he was or why he was. He knew he had to attend to his brother just as his brother would have attended him if it was Jonah lying on his back with a spike impaled through his flesh.

He kneeled beside his brother and looked at him. He made himself look at his handsome face, his closed eyes, and he made himself look at the tip of the stone at his belly. Jonah made himself reach out and he made himself, goddammit, he made himself touch his brother's cold flesh.

He kept his hand there until the nausea passed. Touching his dead brother. Then Jonah came from behind, gripped his brother's armpits and lifted him, pulling him away from the spear. Lifting him into his arms. His brother who had gone dark. Dark to the core like Jonah was going dark to his.

He carried his brother to the ladder, hoisted him up. His heavy-muscled and handsome brother who had meant no harm to anyone but all the same had suffered cruelty at an age long before a boy should know what cruelty was. He hoisted him onto his back. This brother Moses. And he climbed with him, rung by rung, rung by fucking rung. He climbed back to the level of the earth and heaved him onto the wooden platform.

He had to stop. He'd lost his breath. Above him the light was going gray and clouds were tearing across the sky.

He carried Moses on his back across the meadow, through the pine trees, and across the pasture where sometimes bison came to graze and sometimes axis deer and eland and fallow deer and waterbuck and four-horned ram. But none were there now. They knew not to come. They knew to keep their distance. They were hiding in the woods, hiding till this terrible thing passed. This thing that was Jonah Faust.

Twice more he had to stop because he had no breath. Once he stumbled and fell with Moses on top of him. But he rose again and staggered under his brother's weight across the open field back to the hunting cabin, where the paintings were and the drawings and the scribbled notes and the poems and letters, and all the stuff the ghouls and fiends produced in their cells to pass the long hours. Back to the cabin, where he would undress his brother and bathe him and prepare him for what came next. His long dark journey.

185

And then he'd wait for Thorn. The man had nowhere to go. It might take awhile, but when Thorn got thirsty enough or hungry enough, he'd show up. All Jonah had to do was wait.

Big Girl was cantering easily with an elegant uphill gait. Frisco flowed with her, his head high, surfing through a flood of familiar aromas on this familiar terrain, the pollen-saturated air, grass and pine, and far ahead at the horizon was the stark abutment of hard-edged plain against perfect sky, the afternoon light fraying through strips of ragged clouds.

Muscles he hadn't worked on the Miami streets in years were creaky, but with every stride the tightness eased a fraction. It was solace of the best kind. Comfort he hadn't known he'd lost. That wind, that light, that land he once treasured. Strange sensations on such a day. But there it was. Feeling freer than he had in years.

"Quicker this way," Claire called out, riding past him on the left, taking a different angle to the northwest. Her bay's gait as smooth as a marble across glass.

That Claire knew the better course surprised him and made him glad. He'd always half enjoyed this woman, half distrusted her because she'd squandered herself on his brother. Some defect of character on her part, some blind spot. His brother was an imposter, or worse. Frisco hadn't decided exactly how much worse, though he was getting closer every hour of this punishing day.

Ahead he made out the slate-gray roof of the Pintos' home rising above the horizon. The ring of pines that sheltered it. A barn, some junked cars, a speeding windmill.

In Frisco's youth, the Pintos' house had been more his home than Coquina lodge. It's where Frisco learned to ride and shoot and came to understand how a large and noisy family stayed close and happy against backbreaking odds. Learned how chili was spiced, how long it should be simmered, and how to shoe a horse and properly saddle one, how to tell jokes in two languages. And it's where one of the cousins, Javier, showed him how to drink great quantities of beer and not fall down, and Gustavo's eldest daughter, dark-haired Ana, taught him how to kiss and touch a breast with reverence and delight, and one of the Pinto aunts, fat as a barrel, schooled his clumsy feet in the dance steps of that year, and showed him how to slide his hips in a way that still made the ladies smile. All the things his grandparents were too grief-stricken and exhausted by their own losses to bother with.

Trying to catch up to Claire's dust, Frisco leaned forward, put his weight against the stirrups, and urged Big Girl into a gallop. She responded, stretching out, covering twice the ground in half the time he expected, like the horse had caught the bracing scent of the open range, and through her hooves and the lanky drive of her legs she was beginning to understand the possibilities of speed.

Going fast, but still not flat-out. He felt some portion of her holding back, a tightness in that powerful stride as if her limbs were still bound by memories from her early days, all that deprivation, the lonely weeks restricted to her stall, a sad neglect that left her suspicious of those open miles ahead.

From a few hundred yards off, Frisco saw there were no cars in the dusty lot behind the Pintos' house. No clothes hanging from the line, none of the gaudy flags the family displayed on a pole off their front porch, celebrating each change of season, every American holiday and each fiesta from their Mexican homeland. As he pulled alongside Claire and eased Big Girl down to a trot, Frisco saw the small patch of lawn that for decades the Pinto clan scrupulously maintained—gone scraggy with weeds.

They dismounted near the barn and Frisco ran some water in a tub for the horses. No dogs came out to greet them. No cats curled round their legs. A swarm of gnats rode the wind past his head and sailed off to the south.

"They're gone. Everyone left."

"When's the last time you were out here, Claire?"

"Weeks ago, I guess. Back near Halloween. They were having a party."

They left the horses to drink and walked to the brick house. Long and low with smallish windows. A poured concrete patio on one side that Frisco remembered well. It's where they grilled meat and ears of corn and skewers of peppers and squash, and it's where they told long boisterous stories, strummed guitars and sang songs late into the evening, accepting Frisco as one of their own. The aluminum patio furniture was still there. One chair had tumbled onto its side. A crow stood possessively on the chaise. In a corner lay a naked blond-haired doll with neither eyes nor legs.

Claire followed him to the front door. No need to knock. The screen was torn, the varnished pine door stood open. Inside, the musty air was flavored with the onions and garlic and fried grease absorbed for decades into the carpets and wallpaper. Much of the furniture was the same: table lamps, mismatched chairs, a black leather sectional couch, an entertainment unit that covered an entire wall. The screen of the TV was coated with dust. None of the family photographs were on the walls, but otherwise it was just as Frisco remembered. Closing in on thirteen years since he'd been there last. He'd celebrated his twenty-first birthday with the Pintos, a night of margaritas and a roasted pig. And the next morning he'd left Coquina, drove down to Miami and never returned.

"Somebody's here," Claire said. She stood by the front door looking out.

A car door slammed.

"Oh, great," she said. "Donaldson."

Anne Donaldson was speaking on her white cell phone as she came up the concrete walkway. She walked into the house, still listening to the voice in her ear, her eyes lowered. Without a word, she snapped the phone shut and snugged it back into its holster on her belt, and looked first at Claire, then directed her attention to Frisco.

"This pisses me off," she said.

Frisco waited. Claire turned away and began to wander the room, apparently had her fill of Donaldson.

"We're cashing it in," she said. "Game's been called. Why do you think that is?"

"Closing up shop?" Frisco said. "So soon?"

"Governor's orders." She stole a look at Claire, whose back was turned, then faced Frisco. "Any idea why your friend Sanchez would shut this down?"

"He's no friend of mine," Frisco said.

"You got any ideas?"

"How's a lowly street cop fathom the subtle workings of government?"

"You don't quit."

"Quit what?"

"You know what."

"Am I getting under your skin?"

Donaldson made a tour of the living room, not touching anything. Observing the dust on the TV screen, examining the pale squares on the wallpaper where the photos had hung.

"Okay, all right. So I came on a little strong this morning." Donaldson unloosened her ponytail and shook out her light brown hair, ran her fingers through it. "I do that sometimes. A woman in a man's world and all that. I apologize. Okay?"

"Apology accepted," Claire said, turning to the woman.

Donaldson looked to Frisco for his response.

He gave her none.

"Okay, you're probably out here for the same reason I am," Donaldson said.

Frisco waited.

"Something's not right. Something's off. I can't say what it is exactly. The circumstances of the shooting—it's just not kosher. What am I missing, Sergeant?"

"You're the expert. I sat in on a couple of interviews. That's it."

Her eyes roved the living room again; she took a step into the open kitchen.

"They haven't been here for a while. The Pintos."

"Claire saw them at Halloween."

"Was Gustavo around the ranch, doing his jobs? You see him lately?"

"Nearly every day," Claire said. "Coming and going. We haven't spoken in a while."

"Is that unusual? Not talking to him for an extended period?"

"Yes. Normally he'd stop by the barn and say hello. Socialize a little. Not lately."

"Any idea where the Pintos went? They have family in the area?"

"The entire family lived here, three generations," Claire said. "Big sister, Ana, got married, moved away a few years back, but Gustavo's mother, his wife, Angela, and their three grown sons have lived in this house their whole lives. I don't know where they went."

Donaldson opened and closed kitchen cabinets. Same plates as Frisco remembered, same assortment of glasses and mugs and beer steins.

"I'm still hung-up on that map you mentioned, Ms. Hammond."

"Yeah, there was a map. There was most definitely a map."

"Governor denied it. Your husband, Mr. Shelton, no one saw it."

"It was there."

"So they're lying? Is your husband lying?"

"I saw a map."

"Why would your husband and Shelton and the governor deny it?"

"I have no idea."

"Can you tell me anything more about it? Describe it in more detail?"

"I've told you everything. Red markings on a survey map."

"How many red marks?"

"What difference could that make?"

"An estimate."

"A dozen maybe, I don't know."

"You know anything about this, Sergeant? You got an idea about this map?"

He did. He had a very clear idea, but he wasn't about to share with Donaldson. Frisco walked over to the leather couch and sat. A thousand years ago it was exactly in that spot, the lights off, on a moonless night, when he'd first fondled Ana's breast. Ten thousand years. An eon. Thousands of species had gone extinct since then.

"You're not particularly forthcoming, Sergeant. Not much of a talker."

"You're not the first to notice."

"Well, you haven't exactly won my heart, either."

"Don't you have to go write up your report?"

"I'll give you this one, Sergeant. You don't deserve it, but here it is. Call it a peace offering."

Frisco kept his mouth closed, watching Claire stare out at the horses.

Donaldson said, "I asked the Palm Beach County ME for a hurry-up on the forensics, and he was kind enough to put Saperstein first in line. So this is preliminary, but his initial workup suggests your angle-of-entry theory might have merit. The first two entrance wounds were ovoid in shape which as you may know suggests those shots were taken from a distance of anywhere from five to ten feet, and the remaining rounds were fired at a distance a good deal closer.

"The last two left powder tattooing, star-shaped lacerations, which says Saperstein was lying on his back, the shooter leaned over, fired directly into his prone body, touched the pistol to his clothes and the gases released from the fired round went into the subcutaneous tissue and exploded the skin outward in that star pattern."

"And the angle of entry?" Frisco was looking at Claire. Her jaw was working, her eyes ducked down in a distracted study of the floor as if she might be revisiting that moment when she'd found Saperstein's body in the bushes outside the lodge.

"The only persuasive evidence on angle of entry is from the wounds Saperstein took while he was still standing. Shots one and two."

"And?"

"The ME believes the shooter was likely to be taller than Pinto."

"How much taller?"

"Can't be precise with something like that. Best guess, maybe a half foot. And by the way, when I got this, I called your cell, left all this on your voicemail. I guess you don't use your phone."

"I try to avoid it."

"Look, I already apologized, Sergeant. I don't know what else I can do. I was angry this morning. One of my colleagues had been murdered in the line of duty. You should be able to understand that."

"So you're going to tell your superiors about the two shooters?"

"It'll be in my report. Don't see it'll cut much ice. The governor being so goddamn eager to have it over and done."

"But despite that, you'll put it in your report."

"What the hell is it with you, Hammond? What's your issue?"

Frisco turned his head slowly and steered Donaldson's gaze toward Claire. For a moment Donaldson was puzzled, then she grimaced, finally grasping his irritation. She'd been crossing the line again and again, behaving like a rookie. Not that it was in any rule book, but it was unspoken protocol. It didn't matter that Anne Donaldson and Frisco didn't care for each other. They were still cops. And cops talking to cops with civilians present didn't criticize their superiors, and they sure as hell didn't discuss the facts of a case in front of any civilian, especially one so deeply embroiled in that case.

"Anything else, Donaldson?"

"Well, there is one more thing."

He waited.

"How would I locate the hunting lodge? I want to talk to the Faust brothers."

"Why?" Frisco said. "If you've been shut down."

"Just a detour on my way out the exit. An itch I need to scratch."

"I'll draw you a map," Claire said. "From here it's maybe twenty minutes, bad roads. Lots of cattle gates to open and close. You'll need a key for the last one."

"A key?"

"The hunting cabin is inside the game preserve. It's fenced in. I'll put it in the map, where to find the key."

"That would be very kind," Donaldson said, and gave Frisco a chastened nod.

TWENTY-THREE

IT WAS NOT LIKE ANY barbed wire Thorn had ever seen. Bits of sheet metal twisted between two strands of wire, each one shaped into the letter H, with four dagger tips. The barbs were spaced an inch apart. Strung a few inches above and below those two-stranded wires was a single strand studded with six pointed tin stars that twirled like tiny propellers, clittering in the growing wind as if the fence itself were alive, eager to do its work.

It was barbed wire from another era, an antique. When he flicked his fingernail against a strand, tiny plumes of rust sailed into the steady wind. He found a section he could grip without slashing himself and tested its tension. It felt as taut and unforgiving as the day it had been strung.

The fence was at least twelve feet high and ran as far as Thorn could see in one direction, and in the other it disappeared into a stand of pines. Thorn felt sure that when he hiked into those woods, the fence would still be there. But he set off that way just in case.

Such a barrier was far beyond anything needed to keep wildebeests and antelope from straying. It was a monument to some other intention entirely. There was no way any man could climb that barrier. Even if

Thorn had boots and gloves and heavy clothing, that fence would have shredded him to ribbons before he reached halfway. Bolt cutters might have made a dent, but anything less would be insufficient.

He was trapped. Thorn and the wild creatures and a man covered in blood.

Thorn moved along the fence line to the woods. A hundred yards off he halted. In the west the sun had dropped below a dark mass of cumulus and was shining from a slit of open sky along the horizon. Maybe an hour of daylight left.

Thorn watched as the stand of scrub pine and cabbage palm and palmetto brightened. He'd never believed in signs or secret codes sent down by the heavenly stewards. What was unfolding before him was just the everyday magic in the pine flatwoods. The hard flat light threw every limb and leaf and frond into high relief, and every bird and cobweb and sapling in the sharpest contrast imaginable, as if a haze had lifted, the blue smokiness that dulled the world all day long had been whisked away, allowing every green and every brown and all the russets and saffrons to achieve their perfect state.

The vision was so crisp and pure, so perfectly illuminated that for a moment as he watched, it displaced Thorn's thirst and exhaustion and all his aches. He settled on his butt in the tall grass and took a breather as the color, minute by minute, reached its full blossom, then slowly began to back off, dwindling at a slightly faster rate, the light draining away, the bright pigments dulling to sepia, then finally to something close to black and white.

As he was rising to go, a heavy gust stirred the branches and fluttered the leaves and bowed the tall grasses in its path. And it was because of that, the odd confluence of wind and light that he noticed deep within the pine hammock, at the center of all that rocking and swaying, an object that held perfectly still.

Some dark and hulking thing. He squinted and tried to make out its exact contours, but he was too far off to be sure. It was no animal. Way too big for that.

It was on the route he was taking anyway in this wandering exploration, so he set off for the thicket of pines and palms, keeping his eyes on that unmoving thing. He felt like one of those colorblind men recruited in the Second World War to fly along as spotters on aircraft bombing missions. Because of their defect in sight, they weren't fooled by the camouflage used to hide anti-aircraft guns. Their deficiency saved the lives of countless aviators and troops on the ground.

At any other hour of the day, in any other state of mind, Thorn might have passed by that stand of trees without a second glance. Only because he'd been exhausted and stopped to rest, then was drawn by the light and wind, had he managed to penetrate the facade of limbs and leaves and twisting vines.

In the fading light he worked his way to the center of the wooded grove, pushed through the snarl of branches, creepers, and spiderwebs.

And there it stood like some obelisk abandoned by long-departed explorers.

It must've weighed three tons or more, coated with red scales of rust and crumbling blisters of corrosion. Two giant wheels shaped like those on the wagon trains of early pioneers straddled a large cylinder that he knew housed a piston the size of a fifty-gallon drum. The machine sat astraddle two rails as thick as anvils. He'd seen this same engine once before on one of those field trips with that old high school geology teacher.

Thorn circled the motor and circled it again. On what he took to be its rear, he saw a copper plate riveted to one corner, and he kneeled to inspect it. With his fingernail he scraped away a patina of hardened salt and dust, and there was a date and name: 1933, HUMBLE OIL.

He closed his eyes, made himself take several deep and careful breaths. In the past, that's all it usually took to recharge himself. But this time it didn't come close. His body and his spirit had sailed far beyond such easy remedies.

He slipped his hand into his pocket and took out the rudist and rolled it in his fingers, feeling its rounded edges. That once ragged clump of mollusk shells had been smoothed by the centuries, buffed and polished by the restless layers of sand and bits of bone that mounted steadily around it.

On that long-ago excursion, his geology teacher had bused the class to Collier County, an hour west of Coquina Ranch, taking them to a remote spot on the fringes of Big Cypress Swamp, an area called the Felda Fields. It was there in the early forties the first commercial oil well in Florida was drilled. Two miles below the ground was what oil men called a pay zone. But because the reservoir was a measly thirty feet thick, it only managed to produce a few million gallons of crude. Enough to make things interesting, but not the gusher Humble Oil was searching for. At the time when Thorn's class visited, the oil had mostly played out and only a few stripper wells were still operating, the bulky rigs propelled by motors exactly like this one.

It made perfect geological sense. Down in the substrata, over the countless centuries, some portion of that same oil that was discovered in the Felda Fields had trickled eastward along the seams in the bedrock, moving steadily downstream toward a rudist-lined basin deep beneath Coquina Ranch, where it was trapped and held.

But why such a machine had been brought to this spot then abandoned, Thorn could only guess. The business of oil was always changing. Better extraction methods or higher prices could turn old fields new again. A deposit that was once considered unprofitable suddenly acquired great value. Maybe that's what happened at Coquina Ranch.

What was nearly certain was that there was oil beneath this ground, and oil was behind Earl Hammond's death, and it was oil that had brought Thorn unwillingly to this place.

He gave one backward glance at that great machine as he resumed his hike.

As far as he could see, he had no other choice, nowhere left to go except back to the hunting cabin.

TWENTY-FOUR

A HALF HOUR NORTH OF Clewiston, with twilight settling, Sugarman spotted the sign for Coquina Ranch. In the last few miles each ranching operation they passed seemed to be trying to outdo their neighbors with a more extravagant logo. But not the Hammonds. Theirs was barely a sign at all. Just maroon lettering on a modest whitewashed background. No insignia, no fancy crest. And none of the KEEP OUT warnings they'd been seeing plastered around every other turn-off.

Sugarman swung off the highway and into the one-lane dirt road lined by ancient slash pines. The trees were planted so close to the narrow roadway that if he'd wanted to turn around and run for his life, there was no place to accomplish it.

Rusty made a noise in her throat. Not sure of this.

"It's okay," he said. "I know what I'm doing."

"Do you?"

"Trust me. It's not my first time rescuing Thorn."

"What makes you think he's here?"

"I don't know where he is. But this is what we've got."

The road made a hard right and narrowed even more. A half mile ahead, down the corridor of pines, a concrete guardhouse was stationed in the center of their path.

"We're in over our heads, Sugar."

"No, we're not. We're exactly where we should be. Doing the right thing in the right way."

In her lap she made a fist, and stared down at her knuckles like a prizefighter getting psyched for the main event.

"Relax," Sugar said. "Guardhouses are my specialty."

In spite of herself, Rusty smiled.

There was a football game playing on the small TV in the gatehouse. A hundred thousand rabid fans were roaring, and the man inside wasn't happy about missing the next play. He looked like a Mexican with an Aztec warrior or two coloring his genes. On his cheek and forehead were several red welts, inflamed scars that Sugarman had seen a few times before. Ancient cigarette burns.

Sugar didn't mind waiting. And the guard didn't mind letting him wait. He watched the next play, watched the one after that, and watched a little of the Budweiser commercial before he got off his stool and sauntered to the open door.

By then, Sugarman had decided the steel girder blocking the road was about three times as thick as it needed to be to stop an average passenger car traveling at top speed. Maybe they were expecting an invasion of Mack trucks. Or maybe they'd gotten such a fabulous deal on the girder, they couldn't resist. Given another few minutes of waiting, Sugarman could make a decent list of other possibilities. It was one of the ways he'd learned to wait. Observing his immediate environment and trying to decode the decision-making processes of the interior decorator or the builder, or the guardhouse architect. You never knew what you might learn from simple observation.

"What do you want?" The Aztec warrior wore jeans and a black T-shirt, and a chunky nine-millimeter was holstered on his hip. More artillery than one might expect for a cattle ranch. Long ago the Aztec had gotten MOM tattooed on his biceps, but there was still plenty of room for the names of the rest of his family on that muscle.

"I've got an appointment with Frisco Hammond."

"No, you don't."

"Call him. Tell him Mullaney is here."

"If someone at the ranch is expecting a visitor, they tell me. Nobody told me. Which means you're not expected, which means you're not getting in."

He quirked an eyebrow at Sugarman, pleased by his own watertight logic.

Play had resumed on his television set and the guard turned away and went back to his stool. He sat for a minute before the set, then during the next commercial the guard palmed a tiny cell phone from his desk and made a call. He spoke for a few seconds, then snapped it shut, set it down, and went back to the game.

"You think you can back out of this place?" Rusty said.

"I don't believe that's an option."

The man sat through another few minutes of football. Sugarman heard enough of the broadcast to know it was late in the fourth quarter and the score was close. As one who had also frittered away vast amounts of time on TV football, Sugarman was sympathetic to the man's irritation. When you'd burned three hours of a beautiful afternoon watching that steroidal mayhem, and it all came down to the last two-minute drill, it was physically impossible to pull away.

Sugarman waited. Rusty fidgeted. Whistles blew, fans screamed, announcers recited their time-honored clichés. The final two minutes of football ate up twenty minutes of real life. When it was over and the winning coach had been sufficiently interviewed and the beer advertisements resumed, the Aztec brushed off the lap of his jeans, stood up, and swaggered back to the car.

"You still here?"

"Frisco's waiting for me. You know Frisco, right? Browning's big brother."

The Aztec settled the heel of his hand on the butt of his fat pistol.

"You got his cell number?" The Aztec slumped forward to see Sugar's face.

"I do."

"You call him, have him call me. Then we'll see."

"When I call him, all I get is voicemail."

"Well, then, I'd say that leaves you shit out of luck."

Some tough guys were tough and smart. Most were just tough. The Aztec was about to take the exam.

Well-trained security men never stood close beside the door of an occupied car. Cops, highway patrol, for them it was second nature to plant their feet well behind the trajectory of a swinging door. The physics of doing otherwise could be brutal.

Sugarman drew his cell phone from his pocket, punched in Frisco's number one more time, and when the voicemail's robotic voice began to speak, Sugar said, "Well, it's about damn time."

The guard bent forward. Sugar hooked his finger under the door latch and said, "The gentleman monitoring the front gate wants to speak to you."

The Aztec narrowed his eyes, but when Sugar held the phone up to the open window, the man stepped forward into the flight path of fifty pounds of sheet metal.

The door must have banged his knees because the guard buckled forward and whacked his forehead against the window frame. Another scar for his collection.

Sugar shouldered the door open, shoving the man backward to the ground. He was out of the car and had stripped the guard's pistol from his holster before the Aztec finished groaning.

At that point it should have been a simple matter of tying him up with something handy, locating the lever that activated the gate, and driving on into Coquina Ranch, except for the white Mercedes sedan which cruised up behind them and tapped its bumper gently against Sugarman's.

Two men got out of the Mercedes. Sugarman leaned down to the window and told Rusty to stay put. He'd handle this.

At that she unbuckled, got out of the car, and glared at him across the roof.

"I'm sorry," he said. "What was I thinking?"

"Don't worry about me, Sugar."

By then the white guy had gone behind the Mercedes and joined the driver, a black man who Sugarman recognized from somewhere. The two huge men looked at Sugarman, then at Rusty, then at the fallen Aztec.

The black guy grinned and said, "We have us a situation."

The white guy was a head taller than his buddy. In fact, he was bigger than any man Sugar had ever seen up close. He had a pudgy face and apple-red cheeks, and the body hiding inside his baggy khaki slacks and loose white shirt had the bulky solidity of a giant sack of grain. This was a guy you could punch till your fists were bloody and he might not even notice. Yet he moved like the best heavyweights do, with a silky agility that seemed almost weightless.

The black guy hung back as the other man advanced on Sugarman.

"You okay, Hector?" As he spoke, his eyes stayed on Sugar's.

"This man, he ambushed me, Mr. Hammond. Give me a second to catch my breath, sir, I'll take care of business with him."

"Retrieve your pistol from the gentleman, Hector. Then go inside your shed and clean yourself up."

Hammond kept his eyes on Sugarman's face, tipping his head by small degrees to the left and right as if he might be selecting the best spot to sink his teeth.

Sugar handed the pistol to Hector and the guard said something in Spanish about Sugarman's ancestors.

"The name is Sugarman," he said to Hammond. "A friend of your brother's. I just dropped by to have a word with Frisco."

"He told me his name was Mullaney," the Aztec said from his stool.

"You misled my security man to believe your name was Mullaney.

That's the name of the chief of police in Miami. This falsehood caused my associate and me to break off our business dealings and drive back here, which is a considerable inconvenience. Why'd you lie, Mr. Sugarman?"

"Maybe I was stretching the truth a little. I'm a friend of Mullaney's. I thought the name might get somebody's attention."

"Oh, it did do that," the black man said.

"I know you. You're One-Ton Antwan. Dolphin runningback. Nowadays you're promoting casino weekend getaways."

"He knows you, Antwan."

"Yeah? Well, that puts him in the upper quartile of the well-informed."

"Why did you attack my security man?"

"He has a bad attitude and bad manners. His breath isn't that great, either."

Rusty came around the car and slid in close beside Sugar's left shoulder. Hammond flicked a look her way and said, "And who are you?"

"She's with me," Sugarman said. "We're here to see Frisco."

"What do you want with my brother?"

"Look, I'm sorry. I understand this is a difficult moment for you and your family, you're grieving. It's a terrible loss, I'm sure."

Hammond chewed on the edge of his lip. There was something childlike in his menace as if even after all these years living with that body, he still found his superior size and strength a little astonishing, like some teenager who'd been dropped behind the wheel of a car way too powerful for his abilities.

"Want me to call Sheriff Prescott?" Antwan said. "Have these two removed all official and legal-like."

"Look," Rusty said. "We're here to speak to Frisco. We don't want any trouble. My friend was only protecting himself against your thug over there."

"Feisty alert," Antwan called out. "Tough broad on aisle three."

"What's your name, ma'am?"

Browning Hammond dug a hand into his shirt pocket and came out with a toothpick of gold, which he slid between his lips. The toothpick jiggled up and down like some juvenile taunt.

Sugarman cut a warning look her way. Stay cool.

But no, not Rusty, not Taco Shine's half-sister.

She took a half step forward and said, "My name is Rusty Stabler."

Sugarman groaned to himself.

The toothpick stopped wagging. Browning turned to look at his grinning buddy.

"Our situation," Antwan said, "is compounding in interest."

Rusty stayed put, staring defiantly at the two of them.

"You a lawyer?" Hammond asked her.

"No."

"A real estate broker?"

"None of that," she said.

"Your name was on some paperwork I been studying. Rusty Stabler."

"That's right. My name was on some paperwork."

"A few weeks back, Earl showed me those papers, just gave me a peek. I saw your name and I saw the name of a man I never heard of before. A fellow called Thorn. So when Earl passed on, I was mighty curious about what kind of business the two of you were doing behind my back with my own family. So this afternoon I go to the bank, open Earl's lockbox, and let my lawyer take a good long look at that document. He didn't know what to make of it, either. A very strange agreement with your name on it. Rusty Stabler."

"So?"

"You're not a lawyer, you're not a broker. What are you then?"

"I'm the woman you've got to deal with."

"And I'm the man," said Sugar.

But neither of them could take their eyes off Rusty.

"Raise the gate, Hector," Hammond called out.

"How we doing this?" Antwan sidled up to his buddy.

"You take brown sugar," Hammond said. "The woman goes with me."

"No, you don't," said Sugarman. "The lady and I are together. We're staying together."

"Take him, Antwan. Be nice. Don't break any bones he might need later on."

TWENTY-FIVE

CLAIRE CHANGED STATIONS ON THE radio dial, and changed them again. Only football and talk shows and someone selling vitamins. No news, no music that soothed her nerves. Frisco was silent, driving his pickup one-handed, his eyes on the road.

He'd used the ranch's south exit, unlocking the gate with a key from his chain. When she asked why they were using that less-traveled route to leave the ranch, he just looked at her and said nothing. She felt like she was being kidnapped by a stranger. In the last hour after they'd returned to the barn, settled the horses in their stalls, he'd barely acknowledged her existence. He'd walked away without a word. She followed him to the lodge and into the kitchen, where he had a hushed conversation with Deloria.

Claire hovered at the kitchen door, and when she started to stalk away, he ordered her to stop. They were going for a drive. He wouldn't say where. He led her out to his pickup and hadn't spoken for the last ten miles.

South of Clewiston he turned east on highway 80 toward Belle Glade.

"Where are we going?"

"Ten more minutes," he said. "Hold on."

On the outskirts of the shabby town, he wheeled the truck onto a side road that had no sign and bumped down a potholed stretch past rows of trailer homes where the pickers lived and the migrants who'd saved enough to get off the road and rest for a while. Three mutts chased them down the street, barking at the wheels of the truck.

Darkness was gathering. The wind had died. The approaching cold front must have stalled north of them as they so often did that time of year.

He parked in front of a green-and-white mobile home that was neater than any on the street. A flag emblazoned with a Pilgrim holding a roasted turkey fluttered over the doorway.

As they got out, the dogs surrounded them and snarled, but Frisco waded through the pack, shepherded Claire along, and headed for the door. It opened before he could knock.

A short heavy Mexican with bleary eyes and an undershirt spattered with flecks of salsa blocked the way. He stared at the front of Frisco's Miami PD T-shirt, then stepped back.

"You out of your territory, aren't you, my friend?"

"This used to be my area once," Frisco said. "A long time back."

"I don't think I got any warrants on me from Miami. But I could be wrong."

"Is Ana Pinto here?"

"Her name's not Pinto anymore."

"Is she here?"

"What you want with Ana?"

"Tell her it's Frisco."

"Aw, man. I told that woman. I said you'd come and she got all hostile at me. When that woman gets mean, she'll shut up for a week. That's how she is. Goddamn woman."

Ana came to the door with a baby in her arms, two toddlers tagging along. Her black hair was long and straight and her dark eyes full of a resolute calm. She wore tight blue jeans and a T-shirt that hung to her knees. The man in the undershirt padded back inside, and Claire saw him take hold of the arm of a boy who had squirmed into the man's lounge chair. He yanked him out, scolding him in Spanish, swatted the boy on the butt, and sent him yowling into the back rooms.

"How'd you know where to find me?"

"Deloria," he said. "She's worried about you."

"I'm not part of this, Frisco."

"I didn't think you were."

"My father, I told him, no, don't do it. God would judge him and he would burn in hell for this."

"Why, Ana? Why did this happen?"

"It wasn't out of anything but love."

"Love? What kind of love kills an old man like Earl?"

"Gustavo was sick. He wouldn't go to the doctor till too late."

"Sick with what?"

She turned away from him and drew open a drawer just inside the door. When she came back, she held out a sheaf of papers in her hand, and Frisco took them. Baptist Hospital, Miami. He shuffled through them, scanned the print quickly. Lab results, bills, blood tests, scheduled exams with oncologists and other specialists.

"Cancer?" Frisco said.

"His pancreas," she said, touching a shy hand to her belly. "Doctors told him he had only two, three weeks. Not even that, if you'd asked me. At the end he was down to Miami for chemo once a week, but it made him so sick. He wasn't right in his head. In so much pain."

He returned the papers, and Ana set them on the cabinet by the door.

"Where'd your mother go? Your brothers."

"I can't tell you that."

"I'll find out, Ana."

"Don't steal this away. I'm asking you, Frisco. It's all Mama has now. This was my father's gift to her. He meant to do right. You knew him. He was a good Catholic, worked hard all his life, but he lost it all at the end, the hospital, the treatments, he had nothing left, no savings, nothing. Then the devil got in his face when he was sick and confused, and the devil knew he was dying, and he makes my father a terrible offer. What was he going to do? This was his chance to give my mother something and my brothers."

"What devil, Ana?"

She shut her mouth and shook her head.

Her eyes strayed to Claire for a moment, and Ana inspected her with a weary frankness. Whatever she saw made her sigh and stroke the downy head of her baby. She shifted her gaze back to Frisco.

"Gustavo shot Earl dead, Ana. Two bullets in the heart. That's not a good man. That's not doing a good thing."

"It's not simple as that," she said. "Good and bad. Maybe for you it is, but for a man who never had nothing, it was too much temptation."

Frisco looked past her into the trailer.

"I'm sorry, Frisco," Ana said. "Your grandpa was a fine man. He didn't deserve no death like that."

"Tell me where your mother went. The rest of your family."

"I can't."

"I'm going to find out what happened. I won't stop till I do."

"I know that. That's how you always were."

They looked at each other for several moments.

Frisco said, "Does my brother know where you live?"

"I don't know what your brother knows."

"Does the man in there own a gun?"

"He's my husband," she said. "He's not some man."

"Does he own a gun, Ana?"

"He keeps a pistol in the closet."

"Good. You tell him to take it down, load it, stash it away from the kids but somewhere he can get to it quickly."

"Why?"

"You'll know when this is over, Ana. I'll let you know. But until then, have him keep it loaded and close at hand."

Claire kept quiet till they were in the truck and rolling away.

"What the hell were you saying back there? That Browning might threaten that woman's life?"

"That's about right."

Something smacked Frisco's door and he slowed.

The boy who'd perched in the lounge chair was running alongside, slapping at the truck.

Frisco came to a stop and rolled down his window.

"This is from Mama."

He handed Frisco a white slip of paper.

Frisco looked at it for a moment and told the boy to wait. Then he leaned across to the glove compartment, brushing Claire's knees with his arm, opened the glove box, and dug out a handful of peppermint sticks.

"Make sure you share them," he said, and handed them to the boy.

TWENTY-SIX

IT WAS AN HOUR AND a half to Coconut Grove. Frisco took shortcuts across Miami on backstreets Claire had never seen, finally gliding to a stop on a quiet avenue just off Ingram Highway in a neighborhood of old Florida homes with new BMWs and sleek Italian roadsters in the driveways. Lots of oaks and ficus, a fashionably unkempt jungle. This part of the Grove was home to artists and musicians, news anchors and a certain kind of stockbroker who liked funky charm. It was an unusual combination for Miami, where old money mingled with new, and the well-to-do lived next door to thrift-shop bohemians, with everyone sharing the same live-and-let-live creed.

The address on Ana's note was a wood-frame two-story house, white and yellow with a tin roof. In an earlier era it might have housed a hippie commune or a band of Hari Krishnas, but now it had been painted and remodeled to fit in with the neighborhood's elevated status. There were giant banyans on one side and a coral wall running down the other. The garage door was open, and two men in their late twenties were looking under the raised hood of a yellow Corvette while a third young man sat behind the wheel and gunned the engine.

A neighbor was standing on his front porch, holding his newspaper in one hand and trying not to scowl at the boys.

"There goes the neighborhood," Frisco said. "Bunch of Mexicans."

"That's Juan, Gustavo Junior, and Victor."

"Yes."

"What is this, Frisco?"

"I'd say this is the payoff. That house has to be worth over a million, and that car is the cherry on top."

"A payoff for killing Earl."

"The devil discovered Gustavo was ill, he preyed on his vulnerability."

"You mean Browning."

"I hope it's not Browning."

"But that's who you think it is. That's crazy, Frisco. That's impossible."

"So the devil comes to Gustavo and makes him an offer. If you kill old man Hammond, your family will live in style."

"Gustavo wouldn't agree to that. Never, never. No way."

"Ana said he took the deal."

"I don't care how sick he was, he'd never do that."

"I don't expect Gustavo had much choice. It was either accept this reward, or see his family evicted from the ranch. Ana said he did it out of love, but I think there might've been fear, too, and desperation. He knew the end was coming. His own, and maybe his family's. The devil has a lot of bargaining power at times like those."

In an upstairs window a woman in a nightgown peered out into the darkness. She was holding a phone to her ear and speaking listlessly.

"And what about me, Frisco? Am I in league with the devil? Was my job to walk in and shoot Gustavo?"

"That possibility occurred to me."

Claire's face went hot. She jerked forward, clawed at the door handle, got it open, but Frisco reached across her body and slammed the door shut. He kept his arm there until she'd calmed.

"For the moment, Claire, I'm giving you the benefit of the doubt."
She pressed hard against the seat, fuming, unable to speak.

"Reason I'm giving you that leeway is because of the map you saw.
The map the others say wasn't there. But it's other things, too."

"Like what?"

"Well, for one, I think last night Browning was yelling at Gustavo,
not you."

She turned and looked at him.

"I'm talking about your husband. I'm saying it's possible you stumbled into the middle of this. Gustavo was supposed to pull the trigger
and walk away, spend his last days in this house with his wife and his
boys. There's probably some money in a bank account, too. But then
you walked in with the shotgun. That wasn't in the plan. But the devil
adjusted to it. In fact, it had some added benefits. Made the whole
thing neater in a messy sort of way."

Claire shook her head, her mouth rigid.

"You thought Browning was yelling at you to shoot, but maybe he
was yelling at Gustavo. 'Do it for your family.' Maybe this is what he
meant. This house, that car. Do it for this."

Gustavo's wife, Angela, opened the upstairs window and called
down to her sons. They looked up from the Corvette, then turned one
by one to stare across the street at Frisco's truck. Victor marched back
into the house. The other two waited a moment longer as if considering a confrontation, then followed their brother inside.

"We should go," Claire said. "They think we're going to turn
them in."

"Maybe we will."

Frisco pulled the cell phone from his pocket and punched a
number.

"You son of a bitch."

Claire grabbed at the phone but he turned and blocked her with
his shoulder.

"I'm calling Julia Scarborough. You know Julia, your phone friend.

Works at the police department barn. You got her pestering me to come out to the ranch."

"Julia? Why?"

"She's got some basic computer skills."

Frisco dialed, and after several rings Julia answered. He put her on speaker, told Julia that Claire Hammond was listening.

"Claire? You there?"

Claire leaned over and said yes, yes she was.

"You doing okay? I'm so sorry about what happened. It's terrible."

"She's fine," Frisco said. "Now listen. You sitting at your computer?"

No, Julia was outside mucking stalls.

"Okay, do me a favor, would you? Go inside and look something up on the Miami-Dade website."

"What're you doing, Sergeant?"

"Some police work. Don't worry, it's nothing illegal. At least not yet."

A couple of minutes later she came back on.

"I'm ready. Miami-Dade-dot-gov."

Frisco walked her through the steps to the property map. He gave the address of the Grove house.

"Okay, I'm there, got the aerial view," Julia said. "Nice neighborhood. You shopping for a place?"

"Who's the owner?"

"It's a four-three, thirty-three hundred feet inside, eleven-thousand-square-foot lot. Bought last year for a million-two. Owner is an LLC with a business address somewhere in North Miami. It's name is BEG, all caps. You want me to try to track that down?"

"Do that. Call me back. I'll keep the cell on. We need to get a bite to eat."

"It shouldn't take long. Don't you love the Sunshine Law? Everything online. All those secrets, anybody can find out."

"If you have secrets," Frisco said, "it can be a bitch."

Frisco took Claire to Scotty's Landing, ten minutes away, a fish joint on the edge of Biscayne Bay. He left her at an outdoor picnic table and went back to the truck. When he returned, he was carrying a leather cylinder. He set it on the bench beside him, sat down, and had a long sip of his beer.

"I want to go home," she said.

"I don't think that's wise."

"I'm in danger, too? Browning is going to kill me? You're crazy."

"I don't know what that man is going to do. He's not somebody I fully understand."

"So which is it? Am I innocent or was I part of the conspiracy?"

"You tell me."

She looked out at the glitter and tinkle of sailboats tied up in the bayside marina. She felt the rising flush behind her eyes, goddamn tears coming again. She made a fist and hammered it on the table, pounded it a second and third time until several customers turned to look. By then the burn in her eyes had subsided.

She leaned forward across the table, bringing her voice down. "I had no part in any plot to kill Earl Hammond."

Frisco kept looking into her eyes as if waiting for some facial tic to show itself, a signal she was lying.

Julia called back. He put her on speaker again, set the phone on the table.

"Every LLC or corporation has to file a fictitious name form."

"Okay."

"I love this shit. Snooping on people. Click, click, click, get all the dirt."

"I know. You told me once at work how much it turned you on."

"Yeah, well. Anyway, I did a fictitious name search on BEG. State of Florida site. Fill in a little box, a screen pops up, it's all in alphabetical order, click on BEG, it lets you download the original PDF file, the document the person had to record with the state to grab that name. And there it is, the address, the ID number, and the owner."

"Which is?"

"It's an address in Tamarac."

"Tamarac? Wait, let me guess. The name is Antwan Shelton."

"Football player, right? Played for the Dolphins, the guy on the billboards. Always showing off his sexy bare chest?"

"You think Antwan's sexy?"

"Is that what you were looking for?"

"Yeah, I think it is, Julia. Thanks."

"You still there, Claire?"

"I'm here."

"Hey, if you ever need a place to stay, I got a spare room with its own bath and everything. I'd like to meet you finally."

"Thanks," Claire said. "I'd like to meet you, too. I'll let you know."

When the waitress came back they ordered grouper sandwiches, then sat in silence.

Claire watched a couple kissing on the dock. A tall boy and his tall girlfriend. They seemed a perfect physical match, a cozy fit. After the kissing was done, the girl tucked her head against the tall guy's chest and he held her while they looked out at the water. A stand-up cuddle on a beautiful Miami night. Dizzy in love.

She looked back at Frisco and found him watching the same couple. He rolled his eyes to her.

"Young love," he said. "Nothing like it."

"This city can be an aphrodisiac. It can make you lose your head."

Frisco blew out a breath, ducked his eyes, and consulted the back of his hand for a long moment. She'd never seen him look quite so ill at ease. Whether she deserved it or not, she took credit for his brief discomfort. Felt slightly more in control.

She said, "So it's Antwan who owns that house."

Frisco was silent.

"Antwan, not Browning."

"You're around those two all the time, Claire. Can you tell which one is pulling the strings?"

"I know, I know. But it's Antwan's company that owns the house."

"Legally, that's worthless. If he was confronted, Antwan could spin it like he'd done a good deed. He owned this house, it happened to be vacant, he knew Gustavo was sick, so he let the Pintos use it short-term while Gustavo was getting chemo in Miami. Some bullshit excuse. Bullshit is that guy's stock and trade."

"So the fact is, Antwan could take that house back any time he wants. Kick the Pintos out on the street."

"And he probably intends to do just that. Gustavo swapped his eternal soul for a wad of cotton candy."

She watched the cuddlers move down the dock, holding tight to each other.

"So where are we?"

"I want you to make a phone call, Claire."

Frisco finished the last of his beer and slid his stein to the side. He held out his cell.

"Who am I calling?"

"Donaldson."

"Why is that?"

"Tell her what you and I have been doing the last few hours. Everything we've learned since we saw her last. About Ana Pinto, the house in the Grove. Antwan, everything."

"Why don't you do it?"

"She should hear it from you."

Frisco turned and watched a pretty waitress pass by with two pitchers of beer.

"Why?"

"You're a suspect, Claire. It would be an act of good faith, passing on evidence to the lead investigator."

"But that's not really why you want me to call."

Frisco kept his eyes down.

"If I agree to call Donaldson, that proves to you I'm innocent. If I'm collaborating with Browning or Antwan, I'll refuse. That's your gambit?"

"Will you make the call?"

"I can't believe you still don't trust me."

Frisco drew Donaldson's card from his jeans and placed it in front of her.

"You're one brutal son of a bitch."

Claire picked up the phone, flipped it open.

"You've got messages," she said.

"Call Donaldson. Tell her what we know."

It wasn't like her, but Claire was pissed. She punched Frisco's voice-mail and listened to them, one by one. The first five were the string of messages Claire left late last night just after the shooting. In the first one her voice was frantic, pleading, almost unintelligible, she hardly recognized herself. But with each new call her shock and panic subsided, her speech became more plaintive. It was like listening to the ramblings of a dying woman, each message slower than the last, more resigned, more final.

Then a message from someone else, a man, jovial, profane.

"Frisco, you need to hear this. It's Chief Mullaney, a couple of hours ago."

She handed him the phone and he listened, then replayed it.

He set the phone down on the table and said, "You know someone named Sugarman?"

"No."

"How about a guy named Thorn?"

"Never heard of him."

"You're sure?"

"Why? Who are they?"

"It's something about a real estate transaction. Earl signed some papers, made some kind of deal with this guy Thorn. Last night just after Earl was killed, Thorn went missing. His friend Sugarman believes his disappearance is related to Earl's murder. Mr. Sugarman is headed to the ranch to fill me in."

"Earl signed some papers?"

"Apparently he did."

"What? He was selling the ranch to this guy?"

"Or something," Frisco said.

"The radical change."

He nudged the phone closer to her.

"Call Donaldson," he said. "Add those names to your list. Tell her about Sugarman and Thorn. Maybe she's still at the ranch. She can talk to this guy, see what's up."

She dialed the number, holding Frisco's gaze. Donaldson's voice-mail picked up. Claire turned on the speaker, held the phone up for Frisco to hear the woman's recorded greeting.

"Okay, Sergeant. What now?"

"Leave her a message. All the details. Say your name, so there's no doubt who it is. Tell her to call back as soon as she's able to."

When she was done, Claire snapped the phone shut and set it in front of him.

"Okay, you satisfied? Somehow that proves I'm innocent?"

"It helps."

Frisco looked out at the glittering rows of sailboats. He ran a hand through his coarse brown hair and took a long breath, then let it go with a soft whistle at the end like a man summoning the courage to do something he's long dreaded.

He reached to his side and retrieved the leather cylinder. He popped its lid and drew out a large sheet of rolled paper. It rattled in the breeze as he set it on the picnic table. He stretched it out, put his beer stein on one end, and held the other with his hand.

Claire stood up, moved around the table for better light.

It was a survey map with a dozen red circles clustered in one corner. A dotted line marked the boundaries of the property, and the land itself was shadowed darker than the ranches surrounding it. It was a shape as recognizable to Claire as the outline of the state of

Florida. It was Coquina Ranch. And those red circles were all bunched together in the far western quadrant, the fenced area now used as the game preserve.

"Is this the map you saw on the table last night?"

She studied it for several seconds, then looked him in the eyes and nodded.

"You're sure?"

"I'm sure. Where'd you get that?"

"It was given to me by my grandfather when he decided I'd come of age. For me that was thirteen years ago on my twenty-first birthday. In Browning's case, apparently Earl thought that boy needed to mature a little longer. I think your husband got his copy sometime in the last month or so. That's what started this mess."

"What is this?"

"It's the Hammond family test of loyalty."

"Loyalty?"

"Loyalty to the land. To that ranch out there."

"These red marks, what are they?"

"That's oil, Claire. Those red dots are the sites of exploratory wells dug seventy-five years ago. Millions of barrels of crude are down there, about ten thousand feet below Coquina Ranch. A mother lode of oil."

TWENTY-SEVEN

IT FELT AS IF SOMEONE had fired a nail gun into the belly of Thorn's leg muscle. He collapsed in the field he was crossing and tried to stretch it out, but the stretching set off another cramp in his left foot. He relaxed, or tried to. Slowed his breath. In a minute or two the pain eased, and he stood up again.

It had to be dehydration. Except for the half cup he'd squeezed from his shirt, he'd gone almost twenty-four hours without water, made worse by all that alcohol the night before, then sweating in the sinkhole, sweating as he climbed that wall of rock, sweating as he killed a man and climbed that wall a second time, then ran across the plain, sweating as he hiked through the woods.

As he set off again, an ice pick stabbed his right quadriceps, and the slab of muscle knotted hard. In the dark, he held his breath and stood flat-footed for a moment and willed himself to settle down. He concentrated on the call of a barred owl in a nearby tree. "Who, who, cooks for you?"

A mournful question that the owl repeated and repeated again.

"Rusty Stabler," Thorn said quietly. "That's who."

Though the truth was Rusty wasn't much of a cook. Her only true specialty was a cheese omelet. Then again, it was a damn good omelet. With bacon crumbles and spicy salsa and avocado. Damn good.

Thorn thought about that omelet as he stood in the darkness, waiting for the pain in his thigh to subside. He thought about Rusty, her lean, hard body, her restless energy, the two of them in bed coiled together like matching strands of DNA.

After a minute or two, he took an experimental step, then another. Soon he was walking across the meadow, walking steadily without pain in what he judged was a westerly direction.

Out in that open field he tried to get his bearings from the stars, but the clouds were still so dense even the moon was in hiding. Picking his way carefully he set out across that field, the muscles cooperating better now, his stride lengthening. He was guided by a faint and distant light that glowed on the horizon.

He'd never known how dark it could be out on the pineland flats. In that first mile he stumbled and fell three times. He skinned both knees, barked his palms, but got up each time and resumed his march across the plain. It was grassy for a while, then he crossed a patch of barren ground, with crumbled seashells and sand underfoot. It was impossible to walk for long across the unpaved parts of Florida without crunching across the remains of ancient marine life.

He was crossing a rocky pasture when he sensed movement nearby. He halted. To his left then to his right he heard something like the swishing of horse tails chasing away biting flies, then the wet flutter of lips. He strained to see but in that thick darkness could make out no more than the stony ground a yard or two ahead. He extended one hand before him and the other to his side like a blind man crossing a log. He kept going like that for twenty or thirty feet.

The creature he collided with was far bigger and hairier than the antelopes he'd seen earlier. At Thorn's touch, the animal bucked and snorted, let out a bellow that must have been the war cry of its species. Bison or buffalo or some exotic moose or elk. A hundred of them at least, for the darkness rumbled around him as the herd he'd spooked stampeded to the north, one of them butting him to the ground, another stamping his rump, they jostled and jolted and bruised him from every direction. Lying on his side, Thorn tucked into a fetal ball and absorbed a few more licks. In seconds they were gone, leaving in their wake a fragrant swirl of manure and crushed rye grass, and the sharp stink of animal terror.

In the second mile or the third, he skidded down the bank of a ditch, and came to rest ankle-deep in standing water. Squatting down, he cupped some up, brought it to his mouth, and almost gulped before he caught its putrid smell. It was stale piss of one kind or another. Certain animals did that, used the same spot for their latrine, one after the other, covering their rivals' scent in an endless striving for dominance.

For a moment he was tempted to take just one sip. But his thirst, he finally reckoned, was not yet that severe. Thorn wiped his hands on his shorts, climbed up the bank and pushed on. He passed through more glens and crossed meadows of broomstraw and wire grass and a pasture where a chorus of frogs accompanied his passage with tinkling croaks like a hundred plastic combs strummed by fingertips.

Winds aloft skimmed away the clouds, and the half moon that floated into view put a sugar glaze on the scrubland before him. He reached the meadow where he'd been trapped in the pit and saw in the distance the blaze of house lights.

He worked his way forward, located the wooden platform that covered the old well. Saw the tips of an aluminum ladder cocked against the opened hatch.

He drew his pistol, and stood for several moments at the edge of the deck, listening for any human sound. When he was satisfied no one was moving around down there, he lowered the Glock and tucked it back in his pocket.

In the halo surrounding the cabin he saw the red four-wheeler Jonah had been driving, and parked nearby was a compact car with all four doors swung open.

Thorn edged forward to the perimeter of the illuminated area and skirted the cabin, searching for a garden hose, an outdoor faucet, water trough, or cistern. But seeing none of that.

He eased into the shadow of a utility shed that gave him a view of the house's rear. Inside the house there was no movement, but strange music was sifting through the air. It seemed to be coming from the car's speakers, something with flutes and the mournful voices of Indian chiefs crooning on behalf of their ancestral spirits.

A phone trilled inside the cabin. It trilled three more times. No one picked up.

He waited with his shoulder braced against the shed, trying to take the weight off his unsteady legs. Five minutes passed, but nothing moved at the windows. Maybe Jonah was frying up the batch of conch fritters Thorn ordered earlier. Or crushing ice for a pitcher of margaritas.

Thorn knew he was going a little nuts. Lips glued shut, tongue a leather flap.

He stepped away from the shed, following the shadowed path of a pine tree that led toward the house. He stayed within its cone of darkness till he was ten feet from the car. It was one of those hybrid jobs with an ugly shape, an uglier paint job.

Thorn ducked into the front seat and saw the key in the ignition.

He gripped the key for several moments then drew back his hand.

He'd done too much running for one day. And he needed water. Needed it worse than he'd ever needed water before.

The iPod on the passenger seat was like the one Rusty used on her morning jogs. A white cord connected it to a plug in the dash. Thorn picked up the unit and touched its dial. As Rusty had shown him, he made a circle with his fingertip against the smooth face, cranked up the volume, then twisted the knob on the dashboard to push it higher.

He backed from the car, angling across the sandy yard to the four-wheeler. He crouched behind the ATV and waited to see if the music drew Jonah from the house. But minutes passed and nothing happened. A few more minutes, and a lot more nothing.

Only the Indian chanters and the flutes and drums and tambourines echoed across that moonscape. That land of ghostly darkness was dense with ghostly noise. Thorn held the pistol slack at his side and scanned the house from end to end.

For a better view he climbed onto one of the knobby wheels of the ATV. From that angle he made out a living room with couch and chairs, and what appeared to be a long dining room table. There was clutter on the shelves, a heap of clothes in one rocker. A sliver of the kitchen was visible. Old appliances, counters littered with bowls and dishes and frying pans and plates of half-eaten food, cabinet doors swung open. All the markings of a messy bachelor pad. Then his eyes fastened on the kitchen faucet and the glistening ribbon that trickled from its spout.

Thorn worked his jaws, and tried to swallow. Lodged in the back of his throat was a chunk of cinder. He tried to coax some spit into his mouth, but got nothing. He tried chewing on the edge of his hard tongue, and got the same result. He found himself leaning forward to better see the water dribbling.

He was losing it all right. That was clear. His body was in revolt, cells garbling their messages to one another. He'd begun to question his reflexes and his judgment.

With the back of his arm he mashed his raw lips, trying again to manufacture juice inside his mouth. It didn't work. Nothing was going to work but the real stuff.

He jumped down from the tire and mapped his route. Only a madman would barge in the front. Then again it had a certain fittingness. One madman calling on another.

Running in a stoop, he stayed below the level of the windows and stole close to the cabin wall. He worked his way forward to the porch.

He mounted the three wooden steps, then held back in the shadows and tilted his head around the window frame to scout the interior of the cabin. Table lights blazing. Overhead lights on, ceiling fan whirling at full speed. Papers tacked to the walls fluttered in its breeze. On the mantel were a dozen fat red candles of different heights, each with a trembling flame.

Through the kitchen entryway, Thorn could see the running faucet.

Even in his untrustworthy state of mind, he knew it was a trap. Not that it mattered. He was going in. He was going through that door.

Out in the yard the iPod finished its playlist and ceased. After a stretch of pineland silence, there came the slow whoots of a great horned owl reclaiming its share of the night. From some nearby pond or marsh a collection of competing frogs tuned up their orchestra. The marble-clicking-against-marble call of the cricket frogs and the *cheep-cheep* reply of oak toads and dozens of tiny cricket frogs bleating like a lost herd of sheep.

It was an endless war out there in the scrub, every hour of every day. Who would prevail, who would disappear. Who could outsing, outfox, outrun the other.

He drew the pistol from his pocket. Thorn held the handgun for a moment and tried to silence the clamor in his chest. Everything he was doing was out of sync, too fast or slow, the disjointed boogie-woogie of a drunk.

He wrapped his hand around the pistol grip and extended the weapon into a slant of light to see exactly how bad his shakes had gotten. The harder he clenched, the more the pistol quivered.

With his left hand he reached for the knob and saw that hand was trembling, too. He gripped the knob, turned it, shoved the door open, and swung it aside, pressing his back against the exterior wall. Jonah did not spray automatic fire through the wood or at the open doorway. And he didn't shriek and come swinging down from the rafters with knives in both hands and a knife between his teeth.

In the darkness behind him the owls and frogs continued to compete with one another. The only sound inside the cabin was the creaky whirr of the fan.

"People think I got it easy cashing in on my rep," Antwan said. "Making deals, being the front man for this and that. A guy looks at me and thinks I'm cruising down easy street. But let me tell you, brown sugar, it's not like people think. It's hard work being in the limelight."

"I feel your pain."

Sugarman looked across the room at the shattered window. The shotgun's blast pattern had chewed a swatch out of the rock wall. Crime-scene stickers were affixed to the leather couch beside two puncture wounds. There were animal heads on the wall: an antelope of some kind, a bison, a wild boar with yellowed tusks.

He was sitting in a wingback chair beside the couch. He believed his nose was broken, but he hadn't reached up to check because he didn't want to give Antwan the satisfaction.

So far Antwan had punched him three times. Bruised his jaw, loosened a canine. Just recreational hitting, establishing the pecking order. Sugarman hadn't fought back. Not yet. Playing possum, at least that's what he was telling himself. But he wasn't sure he could tolerate much more. Might have to defend the next strike, see what this bully knew about hand-to-hand.

As long as Rusty was okay, there was no urgency. He could hear her talking in a normal voice in the dining room behind them. Couldn't make out everything, but got a word here and there. Telling Browning Hammond about the structure of the business arrangement. How it happened, the history of it, Florida Forever. Like she could reason with him, like this wasn't all going terribly wrong. Hammond wasn't saying much. Just a "goddamn" here and there.

Antwan pulled out his BlackBerry for the fourth time, thumb-typed a message. Waited, didn't get the reply he wanted, and cursed. He slid the device into his pocket and turned to Sugarman again, his big lips curling into a smile, walking over to the wingback like it was time again for another right jab. Then he stopped short and gave Sugar a curious grin.

"I'm trying to figure out which part of you is white. Old man, or old lady. I'd lay odds you had one of them hippie-chick moms. Lived in a commune, milked her herd of goats, grew big old marijuana plants. Along comes a big black dude with nasty manners and she turns all squishy inside. I bet that's your story. You're the love child of a Zulu warrior and a bimbo from Ohio."

"Mullaney knows we're here."

"Aw, man, is that all you got to scare me with?" Antwan said. "Chief of police of Miami? Shit, that's lame. First off, that man's got himself an alcohol problem of great magnitude. Second thing, his plate is full to overflowing—he don't care about your sorry ass. People disappear every day. Drive off, never heard of again, vaporize off the grid somewhere. Happens more than a man would think."

"He's an old friend."

"Well, okay, bring it, baby. Let him send a search crew up here, have a look around, fine-tooth-comb the whole ranch. Nobody's gonna discover no trace of brown sugar or his twiggy. No, sir, Officer, never seen such a person. No, sir. No, sir."

"They'll come looking. It won't be that easy."

Antwan bent in close to Sugar and said, "I think you're still way too pretty."

He punched him square with a left hand. Sugarman's head thumped against the chair. He swallowed the blood, wiped his mouth with the back of his hand. Lips numb, cheeks swelling.

"Look, here's how it is. You been messing in the man's business. He don't like that. Neither do I, cause his business is comingled with mine."

"I see that."

"I don't know what you are, brown sugar, but you ain't no businessman. 'Cause if you were, you'd see how wrong you been, going behind people's backs, trying to take what's theirs without proper remuneration. Am I talking so you understand?"

"Why was Earl in such a hurry to part with his land?"

Antwan took a half step back from the chair and squinted at Sugarman.

"You are one well-informed negro, I'll give you that much. But the thing is, every time you come out with shit like that, you ain't doing nothing but taking another shovelful of dirt out of your own grave."

In the other room Rusty's voice was growing stern. Giving Browning Hammond a lecture in ethics. As a tactic, Sugarman had always liked that approach. Even when you were a hostage, speaking the truth had a way of knocking off balance morally challenged assholes like Antwan Shelton and Browning Hammond.

"Those two guys that kidnapped Thorn, the little one dressed like a derelict and his big preppie buddy, you sent them, didn't you?"

Antwan's grin lost some of its sizzle.

"What did they do with him, Antwan? Where's my friend?"

Antwan dabbed a finger into the corner of his eye and flicked the crumb away.

"I'd just be guessing," he said. "But if I had to put cash money on it, I'd say your buddy Thorn put on his weight belt and went scuba diving without his tank."

TWENTY-EIGHT

THORN STEPPED INSIDE, FANNED THE Glock around the empty
room.

He crossed the bare wood floor, heading behind the couch toward
the kitchen. To his right down a hallway several doors were shut.
Maybe Jonah was down there catching some Z's. Maybe he'd grown
weary of his own pathetic future and exploded his skull with a bullet.
Or perhaps he was absorbed in some old cable TV show. A guy who
gives away a million dollars each week, then sits back in his easy chair
and watches the fun.

The kitchen reeked of rancid grease and rotting vegetables and
damp towels that had been moldering for months. The grout was
green with mildew. Smears of butter and jelly and ketchup and black
grime marked the countertops. Empty tins of sardines spilled over
the brim of the garbage can. These boys had the housekeeping skills
of a drove of feral hogs.

Thorn aimed the pistol at the plates and clutter of frying pans and
pots. He aimed at the faucet and the trickle of water. He didn't rush
to drink. He exercised restraint because he needed to show himself
he was in control. He swung his aim to the door behind him, expect-

ing Jonah to burst around the edge in his weasel grin and grubby clothes.

The pistol barrel wavered before him as if he were shooing away a bug.

The door was empty. In the living room the fan whirred. The drawings tacked to the walls fluttered and rattled. Drawings in Magic Marker and crayon of loony faces and dismembered bodies. Pencil sketches of naked women and couples having Kama Sutra sex. A posterboard decorated with dozens of skulls and a single clown's face. Scrawlings of the doomed and damned.

Thorn lowered the pistol. He turned and went to the sink, bent his head down and slurped. His throat tightened but he fought off the gag. He straightened and swung back to the doorway. Still empty.

From the open window Thorn heard the peeping of frogs in the marsh. Amazing creatures. With no tusks or venom, speed or strength, it was a miracle they survived the constant combat out on the pineland, where every living thing was busy finding any slim advantage. So slow and vulnerable, they puffed themselves up and made their bold squeals to bluff intruders. Managing to survive only with their voices and their guile.

He went back to the water, back to swallowing. A sip and another sip. Taking it slow because that was the advice he'd learned in childhood. The medical folklore of growing up. Don't drink too fast when you're parched. Overwhelming the shriveled stomach could be as dangerous as the dehydration. Old lessons from Kate Truman, the woman he'd called Mother, whose wedding ring had saved his life today, whose lessons were always practical and clear. Never leave dirty dishes overnight because it's harder to clean them in the morning. Don't drink too fast when you're dying of thirst. And always, always turn around and check the empty doorway to see if the killer has appeared.

This time he had.

Jonah's smirky grin had been replaced by a vague stare. He had freshened up. Shaved his head, showered away the hog blood, though he'd missed a red smear on his temple. He looked shrunken inside his brother's snappy blue business shirt. It draped over his bony shoulders like a toga on a child. His eyes twitched around the room and his jaw moved as if he were gnawing on unspoken words. He stood as stiff and uncertain as an understudy pushed onto the stage with insufficient training.

In his hand, however, was one hell of a prop, a Mac-10 with an extended clip.

"You came," Jonah said. "I thought you might."

"I wouldn't miss it for anything."

"Put the pistol on the counter."

Thorn did as he was told. Downshifting into slow motion, he bent back to the water and took another sip and another. It was how you behaved when you were swimming in the ocean and confronted by a shark. You relaxed, went on with your business, no splashing, no sudden moves, nothing that might provoke them. If they wanted you, they could have you—not much you could do to fix that beyond staying cool.

Thorn ran the water over his hands and washed away the piss stink and the dirt. He ran some more water over them and scrubbed them hard. He cupped some water into his hands and bathed his face. Took a last deep drink before turning to face Jonah.

He'd seen Mac-10's before. They were the weapon of choice for South Florida's cocaine cowboys two decades back and were still popular with certain sweethearts who had the burning urge to discharge a thousand rounds a minute.

Thorn cut a look to his Glock, measuring the distance. A couple of seconds to grab, aim, and fire. Enough time for Jonah to sink fifty rounds in his chest.

"You realize Moses gave his life for yours," Thorn said.

"Huh?"

"He was dying, but he screamed that warning to you. Lying there in agony, but that was the only thing on his mind, saving your ass."

Jonah blinked and blinked again as though struggling to recall his reason for being there. Moses had been his meat and muscle and his backbone. Alone, the kid was floundering.

Thorn kept his voice quiet and slow as if speaking into the dreams of another.

"Since I saw you last, I figured out what you wanted to know. The reason you were hired to kill me."

Jonah shifted the Mac-10 in his arms, his finger stroking the trigger.

"You wanted to cut yourself in on the action, right? That was your plan?"

Jonah licked his lips. His eyes faded and brightened then faded again. He was there, not there, then there again as though a searchlight was making slow revolutions inside his skull.

"Look, I'm going to put my hand in my pocket and show you something."

"I'll spatter you on the wall."

"It's what you and Moses wanted to know. I solved it for you."

Slowly Thorn slipped his hand into his pocket, eyes on Jonah's eyes, while Jonah tightened his grip on the Mac.

He dug out the ancient mollusk, and held it on his flat palm.

"It's called a rudist," Thorn said. "It's a fossil."

"You're showing me a rock?"

"Thousands of years ago these creatures covered the seafloor that was two miles below where we're standing."

Thorn kept his hand out until Jonah flicked a look at the shell, then stepped back and reset his hands on his weapon.

"What the fuck you talking about?"

"I found the rudist down in the pit. It came up in the backwash of a well."

"What well?"

"An oil well. That's what formed that pit. An oil well drilled a long time ago."

Jonah mouthed a silent word.

"It's why they sent you and Moses to kill me, Jonah. Why they murdered Earl. Because Earl and I were making a deal to preserve this land. But somebody knew there was oil here and didn't want that deal to go ahead. That's what you and Moses wanted to know. You wanted a piece of the action. You just didn't know what the action was. Well, now you know. It's oil. That's why Moses died. Because of oil."

"Fucking oil?" Jonah rocked his head forward, peering at the rudist.

"If Moses were still here, wouldn't he want to cash in? Wouldn't he tell you to go ahead with your original plan?"

"You don't know anything about my brother."

"I know more than you think."

"Step away from that counter. Do it now."

Thorn obliged, putting another two feet between the Glock and himself. This time he wasn't going to save his ass with a pistol.

"Moses is dead. I'm the one you have to deal with. I'm running things."

"Are you, Jonah? Are you running things?"

"I make the decisions. I do what I want. I don't need anyone's permission."

"You missed some hog blood," Thorn said. "On your forehead."

Thorn reached out as if to wipe it away, but Jonah lurched out of range. His feet were clumsy. He swallowed hard, his facial muscles working, his eyes sliding from Thorn's face to the air around him as though he were tracking the erratic flight of a moth.

"Moses and I talked before he died. I got to know him a little."

"Don't," Jonah said. "Don't talk about my brother."

"He told me something. His last words. He whispered them to me. I had to bend down, get my ear right up to his lips."

"Shut up. You don't know anything about anything."

"You don't want to know what it is? Your brother's dying words?"

Jonah said, "That's it. You're dead. I've had enough of you."

"Moses told me to pass it on. He said it was important, that you needed to know."

An electronic warble came from Jonah's pocket. He reached reflexively for the device, then caught himself, brought his hand back to the Mac, refocused his aim.

"Maybe that's him," Thorn said. "Your boss, the guy who wanted me dead. Maybe this is your chance to let him know who's in charge. Tell him you know all about the oil. See what he says."

"What did Moses tell you?"

The warbling in his pocket ceased.

"It was sad. Very sad."

"What did he say, goddammit?"

"He was whispering. I could barely make it out. I had to lean in close."

Thorn spoke a few words below his breath. A penitent mumbling his prayers.

Jonah drew a half step closer and again the phone in his pocket trilled. When his right hand made the same automatic move to his pocket, Thorn flicked the rudist at his face.

Jonah swatted at it with the stubby barrel of the Mac-10, and in the same motion squeezed off a dozen rounds that chewed up plates and pans and blew apart a section of the pine paneling.

Thorn ducked his shoulder and tackled Jonah around the waist and drove him backward into the refrigerator. Kept his knees pumping as he'd been coached to do on that long-ago high school football field. Keep going forward, keep pushing. That coach, and Kate Truman, and that geology teacher, all those long hours young Thorn had spent trying to learn proper technique, proper manners, trying to understand how the land beneath his feet was fashioned.

Jonah chopped the Mac against Thorn's shoulder, chopped a second time, and Thorn felt his body soften, felt some of the drive drain from his legs. At his left ear the Mac blasted at least a hundred rounds at the ceiling. In an instant he was deaf and faint and something else was droning inside him, a crazed surge that wasn't hate or fear or rage but some poisonous cocktail of all three.

Jonah was a generation younger, the muscles in his arms as supple and unyielding as braided rubber. In a swift pivot, Jonah released the Mac, let it crash to the floor, and seized Thorn in a grinding head-lock, wrenched Thorn's bulk around, and bent him forward and danced across the kitchen with Thorn's skull as a battering ram. It was a rash and childish move, some half-remembered maneuver from the violent playgrounds of Jonah's youth.

Gathering speed, Jonah took two steps, three, four. No fancy judo was required from Thorn. He just went with it, let his arms drop and tangle in Jonah's legs, then clutched an ankle, jerked upward, and sent the young man sprawling.

As their bodies broke apart, Thorn banged a shoulder against the edge of the stove and regained his balance. Jonah stumbled another yard into a clatter of dishes and plates that covered a four-legged aluminum table. The table buckled under his weight, and the plates spilled around him onto the floor.

Thorn searched for the Mac-10, didn't see it, then chose from the stove an iron skillet caked with grease, grabbed its handle and raised it above Jonah's hairless skull like the devil's own sledgehammer and cracked him once, then again.

Jonah remained sitting upright, limp but conscious, his legs stretched straight before him, blood streaming from the gash on his scalp, spilling onto the collar of the well-creased shirt. His head rocked from side to side as if its weight was suddenly too much for the slender stalk of his neck.

TWENTY-NINE

THORN RETRIEVED THE RUDIST, DROPPED it in his pocket. He collected the Glock from the countertop, the Mac-10 from the floor by the doorway. He snapped the release on the Mac and let the big clip fall to the floor. He aimed at the ceiling and held the trigger down to make sure no rounds were left inside. If he'd had sufficient strength, he would have cracked the goddamn thing in half.

His ears were ringing and the fumes of his rage had scalded his throat as though he'd been bellowing at the moon for an hour.

Jonah struggled to stand.

Thorn kept the Glock steady while Jonah staggered to the sink and ran the faucet and lowered his bloody head into the stream of water. When he was done, he used a dish towel to pat himself dry.

Turning to face Thorn, he let his eyes wander downward and saw the stains on the front of his shirt.

"Aw, man. One of the Brooks Brothers."

"Soak it in cold water," Thorn said. "That works with blood."

Jonah looked up and eyed Thorn for a moment.

"What did he say? What did my brother say to you at the end?"

"He said he was fucked. He smiled and he died."

"That's all? That's everything?"

"He wasn't much of a philosopher."

Thorn kept the pistol balanced in his hand. Hardly a quiver at all.

"Well, fucked is right. From day one till now. Fucked."

"What we need," Thorn said, "is some duct tape. Where do you keep it?"

"Duct tape?"

"I'm tying you up, and you and I are going to drive out of here."

"Just shoot me in the head, man. Get it over with."

"I'm over my quota already. Duct tape, where is it?"

Jonah's shoulders slumped and he waved a lazy hand toward the door.

"Back bedroom."

"Lead the way, Jonah. Be careful."

Thorn tagged behind by several steps. A slow march through the living room. Several of the candles had guttered out. The papers on the wall were rattling like a field of brittle grass before an approaching storm.

"What's this? Your collected works?"

Jonah halted in front of the poster with rows of skulls. In the top left corner a single circus clown in pasty makeup was grinning wildly.

"These were done by monsters. Gacy, Dahmer, Manson, you know, the heavyweights. Doodling in their prison cells. Moses and I sold this stuff. It's how we made our spending money."

"Oh," Thorn said. "Like a paper route."

"Bunch of whackjobs," Jonah said. "These are very sick fucks, sicker than me. I wasn't sure before, but now I know. Totally sicker than me."

Jonah led him down a narrow hallway to the last door. He opened it, stepped inside. Thorn hung back in the corridor and waited. The Glock was centered on Jonah's back. Thorn fighting the urge to end this now.

Jonah walked across the room to a dresser, keeping his hands extended to the sides for Thorn to see as he reached out and took something off the dresser.

"Duct tape," Jonah said, turning around and holding up a roll. "All that's left."

Thorn stepped forward through the doorway. There were twin beds, side by side. A lamp burned on a table between them. Moses was laid out on top of the blue bedspread. He was wearing a fresh pair of slacks, a crisp white shirt, his hair combed flat. His hands were folded together over his stomach, concealing the puncture wound.

On the second bed lay a naked woman. A brunette, average build. Her legs were spread wide, ankles bound to the bed posts with silver duct tape, her arms stretched out as though she were making a swan dive into a bottomless pool. Her wrists were taped to the frame. A single strip covered her mouth. Her eyes were open but empty. Thorn saw no rise and fall of her chest. Across her throat a bruised and bloody crease dented the flesh as though she'd been throttled with a lead pipe.

Jonah had backed into a corner of the room. His eyes were ticking back and forth between his dead brother and the woman's naked body. Thorn stepped fully into the room. There was an odor he couldn't name and didn't want to.

"Who is this?" Thorn said.

"Her name is Donaldson. She's a cop. She tried to arrest me."

"You did this?"

The phone in his pocket sang out again. But Jonah made no move. He held the roll of tape in his left hand. His right was pressed flat against his heart as if he were pledging allegiance to some dark and secret nation.

"I had to see," Jonah said. "I had to see exactly how fucked up I am."

Thorn felt his finger tense against the trigger.

"I'm not a monster," Jonah said. "I thought I was, but I'm not."

"You might want to reconsider."

"No, see, I touched her after she was gone. I tried, I really did. But it didn't give me a thrill."

"It's not supposed to."

Jonah's eyes wandered from the dead woman's body to Thorn.

"But how do you know until you try? How do you know for sure?"

Thorn had no answer for that. It was one of the Zen koans he hadn't gotten to yet.

"Let's go," Thorn said.

"Where?"

"Out of this room."

Jonah walked past him into the hallway. Thorn took one backward glance at the woman on the bed, then shut the door and told Jonah to keep walking.

When they were in the living room, the phone in his pocket trilled again.

"Answer it," Thorn said.

Jonah drew out the glossy red phone and looked at its screen.

"Who is it?" Thorn said.

"He's asking where the fuck I am."

"Asking? How's he asking?"

"He's texting me. You know about texting."

"I should but I don't."

Jonah held up the phone and Thorn stepped closer.

"See," Jonah said. " 'WTFUB'—where the fuck you be? He's always asking that. You want me to hit him back?"

"Who is that?"

"Guy you told me you saw in a bar on TV. You know. One-Ton Antwan."

"That's who's running the show?"

"He's the man. They don't come any badder than that zombie."

"Ask him what he wants."

Jonah thumbed the tiny buttons.

"He always gets back quick. Man's very hyper, got blood-pressure issues."

The device made an electronic tinkle, and Jonah looked at the screen.

"He wants us to come to the lodge. Me and Moses. Got a job for us."

"What job?"

"The way you say it is, 'WTF4?'—What the fuck for?"

"So say it."

Jonah typed the letters, and a second later when the phone jingled again, Jonah held it close and said, "He's got some garbage needs to go to the dump."

"What garbage?"

"I can ask him, but he won't say."

Thorn felt the skin on his neck prickle. "Ask him: What garbage?"

Jonah danced his thumbs on the keyboard. A few seconds passed, the phone remained quiet, and Jonah said, "I told you. Antwan doesn't share his business dealings. He's one cagey primate."

Jonah settled on the couch across from a crude drawing of a topless woman with large round breasts. He looked at it for a few seconds, then winced.

"This whole fucking disaster, man, it was my idea. I mean if we'd just smacked you, tossed your body in a canal, Moses would be alive. But I wasn't satisfied. I wanted more cash flow. Fucking money, man, that's the root of all evil."

"No," Thorn said. "It's only one."

Jonah reached to a side table and touched a finger to a small white cell phone.

"Who are you, Thorn? Some kind of kingpin?"

"What're you talking about?"

"You're some kind of big deal, aren't you? I mean even Claire Hammond knows you."

"Is that right?"

He tapped the white cell phone again.

"This is the cop's."

"So?"

"After I killed her, I mean, it's like I had to see who she was, so I went through her stuff, her wallet, her purse and shit. Listened to her messages, one from her husband, sounding worried, wanting to know when she's coming home. And, hey, then there's one from Claire Hammond. She mentions your name, Thorn."

The device in his lap played its jingly tune again.

Jonah read the text and said, "Okay, so I was wrong."

He typed something back and after a second the phone jingled again.

"What the hell're you doing?"

"Antwan wants to get rid of some people at the lodge. I asked him who it was, and all he said was a couple showed up, sticking their noses in his business. A guy he's calling 'brown sugar' and the guy's squeeze, a twiggy."

"Brown sugar?"

Thorn grabbed the shoulder of Jonah's shirt and hauled him to his feet and pushed him toward the front door.

"Hey, back the fuck off, man. What's going on with you?"

"We're going to the lodge."

"I'm not going to any lodge. I'm staying here. I'm staying with Moses. I'm going to have a funeral."

"Get going."

Thorn shoved him toward the door.

"I said no. I'm not deserting my brother. Fuck the lodge."

Jonah dodged to the left behind the couch and was halfway to the kitchen before Thorn could raise the Glock. But again he couldn't shoot. Not moral hesitation, but necessity. The asshole knew the way out of this landlocked maze.

Thorn started across the living room, calling out to Jonah.

He was passing by the Gacy poster when Jonah popped into the doorway holding the Mac-10. His shit-eating grin was back.

But only for a second. That grin died quickly on his lips. Thorn dropped him with the first shot to his chest, watched him fall, then stepped close to put the second through his tortured brain. Granting Jonah his final wish.

With the toe of his shoe, Thorn nudged his shoulder. Jonah was gone.

Thorn kicked away the Mac-10, and it skidded across the hardwood floor.

There was no clip in the slot.

THIRTY

FRISCO HAD NEVER TOLD THE story, never been tempted to tell it. Since the night Earl Hammond revealed it to him, Frisco kept it locked up with most of the other memories of his childhood on Coquina Ranch, inside a dark vault in his chest. Though he'd hauled it around without complaint all these years, he knew the knowledge had made him colder, less trusting of men who held the reins of power.

In silence and in no particular hurry, he drove west out of the orderly network of streets and roads and avenues that spanned Miami, all the roadways broad and lit, straight as rulers, and numbered north and south and east and west. Most of the city was mapped that way. If you knew an address, you could drive directly to it. Good for cops and taxi drivers, good for tourists. But soulless and dull. In a way that's what Earl Hammond's story was about, those roads, all the other cars packed tight around him.

"You ever hear of the Trilateral Commission?"

They were stopped at a light, 8th Street and 107th Avenue. Claire turned down the jazz station she'd been listening to.

"Some kind of Ayn Rand phony cabal? The twelve men who run the world?"

"Well, that particular cabal exists, the Trilateral Commission. David Rockefeller started it in the seventies. Supposed to foster international cooperation. They have official meetings, put out papers, that kind of thing."

"Is this about Coquina Ranch?"

"It's about the second half of that story Earl was telling you."

She was cupping Frisco's cell phone in her hands. He could see its slow green pulse like some otherworldly creature calmed by her touch.

"Trilateral Commission is just one of many. There's Bohemian Grove, a summer camp for the rich and famous out in California. The Carlyle Group, Davos, Bilderberg, the Jerusalem Assembly. Skull and Crossbones. A couple dozen of them. Lots of overlap, same guys, different campfires. Ex-presidents, sheikhs, people you've never heard of. The global elite. The Four Hundred who matter."

"Sitting around, complaining about their prostates," Claire said.

He smiled.

"Prostates are not unimportant."

"So you're saying Coquina Ranch is one of those?"

"It was never supposed to be."

Claire was silent while Frisco gathered himself for a moment.

"That night little Earl went back to bed, but it was too much for him. For godsakes, Ernest Hemingway, his hero, was sitting out there a half mile away. The President of the United States is there. Earl fidgeted for an hour, couldn't get to sleep, so he rolled out of bed and stole back down there. He knew every twig and branch out in those woods, so it wasn't hard to sneak around. In the daytime when the campfires weren't in session, he played in those woods, pretended he was part of the gatherings. One of the gang.

"By the time he returned, the cast of characters had changed. Hemingway was gone. Hoover had left, too. Edison and Ford were still there, and another man had joined them. An old codger, frail as Edison, in his eighties."

Frisco steered into a service station, pulled up to the full-service pump, and let an elderly Cuban gentleman fill his tank with gasoline that cost fifteen cents a gallon extra for a little old-time service. He wanted to do the story justice, but it sounded bland as he related it to Claire. None of the color or the smells that he could picture in his mind. The dying campfire, the men huddled close. That story had been in the vault too long and lost its flavor.

"Earl found out later who the old guy was. Rockefeller."

"John D.?"

"Yeah, he had a winter home in Ormond Beach and he'd gotten to be friends with Edison and Ford, met them at the ranch a few times. They shared a love for Florida. They'd go camping together, in their straw boaters and sport coats, a bunch of eccentric outdoorsmen. Rockefeller was a serious golfer at a time when playing a round of golf was like hiking the backcountry. He'd been retired from Standard Oil for twenty years, his wife had died. That was the time when he was giving his money away in huge chunks."

Frisco paid the Cuban man for the gas and pulled back into the traffic. He glanced again at his cell phone flashing in her lap.

"What's wrong?"

"Nothing," he said. "I just haven't had much practice telling this story."

"You're doing fine."

Frisco cracked his window, let in some cool night air.

"Well, what little Earl heard that night, he didn't understand. It took him years to put it together, to grasp what an outrage he'd witnessed."

Claire was quiet, watching Frisco speak.

"It was just talk, nothing concrete, no papers drawn up or anything like that. None of that came clear till later. But Earl Junior was certain the seed was planted that night. The Depression was just taking hold, and here were these men, captains of industry, they got all the money in the world, and they couldn't stop looking for business opportunities. It was in their blood, it was who they were.

"The plan was simple. Start a company, call it something innocent. Rockefeller proposed the name that night, and that's the thing Earl remembered. National City Lines. A year or two later Firestone came into the deal, and Alfred Sloan with General Motors. Rockefeller used his West Coast branch, Standard Oil of California, as cover. A year or two after that campfire, National City Lines started buying up streetcar systems, all the electric mass transit. Trolleys, trains. They bought more than a hundred. Tulsa, St. Louis, Philadelphia, Los Angeles. Then they just stepped back and let them fall apart, raised fares, cut service, fired mechanics and conductors, didn't maintain the rail lines, let it all rust. Found every goddamn thing they could to undermine the business. A decade of neglect and sabotage until automobiles and gasoline-powered buses started looking pretty attractive to commuters and politicians. Just a simple plan to get everybody out of electric trains and into gasoline-burning cars, so all the men sitting around that fire could get a little richer."

"Goddamn."

"Yeah."

"That's it?"

"When he got old enough and put it together, Earl Junior hated the idea that National City Lines was born at Coquina Ranch. Hated that his own father had collaborated in a way. It was corruption of the worst kind—moral, ethical—and it was unpatriotic. Everything Earl despised."

"It's what competitive people do," Claire said. "Same in sports. Find your opponent's weakness, exploit it. It's the way the world works. Push hard, take advantage. Go for the throat."

"Part of the world works that way, I guess."

"I'm not trying to justify it."

"There's referees on the football field, and there's cops on the street, but tell me, Claire, who's watching the guys sitting around the goddamn campfire?"

She was silent, staring out the windshield at the faint lights of ranch homes in the distance. Frisco had never realized how angry that story made him.

"I'm sorry I barked," he said.

She waved her hand, blowing it off. "So where does the oil fit?"

"Geology was one of Edison's hobbies. The guy had a million hobbies. All that time he spent on the ranch, he and Ford were poking around, damming up streams, digging in the dirt like a couple of kids, excavating fossils. Eventually he sold Earl Senior on the idea of setting up a few exploratory wells. He thought the topography looked right. Earl said fine, be my guest. All a big joke.

"That's how it started. Wildcat crews showed up one day, rigs got built, wells drilled. I don't know who footed the bill. Probably John D. They hit some oil, hit it again, all in that one area on the western border where the red circles are. But Earl Senior lost interest. He didn't see the point. Why wreck his sanctuary? The ranch was selling cattle to Cuba at the time, making good money. He thought of the oil as a retirement fund. He could tap it one day if he needed to, like hocking the family silver. He wasn't opposed to drilling.

"Earl Senior sat on that survey map till he was an old man, then he picked a time when he thought his son was ready, and passed it on to Earl Junior as part of his initiation into the Hammond patriarchy. When Earl Junior was running things, first chance he got, he built that fence around the oil land. Had the bore holes filled or covered. Wanted no part of it. Just that one night hearing Rockefeller talk about destroying the cheap, easy transportation system of the common man, that sealed it for him."

"So that prisoner-of-war thing, that was a lie?"

"A cover story, yeah. I always thought that fence was more symbolic for the old man than anything. A way to close up that area like it never existed. I think it's why Earl agreed to let Browning go ahead with the safari deal, let wild animals roam on that land. Probably hoped Browning would get hooked on the hunting preserve, he'd fall in love with that land, one day it might keep him from drilling."

"When you were twenty-one, Earl gave you a copy of the map, leaving it to the next generation to decide."

"Like I said, a test of loyalty."

"And that's when you left the ranch. Went into Miami and never came back."

"That's right."

"You never fell in love with that land?"

"I didn't say that."

"Then why leave?"

"The job description didn't suit me."

"You mean the campfires? Hosting all the hotshots?"

"Never been all that fond of hotshots."

By then they'd moved beyond the urban sprawl and the fuck-you-I'm-packing-heat traffic of Miami. There were faster routes back to the ranch, but Frisco was in no hurry. He took the north turn off Tamiami Trail, passing by the Miccosukee casino that had risen in the last few years on the edge of the Everglades. Thousands of cars and tour buses filled its enormous lots. They traveled a mile beyond the casino's glow, entering the dark prairies again. There was an hour left to Coquina Ranch.

"Why did Earl only tell me the first half of the story?" Claire said.

"It's the way he wanted Coquina Ranch remembered, the romantic version. Powerful men hashing out things, arguing about the greater good, oddball get-togethers, Hemingway mingling with Hoover. It's how he ran those campfires all his life. Kept them personal, philosophical, like college bull sessions. Any business talk started up, anything with a dollar sign, Earl would squash it. He was ashamed of the second half of that story. That's the ranch's dark side. A bunch of greedy bastards conspiring."

"He wanted me to be proud of the ranch. Even if it was only half the truth."

"The fact that he told you any part of that story amazes me."

"Yeah?"

"Earl was a decent man, but he was a Hammond, in most ways as hide-bound as the rest. Like keeping the men-only rules. Only reason he told you that story is because he must've seen something in you he hadn't seen in a woman before, not even Rachel Sue. Something he trusted."

"Well, he was wrong," she said. "I let him down when he needed me most."

"Knock it off. Earl saw who you are, that's why he opened up. He was right. That's damn well who you are—someone he could trust to do the right thing."

"And you? Do you finally believe that?"

He looked at the green light blinking in her lap. "I think my brother is a goddamn fool. That kid's made only one good choice in his entire life. And I don't believe he even recognizes it."

She sighed, then reached out and turned the jazz station back up and listened to the music for a few miles until it began to fade, and turned into static as they moved farther into the countryside. She snapped it off and leaned her head against the seat.

Frisco kept the truck at the speed limit while the ten-wheelers boomed past. It was several miles before she spoke, her voice with its edge again.

"I need to fill in some blanks."

"Okay."

"Who shot Saperstein?"

"My guess is one of the Faust boys. The little guy with the grin. Last winter Browning came into Miami, we had lunch. He brought those two along. That little twit wouldn't take his eyes off me."

"Jonah," she said. "He's the mean one."

"What I think is, they strong-armed Gustavo, got him to the lodge. Jonah's holding the pistol, the three of them walk up, Saperstein stops them. Jonah nails him and keeps on shooting. Making a point for Gustavo, showing him how serious this is. Then he reloads, hands the pistol to Gustavo, shoves him toward the front door. That's the film I got running in my head."

"Not Browning?"

"Browning's inside with Antwan and the governor. They're looking over the map, figuring out their next move, how long it'll take before they can start drilling. Divvying up the profits. Doing it all in front of Earl. It must've broken the old man's heart."

"I heard them hooting in there. Laughing like loons. Not Earl, but the others."

Frisco nodded and blinked hard as if trying to erase the image.

"And Sanchez? He's in it, too?"

"What do you think?"

She considered it for a while, then said, "On the hunt yesterday, he wounded a wildebeest then claimed he was too tired to go after it. I grabbed the shotgun, and after I brought the animal down, he wanted his picture with the thing like it was his."

"Which only proves he's a sack of shit."

"Browning makes fun of him. Says he's dull normal. Like a trained seal."

"Let's try this," said Frisco. "Sanchez is an innocent third party. His job is to give the scene the stamp of approval. An eyewitness nobody questions."

"Unless he's one hell of an actor," Claire said, "the way he broke down after Earl was shot, that was real. He was in shock, he still looked that way getting on the chopper."

"Yeah," Frisco said. "He thinks he's coming to Coquina Ranch for the usual male bonding, drink some whiskey, maybe hear about a business venture, then boom, people die in front of him. A few hours later, back home at the governor's mansion, he thinks it over, he realizes he's been used. What does he do? Does he call the attorney general, his FDLE people? No, he shuts the investigation down, which tells me he got over his shock pretty quick and decided he wanted a slice of the action. Maybe he was in it from the start, but at this point, it doesn't matter. Any way you cut it, everybody's hands are dirty. It's a daisy chain of guilt."

"I don't know, Frisco. Why can't it be just what it looks like? Gustavo is sick, dying, angry at being fired, his family is evicted, and he does all this on his own."

"You want to believe Browning is innocent. So do I. He's your husband, he's my brother."

"I do. I want him to be innocent."

"You saw the map, he denied it was there. That's not enough for you?"

"That map," she said.

"Yeah?"

"Does Browning know you got one, too? Your rite of passage."

"I'm not sure, but I expect he does."

"Then that whole thing, denying it was there, he's got to know you see through him."

"He's daring me."

"Daring you to expose him? Christ, you're a cop. He has to know you won't cut him any slack."

"He's a cocky bastard, always has been. He knows the evidence is too slippery. There's nothing to hold on to. Where's the proof of anything?"

"Ana Pinto. Her mother and brothers. They know what happened."

"A bunch of trailer-park Mexicans making wild claims against the governor and Browning Hammond? Justice may be blind, but it ain't that blind."

She fiddled with the radio again, moving up and down the dial. Got a lot of Spanish, a religious lunatic, more static. She snapped it off and rearranged her long legs.

"The way Browning was at lunch today . . . I've never seen that man before."

"The toothpick."

"And the Bible verses, mocking Earl. I wanted to tear his eyes out."

Frisco watched the lights of Clewiston appear in the distance.

They were quiet for a while, then she said, "In your version, Gustavo was supposed to shoot Earl, just get in his truck, drive down to Miami, and hide out. Live there for whatever time he had left."

"That may be how they sold it to him," Frisco said, "but no way could that work. By morning his face is on TV, his neighbors in the Grove recognize him, he's busted. Gustavo wasn't a sophisticated man. He'd lived out on the ranch all his life, he thought Miami was this big complicated city, he could just go there and disappear. He was being scammed, start to finish."

"I knew something was wrong with him. He was avoiding me."

"Hey, if somebody's at fault, it's me. I should've sat Earl down years ago, told him not to show that map to Browning. I saw this coming, or something like it. Browning's world view is pretty simple. If there's oil on the land, then by God, you pump out every drop. That's just what you do. Browning failed the loyalty test, and Earl couldn't accept it."

Frisco glanced her way, but Claire was preoccupied with the seam on her jeans. Picking at it with a fingernail. He could smell the heat her body was giving off, a brew of scents, the dusty straw of the barn, the lather of horse and saddle oil, and whatever soap she'd used hours ago, something with vanilla. He kept his eyes on the highway shooting straight ahead into the night.

"For a long time I've felt like I was losing Browning," she said. "That we were drifting apart."

"I don't need to hear this."

"Well, I need to say it, so shut up and indulge me."

Frisco closed his mouth.

"Last summer just before she died, I went to Rachel Sue and told her I was worried about my marriage. I asked her if she had any idea how I could do a better job of pleasing Browning."

"This should be good."

"Pies. That's what she said. 'My boy likes pies. Fruit pies are best— blueberry, apple, but pecan is good, too. With Browning, you can't go wrong with pies.' "

Frisco chuckled. He looked over at her, but she was staring out her window.

"I never was any good with pies," she said.

He turned his eyes to the road and reset his hands on the wheel. They rode in silence for several minutes, until Frisco's phone buzzed.

Claire lifted it, squinted at the screen. "You want to talk to Donaldson?"

"Not really."

"You probably should."

She handed him the phone. He let it ring a couple more times before he flipped it open.

"Okay," Frisco said, "so what is it now?"

"Who is this?" a man's voice asked.

"Whoa," Frisco said. "You first. You called me. That's how it works."

The man was in a hurry, speaking fast but precisely.

"Somebody named Claire Hammond left a message on this cell phone. My name was mentioned in the message."

"Is that right? And your name is what?"

"Thorn."

"Thorn," he said. "Okay. Put Donaldson on. Let me talk to her."

"Donaldson is dead," Thorn said.

Frisco looked over to Claire and said to Thorn, "She's dead?"

"Now listen to me. I'm lost somewhere on Coquina Ranch. I need directions. And I need them now. Can you help me or not?"

THIRTY-ONE

A WOMAN CAME ON THE phone, said her name was Claire. She was taking over because Frisco needed to concentrate on driving.

"Now what's your situation, Mr. Thorn?"

Thorn told her his friends Rusty and Sugarman were being held at the lodge, and he believed they were in imminent danger.

"How do you know that?"

"I don't have time to explain. I need directions. I need them now."

"Describe where you are. What do you see around you?"

He told her he was on a one-lane logging road with cattle gates every few hundred yards. Tall pines running along the edge of both shoulders.

"Is there a pond on your right or left?"

"I don't see one."

"Keep driving."

He drove another quarter of a mile, switching on the brights.

"Left. Up ahead, there's a pond, yeah."

"Left?"

"Yeah, on the left."

"Okay, that's Curry Lake. You're on Telegraph Grade Road. Turn around. Make a U-turn, you're going the wrong way."

"Gas gauge is touching empty," he said. "I need the most direct route. Even if it means ramming through the fence."

"I'll get you there," she said. "Stay calm."

"How far away is the lodge?" Thorn said. "How long is this going to take?"

"From where you are," Claire said, "maybe twenty minutes."

"You know anything about texting?"

"What do you mean?" He could barely hear her voice over the violent squeaking of the Prius as it bounced across the rutted road.

"Text messages keep popping up on Jonah's phone. I think Antwan Shelton is getting suspicious."

He heard Claire Hammond speaking to the driver, explaining the situation.

Thorn said, "Antwan keeps asking, 'WTFUB?' Where the fuck am I?"

"Don't answer him," Claire said. "We'll be at the lodge soon, before you can get there. The man you spoke to a minute ago, that's Frisco Hammond, he's a cop. He and I are going to take care of this."

"I don't want Antwan to get nervous and make a run. Do you know texting or not?"

"Some," she said.

"So give me something. I need something to keep him calm."

Claire said, "Type 'KC', that's 'keep cool.' Then 'TTFN.'"

"What's that?"

"Ta-ta for now."

"Is that something Jonah would say?"

"It's pretty standard."

"I don't want to tip this guy off."

"'TTFN,'" Claire said.

"I'm coming up to another gate," Thorn said. "An intersection of some kind."

"That's Possum Road. Open the gate, go through, take the left."

"Am I still in the game preserve?"

"Yes."

"Well, that would explain the five hundred buffalo standing in my way."

"You got a gun?"

"I do."

"Fire it in the air, they'll move."

He honked his horn instead. Half the ammunition from the clip of the Mac-10 was already gone, the rounds Jonah fired into the kitchen wall. And by God, Thorn was not about to waste another shot until he had something a whole lot better than buffalo in his sights.

" 'TTFN'?" Antwan said. " 'TTFN'?"

He looked at Sugarman, looked again at his BlackBerry.

"Faust boys don't say 'ta-ta.' I been back and forth with those two for years, and I never saw one 'ta-ta.' Not one. I smell something here. I do believe we have some form of putrefaction."

Antwan stared at Sugarman.

"Can't help you," Sugar said. "My nose is all clogged."

He was still in the wingback. Another tooth was loose. A molar on his lower right side. Damn, he hated the dentist. Hated the idea of a bridge. He wasn't sure if at his advanced age the molar would ever tighten up again, or if Antwan Shelton had loosened it for good. Either way, he was pissed. Beyond pissed.

But holding back because he could still hear Rusty and Browning Hammond going back and forth. Fairly civil, at least no obvious rancor, though it sounded like Browning was starting to get a whine in his voice. Complaining that no one took him seriously, everyone undermined him. People messing in his business.

Which wasn't a particularly good sign. Like he was building his case, lathering himself up about the unfairness of the world, giving him the right to strike back.

Sugarman scanned the room for the hundredth time, looking for weapons. He hadn't ruled out going hand to hand with One-Ton, but only as a last resort. The guy had bulked up since his running-back days. Saddled himself with an extra fifty pounds, which meant he outweighed Sugarman by a hundred.

He made another sweep of the spacious room, decorated in a manly style, part library, part trophy room. Assorted lamps, wood carvings on the shelves, some family photographs, and a couple of paintings that showed different views of the pinelands. Books, vases, a gun case with steel bars. There were the animal heads on the wall. A fireplace, but he saw no poker or scoop, or any of the usual brass implements he might bash Antwan with.

He took a longer look at the animal heads. At the mounted antlers, the feral hog's thick yellowed tusks, the twisty horns of an antelope. They were hung low enough on the wall to reach, but it was a very long shot. Very long.

Browning strolled into the living room tugging Rusty with him. He had his right hand clamped to her arm just above the elbow. The pressure he was applying had stiffened Rusty's back and drained the color from her face.

"Hey." Sugar rose from the chair. "Let her go."

Antwan danced into view and crushed Sugarman's jaw with a right hand so hard the lights in the room flared and went dark and Sugar found himself sitting in the wingback chair again with a woozy warmth flooding his body.

"I told you, negro, mind your P's and Q's. Didn't I say that half a dozen times already? Didn't I give you ample warning? You not listening to the coach, brown sugar. Tighten that chin strap and stay the fuck still."

Browning stood to one side, sucking on his gold toothpick, while he appraised Sugarman's damaged face with dreamy interest. Rusty flinched at the sight of him and started to speak, but Browning tightened his grip on her arm and she sucked in a gasp instead.

"You about finished, Brown?" Antwan said. "Get what you need, did you?"

"Call the Faust boys."

"One step ahead of you, brother. They're on their way. Or somebody is."

"Somebody?"

"Got a text from the Faust brothers. Didn't sound like the manner in which they usually communicate."

"What're you saying? Somebody else has their phone? The cops?"

"Well, we'll know when they get here, won't we?"

"This is falling apart. Too many loose ends."

"Unraveled a little, granted. But if we keep our eyes on the prize, Mr. Hammond, sir, I think it'll all turn out just fine and dandy."

Antwan grinned and bobbed his head in that fawning way that slaves once curried favor with their masters. A spoof that Hammond, in his distracted condition, didn't seem to notice.

"Frisco knows the truth, I think Claire knows, too."

"What if they do, Brown? Think about it. Even if they know everything down to the last itty-bitty detail, they still got nothing. Not a damn thing. Governor of the state of Florida was standing right here. Ain't a judge and jury in this great land of ours wouldn't trust what that man says. Gustavo Pinto shot your poor old granddad in a state of severe disgruntlement. That's the end of it."

"The Pintos," Browning said. "They're hanging out there, too."

"It's on my punch list. I always had a soft spot for those Mexicanos. I'll swing by there tomorrow in a big stretch limo full of tacos and bean dip, and we'll all go for a nice long drive in the country. I got it covered, A to Z. You worry too much, Brown. You got to work on that breathing, man. Slow it down, in and out, stay limber."

"All right, all right."

"So we're done, then?" Antwan grinned at Sugar. "We're finished with this nuisance?"

Browning was eyeing Sugarman with the weary disinterest of a meat packer on the assembly line. "Yeah, we're done," he said. "But not in here. Take them to the barn."

"Well, in that case, can I trouble you to unlock that cabinet, select me a weapon?"

Browning's wrinkled brow and anxious frown had smoothed, his mood lifting with such speed it seemed as though Antwan's pep talk might be a customary part of their arrangement. Like these two had been studying from the same playbook for so long now they were doing a strange tango of give and take, pivot and slide, dip and swoon. In perfect balance, neither of them seemed fully responsible for any given act.

Browning turned and headed for the gun cabinet. "What's your pleasure, Antwan?"

"Always had a fondness for that Sig Sauer Mosquito, one with the silencer."

"What're you, stupid? The cops have the silencer."

"Just funning with you, Brown. Just funning, keeping things light is all. The Sig is good. Don't need no silencer this time around."

THIRTY-TWO

MILE BY MILE, CLAIRE HAMMOND guided Thorn to the gate in the barbed-wire fence. He got out of the car, found the padlock lying on the ground. He threw open the twin doors and drove through, left them standing wide open.

Let the deer and the antelope roam.

A warning light was flashing red on the instrument panel. Low fuel.

"How much farther?"

Claire said, "Ten minutes, but Frisco wants you to wait. Don't go barging into this. We're just turning into the ranch now. We'll be at the lodge in five."

"I'm not waiting. Give me directions."

"No," she said. "I can't do that. It could be dangerous."

"Give me the goddamn directions. These are my friends."

She clicked off.

Thorn continued down the same one-lane cattle path. It seemed to be as close to a main road as the ranch had.

He fumbled with the phone till he found the redial button and called her back.

She didn't answer.

———

Frisco took the main gate entrance, which was the shorter route to the lodge. Hector Ramirez stepped out of the guardhouse and stood in the headlights, staring at them through the windshield.

Frisco leaned his head out the open window. "It's me, Hector. Open the gate."

"Can't do that."

"Open the goddamn gate, Hector."

"Mr. Hammond said no one comes in."

"*I'm* Mr. Hammond."

"I know who you are. I work for the other guy."

"Open the gate, Hector. This is serious. There's an emergency."

"Can't do it. I got orders."

Claire's phone rang again.

Frisco got out of the truck and walked slowly around to the front. But Hector drew his pistol and told him to stop. Frisco kept coming, holding out his hand for the gun.

As Frisco closed in, Hector stepped back and fired once and Frisco stumbled sideways into the doorway of the guard shed, clutching at his thigh.

Claire scooted behind the wheel, slammed the truck into gear, popped the clutch, and rammed Hector against the heavy girder blocking the road. His head rocked back in agony, but he still managed to lift his pistol and aim at her. She revved the engine harder until his weapon wavered, then fell from his hand.

Gripping Rusty's arm, Browning Hammond dragged her along to the gun cabinet. She looked back at Sugarman, her eyes sending a signal of some intent. She was going to make a break, though Sugarman couldn't imagine how.

Antwan Shelton was grinning at him as if he'd intercepted Rusty's look.

"Ya'll some kind of tag team, are you?"

Looking at Antwan's taunting smile brought it back to Sugar. During all those hours watching football, plenty of times he'd seen One-Ton strutting in the endzone, all swivel hips and bluster, celebrating another touchdown, and he remembered the last day of the running back's career, riding on a motorized cart off to the locker room, his knee in a brace, one final mustered grin and wave to the cheering crowd.

Sugarman couldn't remember if it was the right knee or the left. He tossed an imaginary coin, and chose the right.

"You've never done anything on your own, have you, Antwan?"

"Shut up, brown sugar."

"People open the holes, you run through. You're a leech, that's all. Browning supplies the blood; all you do is suck."

When Antwan stepped in, drawing back his fist for one more blow, Sugarman slid down in the wingback, and snapped the heel of his shoe against Antwan's right patella. It must've been that knee that ended his career, because Antwan's grin evaporated and his face went slack.

After half a second he caught himself and managed to plant his feet and take another swing, but Sugar ducked beneath his fist and shot a second kick to the same knee. It buckled inward and Antwan went down roaring.

Sugar swung around, expecting Browning to be bearing down. Expecting almost anything but what he saw.

Browning had released his hold on Rusty Stabler, and she was standing directly in front of him slapping his face. First her right hand, then her left, knocking his head an inch or two in one direction, then an inch or two in the other. Browning seemed bewildered, as if the slaps had set off some involuntary response, a stoicism learned on the practice fields of his youth. Enduring the sadistic discipline of an angry coach.

As Sugarman crossed the room, Browning's spell seemed to lift. He blinked. Saw her standing there before him, not his coach, just a trifling woman, then saw Sugarman approaching, and he growled and cocked a massive fist. Rusty didn't try to dodge the blow. She stepped in close and whisked the gold toothpick he'd been sucking on all evening from his lips and stabbed it into his right eye like some ruthless trick she'd learned from Taco Shine and his gang.

Browning staggered backward against the gun case. He pressed both hands to his face while blood flowed through his outspread fingers, a low howl rising in his chest. He lowered his hands and stared at the blood with gloomy fascination.

Sugarman attacked him from the rear. Jumped onto his back, used a chokehold he'd employed a dozen times as a patrolman. With drunks and enraged husbands and child beaters it never failed. But this ox of a man shrugged him off with a sloppy swing of his arm like he was backstroking across a quiet pool. Sugarman tumbled sideways onto the couch.

Across the room Antwan got halfway to his feet, cursed, and sagged to the floor again.

Sugarman headed to the trophy wall, reached up and gripped the antelope's antler, twisted it hard, but it wouldn't come free. The boar tusk was a different matter. The taxidermist's glue was old and brittle, and the tusk snapped off like ripe fruit from the branch.

Browning had turned away from them and was fitting his key in the lock of the gun case. He swiped at the blood on his face with one hand, struggling to see. Sugarman raised the tusk a foot above Hammond's back and rammed its point into the muscles of his right shoulder.

Huffing as though he'd merely been bumped by some discourteous passerby, Hammond came around slowly with a pistol in his hand.

Sugarman backed away, dropped the tusk. Hammond motioned the pistol at Rusty.

"Over there," he said. "With your boyfriend."

Rusty circled the couch and came to Sugarman's side.

Antwan was on his feet, his hip propped against the wingback.

"Gut check, Brown. Come to Jesus, brother. That thing in your eye, man, it's a fucking splinter is all. Get it out of there. Go on, dig it out, you can do it."

"It hurts, Antwan. I'm going to pass out."

"Sure it hurts, Brown. But that don't bother us. We're fucking warriors. Hurting is what we do. We give it, we take it, that's who we are, man. We not pussies like other folks. We been down in the trenches, the fucking war zone. Pull that splinter out of there. Pull it out now."

With his left hand Browning reached up and pinched the tip of the toothpick and plucked it from his eye. He wobbled for a moment, whimpered. When he'd recovered, he held the toothpick up, showing it to Antwan.

"You are one tough motherfucker. You just earned my renewed respect and admiration. Now lick it clean, boss. Show 'em who you are. Lick that blood off, make it disappear."

Browning's head hunched forward as if he were shouldering a bag of cement.

"Show 'em, Wild Dog. Show these girlies what we're made of."

Browning Hammond swallowed hard, then slid the toothpick between his lips and sucked it clean and dropped it into his shirt pocket.

"That's my boy," Antwan said. "That's my big beautiful boy."

"All right, let's go."

"Hold on, Brown, you gotta give me your belt," Antwan said. "I need to take a couple of wraps around this knee, brace it up a bit. I think I got me some ligament damage."

"You stay here," Browning said. "I can handle these two shitheads."

"No way, man. I don't care if I have to hop one-legged from here to China. I'm gonna to have me a piece of this action."

Thorn was operating on battery power. The car's instrument gauge was lit up, five lights flashing, warning him of imminent meltdown.

Everything that could possibly go wrong in that little car was about to do just that.

Claire was on the phone again. She'd called. There'd been some kind of trouble at the front gate. She didn't say what, and Thorn didn't care. But they'd been delayed and she wanted to let him know so he could wait for them. Wait for Frisco. He was a cop. He knew what to do in circumstances like this. Right, Thorn said. Right, he'd wait for Frisco. Just get him to the lodge and he'd wait there.

She directed him down one dusty road after another until he came to a narrow bridge.

"You're about two hundred yards away."

"I see it. A barn or something. There's lights."

"A barn, a corral, a parking lot, then the lodge. Wait for us. Frisco's got the front gate open. We'll be there in five minutes."

Thorn snapped the phone closed. He shut off the headlights and rolled quietly through the night, his battery almost dead.

THIRTY-THREE

THORN SAW FOUR PEOPLE COME out of the lodge, then walk across a narrow bridge. He brought the car to a halt in a clearing at the edge of the barn. He reached over to the passenger seat and picked up the Mac-10, checked that the clip was secure.

He opened the door and got out.

The group of four was silhouetted against the glow coming from the windows of the house. Thorn cut toward the barn, skirting patches of light, staying in the darkest shadows. A light breeze carried the croaking of frogs and the whinnies and snorts of horses in the barn.

There were three men, two of them very large. And there was a woman, medium height. He moved closer to the barn to put the dim light directly behind the four of them.

In the lead were Rusty and Sugarman. In that gloom he couldn't make out the expressions on their faces, but he could tell from the way they were stiffly shuffling ahead of the two large men that they were prisoners and there were more than likely guns pointed at their backs.

He waited by the far corner of the horse barn. They crossed a dusty parking lot and entered an adjoining corral. Forty or fifty feet away. He wanted to let them pass, then he'd come at them from behind. If they kept on the same path, that would happen in less than thirty seconds.

They came forward a little farther, then a flashlight with a dull beam shined on the Prius, and after a second or two it shut off.

A man's voice called out, "That you, Moses? You there, Jonah? You boys get your asses out where I can see you."

Thorn waited, hearing the horses bumping around in their stalls as if they could sense the rising tension beyond the barn.

"All right, then," the man said. "I do believe we have us an intruder."

Thorn waited. The four of them had halted in the center of the corral.

"You sent me a message, Mr. Ta-Ta. Said to keep cool. Well, I am. I'm here being ever so cool. Just like you said. Are you cool, too? Mr. Ta-Ta. You hear me? How cool are you?"

The flashlight came on again and swept across the front of the barn.

"Okay, then. I'll tell you what I'm going to do, Ta-Ta. In five seconds I'm going to fire a bullet into the skull of one of these fine folks, these poor innocent civilians. Then we'll see just how cool you are."

Thorn heard a car's engine coming down the same road he'd traveled a few minutes earlier. Almost as quickly as he heard it, the motor ceased. His backup was arriving.

The man with the smartass voice began to count. He made it to three before Thorn stepped away from the barn.

"Okay," Thorn called out. "I'm here. Mr. Ta-Ta has arrived."

"Well, now, look at this, Wild Dog. We done accumulated ourselves enough folks for a good old-fashioned square dance."

"Step out here," another man said. "Show yourself."

"They're armed," Sugarman called.

Thorn saw Sugar's head jerk to the side. One of the two had clipped him.

Thorn stepped forward, the Mac-10 aimed at the group. He kept coming until he was twenty feet away, then he halted. He could just barely make out their faces.

"Well, looky there. That wouldn't be the Faust boys' Mac-10 automatic weapon, would it? What'd you do with my little buddies?"

The big man said, "Who the fuck are you?"

"My name is Thorn."

The big man looked at the black man.

"And you would be Browning Hammond and Antwan Shelton."

"Well, I'll be double-dog damned. What you doing still walking around alive?"

"You sent children to do the work of men."

"Hey, brother, that's some kind of shirt you're wearing. What happened to you? Come in second place in a shootout?"

"You're the fucker that's trying to take my land," Hammond said. "You and this woman were conspiring to steal what's rightfully mine. What's been in my family for generations."

"No," Thorn said. "We were trying to preserve it."

"Preserve it?" Antwan chuckled "There ain't a fucking thing anywhere around this godforsaken place worth preserving."

"There's oil," Thorn said.

"Oil," Rusty said. "Aw, Jesus Christ. That's it."

Thorn stepped closer, saying, "Must be a whole lot of oil if you're willing to kill your own flesh and blood."

"Shut up," Hammond said. "Everybody shut up."

He took a grip of Rusty's hair and hauled her forward. His pistol jammed into her cheek.

"Now put down that weapon, Mr. Thorn. Drop it at your feet. We'll go inside and we'll hash this out. There's got to be some way to make everybody happy and go our separate ways."

"Don't do it, Thorn," Rusty said. "Don't do it."

"No, don't do it," a woman said.

She came from Thorn's right and walked to the edge of the group. Tall and thin with long hair.

"Well, do-si-do," Antwan said. "Swing your partner left and right."

"I know this looks bad, Claire."

"Let her go, Browning. Let the woman go."

"It'll be over and done in just a second. Then it'll be okay again."

"Let her go, Browning."

"Look, I got to get to a doctor," he said. "This is bad, Claire. It's my eye. I've been blinded."

"Hold on, cowboy," Antwan said. "We about got this settled. Don't go all soft and cuddly on me now."

"I'm hurt, Claire," Browning said. "I need help."

"Yes, you do. You've needed it for a long time."

"Enough of this shit," Antwan said. "Put the Mac down, Thorn."

"Yeah," Browning said. "Put it down before someone gets hurt."

"Let's try that counting thing again," Antwan said. "Ready, set, here we go. One, two, three . . ."

The horse was bigger than any Thorn had ever seen. It broke from the barn door at full gallop. On its bare back was a man in a gray T-shirt and jeans, leaning low and hauling ass right at Browning Hammond and Rusty.

All four of them stood immobilized as the horse charged like a shadowy apparition from some Arthurian tale. Browning Hammond released his grip on Rusty, raised his pistol to fire, but he'd responded too slowly, for the horse was on him and knocked him to the side, and the rider reached out with one arm and scooped Rusty around the waist and carried her off to the far end of the corral and put her safely down. It took a moment for everyone to recover, to register the immensity of what they'd just witnessed.

Sugarman was the first to regain his senses. He swiveled to the right and delivered a stomp to the side of Antwan's knee, felling the man into a groaning heap before he disarmed him with quick and professional ease.

Browning Hammond looked around at the gathering, watched his wife marching toward him. He groaned once and raised his pistol, turning it to his temple, but Claire Hammond moved swiftly to his side and peeled the weapon from his grasp.

"Oh, no, Browning. You don't get off that easy."

With a shaking hand the large man covered his ruined eye and sank to his knees in the white glowing dust of the corral.

THIRTY-FOUR

THERE WERE FIVE OF THEM around the campfire on that chilly March evening. The pine logs were erected in an elaborate square that reminded Thorn of a miniature version of the kind of fortress Davy Crockett and his boys might have whipped together on the edge of the wilderness. Sparks swirled up into the dark evening as if a band of Iroquois warriors had attacked the fort with flaming arrows and were circling on their horses, whooping with crazed delight as the pale faces fired their flintlocks.

Okay, so Thorn's imagination was a bit overstimulated by the Chianti and the stories Frisco had been telling, listing off some of the notable people who'd gathered in this very spot. A few of those folks even Thorn had heard of, most he hadn't, though Sugarman seemed to know them all, saying "wow" and "really?" and "man, oh man" over and again.

At a lull in the conversation, Sugar drew his small Canon camera from his shirt pocket, but Frisco waved him off.

"No photographs, sorry."

Sugarman lowered the camera.

"Really? That's a rule?"

"Yeah, always has been," Frisco said. "No photos, no recordings, no videos."

"So where's the proof any of those people were actually here?"

"There is none."

"Hemingway, Edison, Ford. It could all be fiction."

"It could be," Frisco said.

"Any other rules we should know?" Thorn said.

"No mention of prostates," Claire said. "Other than that, anything goes."

"Not very challenging," Rusty said. "I've never had any desire to discuss prostates."

"I think we're breaking that rule already," Sugar said.

Frisco was silent. He sat on a stump, staring at the campfire, sipping a beer from the bottle. The night was cool. One of the final fronts of the season had plowed through yesterday and left them swimming in air so pure and perfect everyone was a little dizzy. Soon the seven months of summer would begin, hurricane season with all that waiting and watching.

"Thomas Edison. Right here?" Rusty patted the rock she was sitting on.

"Right there," Frisco said.

"Did you know that Edison found the smell of cooking food revolting?" Rusty said. "He couldn't go anywhere near a kitchen. He liked to eat just fine, but smelling it while it was being prepared, that turned his stomach."

"Where'd you hear that?" Claire said.

"I read a biography last week."

"She was getting ready for tonight," Thorn said.

"An overachiever," Frisco said.

"Nothing wrong with overachieving," said Claire.

"What blows me away is Hemingway," Sugarman said.

"Exactly where you're sitting," Frisco said. "He made a fool of himself that night."

"Insulted Hoover," Claire said. "Insulted Henry Ford."

"Full of himself and drunk as usual," Frisco said. "Apparently he saved all his good stuff for the books. Nothing left over for real life."

Claire said, "Ringo Starr and the Maharishi. Those were guests of Frisco's dad. Earl Three."

"Be still my heart," Thorn said. "Not the Maharishi."

"Right there." Frisco pointed. "Yammered all night about his prostate."

"Have a little respect, Thorn," Sugarman said. "This is hallowed ground."

"How hallowed could it be if we made the cut?" Thorn stretched out his legs into the dancing light.

"Can't take this guy anywhere," Sugar said. "I apologize. Thorn doesn't know the meaning of the word *reverence*."

"That's not true. I revere lots of things. Just not that many dead people."

"So that's it? You just sit around and talk? That's all there is to it?" Rusty kicked a sputtering cinder back toward the bonfire.

"That's it," Frisco said. "Sit, talk, drink a little. Pretty simple."

"Are we allowed to talk about what happened?" Sugarman said. "Antwan, the governor, and all that."

"Do you want to?" Rusty said, giving Sugar a hard look. "Really?"

There was silence for a moment as everyone drifted off into their own recollections of the aftermath. Twenty to life for Browning and Antwan seemed light to Thorn. And simple impeachment for the governor seemed lighter still. In some law-enforcement quarters there'd been lingering questions about the deaths of the Faust brothers, suspicions that some unnamed third party had been involved. Though lately that fervor seemed to be dying out as a string of new atrocities in South Florida moved to the head of the line.

One of the logs crumbled, and gold embers whirled away into the air and winked out against the starry sky. Thorn listened to the frogs out in the brush, their mad peeping, and to a distant owl and some crickets and the flap and squeak of a heron rising into the darkness.

For a moment he had a vision of other campfires blazing away in other outposts far from the busy hives of cities. Campfires sprinkled around the globe where men and women were engaged in similar ceremonies, honoring the wilderness as their elders had. Trying in this way to stay attuned to the dwindling frontier, where the old lessons were still the lessons that mattered most, where it was possible for a moment, in the scattered halo of the flames, to recall the legends and testaments of one's youth and believe in them again with full faith and pleasure.

"Why don't you tell us the one about that rattlesnake, Thorn," Claire said. "Your brush with the wild hog."

"It's true," he said. "It really happened."

"Any photographs?"

Everyone chuckled.

"Okay, so tell us. Convince us," Frisco said. "Make us believe."

"All right." Thorn had a gulp of the Chianti, then set his glass on the log beside him and brushed off one leg of his jeans. "I was running from Jonah. Ran three miles across some pasture land and came into a stand of pines and cabbage palms."

"Three miles? You ran three miles without stopping? An old fart like you?"

"Yeah, right after I climbed the walls of that sinkhole."

"And then you sat on a rattlesnake."

All of them laughed. They didn't believe him. Thought he was exaggerating. Thought he was embellishing his small part in the larger tale. No matter how hard he tried, there was something about the way Thorn told a story that always made people believe he was joking. Like the night he was praising Rusty at the party, same thing, everyone hooting at his earnestness.

He touched his pocket, the lump of the diamond ring. He'd been carrying it around for the last few weeks, looking for the perfect time to spring it on her. He glanced around at these people, this place. But something told him no, maybe not tonight. Not just yet. Get Rusty alone, go down on one knee, give her something goofy and romantic to remember. Something she might tell later at a campfire when she wanted to get a good laugh.

X